# Smoke & Whispers

# SMOKE & WHISPERS

## MICK HERRON

**ISIS**
LARGE PRINT
Oxford

First published in Great Britain 2009
by
Constable
An imprint of Constable & Robinson

Published in Large Print 2009 by ISIS Publishing Ltd.,
7 Centremead, Osney Mead, Oxford OX2 0ES
by arrangement with
Constable & Robinson Ltd.

**British Library Cataloguing in Publication Data**
Herron, Mick.
    Smoke and whispers
    1. Police - - England - - Newcastle upon Tyne - -
    Fiction.
    2. Detective and mystery stories.
    3. Large type books.
    I. Title
    823.9'2–dc22

ISBN 978–0–7531–8474–5 (hb)
ISBN 978–0–7531–8475–2 (pb)

Printed and bound in Great Britain by
T. J. International Ltd., Padstow, Cornwall

To Juliet Burton

# Acknowledgements

It's a common complaint that authors take liberties with geography. In this instance, geography has taken liberties with the author. Some locations in this novel will have been redeveloped out of recognition by the time of publication — mostly, I hope, for the better — but they're described the way I found them in the winter of 07/08.

The scenes set inside the derelict Jesmond Picture House were written before I saw Richard Shepherd's spooky photographs of its interior. They can be viewed at http://www.shepy.co.uk/myphotos/main.php, and provide convincing evidence that Sarah exaggerated the cobwebs.

Arimathea House does not exist. Incarnation Children's Centre in New York does. Journalist Liam Scheff's reports on what happened there suggested one of the main planks of this novel (http://www.altheal.org/toxicity/house.htm).

XYZ are Sarah Jones, Matthew Jones and David Jones (http://www.myspace.com/xyzfolk).

Last Orders are Matthew Jones, David Jones, Kevin Lees and Joe O'Connor, with Maz O'Connor providing vocals (http://www.myspace.com/lastordersfolk).

Love and thanks to my mother, to Anne and to Mick for some long city walks.

And thanks too to Tony Smith, for a lot of learning, a little software support, and at least eleven years of squash.

Mick Herron
August 2008

# CHAPTER
# ONE

It was dark, but there were stars upon the water. They reflected from the lights strung on the bridges, from the windows of the still-lit buildings, from the yellow shuttle-bus pulling away along the quay, but most of all from the searchlights on the police launch: dabs of light that pricked out the body bobbing on the river like a chalk outline on concrete.

Small groups on the Gateshead Millennium Bridge watched events unfold.

"There was a time the city would have been fast asleep by now."

"Welcome to the 24/7 society." The speaker scratched his nose. "Welcome to the twenty-first century, in fact."

Fairfax looked at his watch, in retrospective validation of his comment. 11.24. On the far bank the Sage's glassy surface threw back distorted impressions of Newcastle: loopy cartoon buildings shivering in a February wind. He said, "The CC coverage might've picked it up. If it came from a bridge."

"Suicide TV."

"The operators call it JumpWatch." Fairfax buried his hands in his overcoat pockets. "That's if it came from a bridge," he repeated.

1

But if CCTV had picked it up, they'd have known about it sooner. An alert would have been sounded; the launch dispatched more quickly. Instead, the body had just floated quietly into view, and left to its own devices might have made it to the open sea. A pedestrian had spotted it, and belled the nines, as they used to say. From a mobile. Which speeded things up, if that mattered to the body.

"Said he thought it was the seal at first."

"He thought it was what?"

"The seal. It often comes up here. Splashes about in front of the Baltic, draws a crowd. Didn't they have a whale in London once?"

"It died," Fairfax reminded him. "And it's too cold for a seal."

"They live in the sea. I'm guessing they like the cold."

In which case, it had come to the right place. Any colder and it could have put a T-shirt on and gone clubbing.

An unborn pun drifted away across the river. The body was that of a woman, Fairfax thought. Already, the business of establishing identity was under way.

Downriver, more light bled from the buildings lining the water: hotels, restaurants, bars — even closed for business they leaked electricity into the night, as if scared of the dark, or the predators it used to bring. But that city was long gone, or at least banished from its old haunts. The quayside wore new clothes these days; its warehouses torn down; the cranes that lined the waterfront just a memory. The rats chewing on its

2

leavings were of an entirely new order; wore suits and power haircuts, and slit each other's throats quietly in boardrooms, rather than noisily over snooker tables. The stakes were of an order that even the eighties' sharks had never dreamed of. That stretch of land between the Baltic and the Sage was reputedly the most expensive in the country. All of which, Fairfax supposed, should have altered his lot beyond recognition: coppering the city was not the job it had been twenty years ago. But in the end coppering always boiled down to the same thing, and sooner or later you had a body in the water.

On whose surface the borrowed stars twinkled, small flashes of illumination just that little bit younger than their sources on the bridges. Come morning they'd surrender to the larger glare of day, by which time a lot more light would have been cast on the body. It would have been recovered, for a start; would have gushed water like an old mattress as it was hauled on to the launch, and with torches shone upon it would appear fragile and monochrome: black hair, white skin, black jacket. Empty eyes. In too many ways, that was the whole story right there: the body, once retrieved, had empty, finished eyes. But it was all just beginning, too. Come morning, DI Andrew Fairfax would have learned more: scraps of knowledge pieced together from an unwrapped body on a slab; from clothing and pocket contents, driving licence and credit cards, all chipping in to produce an identity, even if its owner was no longer around. Zoë Boehm. Private inquiry agent, according to a sheaf of business cards in her wallet.

Forty-six. Formerly of Oxford. No footage existed of her launching herself from the suicide's favourite, the High Level, but she'd drowned all right, even though she'd received a blow on the back of the head first. A wound not necessarily inconsistent with a high fall into water.

Come morning, all of that. At the moment, what Fairfax had was a floating body.

He said, "Valentine's coming up."

Valentine's always saw a needle in the suicide figures: the first Monday of the New Year was the divorce lawyer's favourite day, and all those filed papers would be turning up on doormats round about now, just as shop windows filled with heart-shaped balloons and cuddly bears. Everywhere the newly-single looked, they'd be seeing red. For some, it was the last straw. But then for some, the last straw was the first within reach, as if the whole bundle had been handed to them the wrong way round. For some, not much encouragement was needed to go jumping to conclusions.

Which Fairfax was doing himself. Whatever the statistics said, there were always anomalies. Accidents kept on happening, and murders never stopped.

"Well, we'll see," he said.

A hook on a stick snagged the body, and the heavy process of dragging it on to the launch began.

# CHAPTER
# TWO

Fires have to be tended carefully, in case they go out; except those that have to be fought fiercely, in case they don't. Which was a way of saying that events could be one thing or could be another. There was no way of telling without getting close.

There'd been a body in the water. That had an end-of-story feel to it, but still: she had to get close.

She'd come to Newcastle on a stopping train, and when she alighted beneath the high arched spaces of the station, what mostly struck her was the cold; a five-degree drop en route, and it hadn't been warm to start with. Carrying only a holdall, she picked her way through people hauling suitcases on wheels — edged past others on benches, holding gently steaming cardboard cups — and found the exit, where she paused to check the map she'd downloaded that morning. Nearby was a bar whose tables spread on to the concourse. A group of young men in short-sleeved shirts sat at one, hoisting glasses in a toast that mostly consisted of vowels.

Short sleeves, she thought. Jesus.

Taxis waited outside, but she wasn't going far. She turned right. Her route took her past a large hotel and the Lit & Phil, then a confusing array of traffic lights and road signs before bending to the right between what appeared to be matching warehouses: big wooden structures with metal shutters blinding their doors and windows. Cars hurried past, looking for a motorway. She reached a corner, checked her map, and turned right again, down a high-arched tunnel under the railway line. At the far end, where the road turned cobbled, she found the Bolbec Hotel. Above her a train rattled north.

And somewhere in front of her, unseen from here, flowed the river, down which the body identified as Zoë Boehm had floated the week before.

A fire that had definitely gone out.

Number 27 — second floor — had that twice-breathed air of all hotel rooms, and was decorated to suit an era long expired. Ranks of fleur-de-lys marched up and down the wallpaper, and curled round the lampshade's fringed hem. The colours that weren't green were either cream or red, and the carpet's reds were interspersed with deeper reds; not so much a pattern as a palimpsest, though what stories her hotel carpet hid, she didn't want to know. The bathroom was tiny. Sarah put her bag on the bed, used the loo, then washed her hands and face. The activity splashed colour into her cheeks, and she thought, observing the reaction in the mirror, that she looked suddenly older: a more weatherbeaten, less maintained Sarah Tucker. Back in the bedroom she turned the lamp on and the overhead

6

light off. The room's colours changed; became warmer. Sitting on the bed, she pulled out her mobile.

"Russ? It's me. I guess you're not back yet." She paused, her words drying up in these unfamiliar surroundings. What did she want to tell him? That she'd arrived safely: "I got here okay. Train a bit late but . . . And I've checked in at the hotel, the Bolbec Hotel. I'll let you have the number later, but you've got my mobile." Well, of course he did: they'd been living together three years. From somewhere below the window came a shout that might have been ecstasy as easily as pain. "I'll try to call later. But I'll probably have an early night. Love you. Bye."

For a moment she sat wondering if Russ had been there while she was speaking, though why she should think that, she couldn't say. Russell wasn't terribly happy that she'd come away — well, that was unfair; wasn't happy about the ordeal she was about to undergo — but he knew it had to be done, and would have come with her if she'd asked. She hadn't. This was something she had to do alone: again, she couldn't have put the why into words. Something to do with taking leave, she supposed. The friendship she'd shared with Zoë had been mostly celebrated in its absence, but there'd been a bond between them which you couldn't have forged with evenings in wine bars, or shopping for shoes. Not *had been*, she corrected herself. *Was*. There *was* a bond between them until the world proved otherwise, which it would have the opportunity to do very soon.

She made another call. "I'm supposed to speak to an Inspector Fairfax. Detective Inspector." She waited. "When will he be there?" It was after six. Policemen went home too. She was put through to his voicemail, and told it who she was. "I'm the friend of, of Zoë Boehm's. The woman whose body was found. Whose body you think was found." The river lapped quietly, not far away. She looked at her watch again. It had little new to tell her. "I'm told there's still not been a formal — that you need an actual identification made. By someone who knew her." She thought: Why am I telling him this? He already knows. Arrangements had been made. Sarah had spoken to officers from three different forces. She recited her mobile number. "I'll be there in the morning. Thanks."

That done, she unpacked her bag. It didn't hold a lot; what she was wearing was going to have to see her through tomorrow. She'd worn black jeans for the journey; black boots, white blouse, a black V-neck, and probably resembled an off-duty nun. Her coat was on a hanger now. It was thigh-length, very dark blue, and from midway up buttoned diagonally towards her right shoulder. She'd loved this in the shop, though had wondered since if it didn't look vaguely military. But no one saluted when she wore it, and Russ claimed it looked good on her.

Perhaps she should call him again. She could do with hearing his voice. Thinking so, she touched the diamond ear studs he'd bought her last birthday, when she'd turned forty. It had felt okay, on the whole. The studs had helped.

. . . They'd never argued much, and Sarah took more pleasure in this than she would have done in the opportunities for letting off steam argument allowed, or the traditional ways of making-up it fostered. But they'd had disagreements, and her being here had provoked one. "There must be somebody else," he'd said. "Family. Didn't she have family?"

Russell was tallish, dark — thinning a little on top — and had kind brown eyes. He didn't swagger; didn't roll. He was doing neither now, but his words had been gathering momentum for hours. Sarah was sure he'd tried to block them, but it must have been like holding a door shut against an incoming tide.

"I don't think so."

They were in their kitchen, sitting at the large wooden table which bore the scars of years of farmhouse work. Both were city-bred, and neither went out of their way to fake rural credentials, but the table had been here when Russ had bought the house, and no way was he getting shot of it. Here in this same kitchen Zoë had once arrived, trouble trailing at her heels. That was the first time Russ had met her. It had been a memorable occasion.

And now he'd said carefully, "You don't *think* so?"

"Russ, you know how it was. We didn't have an . . . ordinary friendship."

"You mean, the kind where you stay in touch and share details about each other's lives like, for instance, whether you have family or not?"

"She saved my life."

He reached for her hand, and she gave it. "I know," he said. "I'm sorry. I'm not trying to make this harder for you. And I'm sorry as hell about what's happened, you know that."

She did know that. He had held her while she cried.

"I'm just worried it'll upset you more. Identifying her . . . remains."

"It'll upset me ten times as much if I don't know for sure."

"Don't know what for sure? That she's dead?"

"Yes. That she's dead."

"It was in the paper, Sarah. There was ID on the body."

"But no one formally identified her."

"They don't need that these days. They can do a dental check. DNA. Whatever."

"I need to know for myself, Russ. Reading it in a newspaper, or some kind of official letter — it's not enough. I need to *know*."

Because Zoë had been slippery in life, and there was always the hope she hadn't lost this quality in death. There was a certain statistical foundation to this. Death happened to everybody, but could only happen to Zoë once. That made the odds *Everyone else: Zoë*. If you approached the issue from this direction, you'd obviously want proof before you began to mourn.

But these weren't terms to use with Russ, who would doubtless find a way to dismiss them.

Before she could find an alternative argument, he was talking again: "Sarah, I loved Zoë, okay? I mean, I didn't know her well, but I didn't have to. I owe her a debt I'll never be able to repay. But . . ." He reached out; added his other hand to the one that was already holding hers, and stroked her fingers. "But the way she lived, what she chose to do with her life — I'm not saying it was always going to end this way. But I don't want you being drawn into it again."

"It's not a question of that. It's not about being *drawn in* — what would that mean anyway?"

She meant what she said: what did it mean? If Zoë was dead, and Sarah satisfied herself of that, how did it implicate her? Did Zoë being dead mean part of Sarah would die too? Is that what Russ meant?

He said, "Sarah, you only know her body's been found because you saw it on the web."

It was true. In the absence of phone calls, in the absence of letters, in the absence of anything resembling regular keeping-in-touch, Sarah had developed the habit of Googling Zoë occasionally, to see if she was cropping up in newspapers. Perhaps, she now thought, she'd always been expecting something like this. To fire up a search engine, and have the first thing it rolled over be Zoë's body. *Found in the river Tyne last night has been identified as one Zoë Boehm* she'd read. The river Tyne. She'd looked from the list of references eating up her screen to the postcard on the desk in front of her, and thought how strange it was that these connections could be made so easily; so flippantly, almost. *Found in the river Tyne.* The same Tyne flowing through Zoë's postcard, which had arrived the previous week.

"I don't know what difference that makes," she told him. And told him, too, that she'd made her mind up; that this was something she was going to do.

Russ had this quality: he knew when to stop making objections.

She'd brought the postcard with her. It lay on the laminated sheet on her bedside table, the one explaining how the telephone worked; where to go when the hotel caught fire; what time breakfast was served. All useful information, but she'd have preferred this clarity to be transferred to the postcard; its message set out in simple, basic terms, perhaps with a telephone number attached, or a list of available times.

Once, years ago, Zoë had arrived when Sarah was in big trouble. "I can't just walk away," she'd told Sarah. Neither could Sarah, now.

Having arrived, having unpacked, having made her calls, Sarah felt somewhat paralysed. It was a not unfamiliar response to unfamiliar surroundings: should she stay here, where the few possessions she'd brought at least allowed her to feel she'd made a mark, or head out and lay claim to somewhere else? If Russ were with her, there'd be no contest. Alone, and in a city not different enough to feel exotic, the temptation was to hunker down: stay in her room, read, get through tomorrow when it came. Go to bed early. Have a bath. Options unfolded like a flower, all of them safe and time-consuming. She wandered into the bathroom, to reflect a while.

12

The face that looked back at her was the one she'd grown into, with even the changes that time had wrought seeming expected, as if they'd always been buried beneath the skin, waiting for the right moment to appear. Lines at the eyes threaded outwards, and on bad days her chin would sag if she didn't hold her head at a tilt. But holding it so gave her a defiant edge, which made her feel more confident, and thus better able to cope with a fat day . . . Her brown hair, which she now wore short, tufted in a way that could look artfully achieved, but was mostly down to its having its own ideas about how it should grow. That was the process in a nutshell, really. Your body did what it was going to do. You took steps in mitigation, but the face you were growing into was already there.

What she thought now — an attitude she'd achieved these past few years — was that hers wasn't a bad face, and allowing for the age-old default female setting of wishing she looked completely different, she was happy enough with it, except for the chin, and perhaps those lines at the eyes. And now she reached into her handbag, withdrew her spectacles case, and put her glasses on. Okay: this, maybe, her face hadn't been prepared for. Evolution took slow steps, as she understood it. Aged thirty-nine, she hadn't worn glasses; aged forty she did. Maybe, in another ten years, she'd have grown used to the way they made her look, but she wasn't banking on it.

Russ liked them. He said they made her look "studious, but still up for it". Russ could be depended upon to say the right thing, particularly if he'd had a fortnight to prepare.

But this was ridiculous: standing here hamstrung in a hotel bathroom. She brushed her hair. She'd go out. At the very least she'd head down to the bar, and have a drink. It was surprising, actually, that it had taken this long to notice she hadn't had one yet.

At the doorknob she paused, and looked behind her. She'd planned to ask for the room Zoë had had, but when it came to the crunch, found herself unable — how would she frame the request? Hold herself out as another private detective? Did the staff know that's what Zoë had been? Or even, come to that, that Zoë had been pulled out of the river a week ago? She'd checked out of the hotel before that happened. Ludicrous to think the staff kept a check on erstwhile guests; possible, too, that Zoë Boehm hadn't used her real name when checking in. Sarah herself wouldn't have known she'd been here had it not been for that postcard.

*I'm in this mausoleum called the Bolbec Hotel. I swear at nights you can hear the mice laying plans.*

The picture showed the Gateshead Millennium Bridge after dark; a graceful arc reflected in the water; an oval the river might pour through.

Unlike Zoë to drop Sarah a line. But was it unlike Zoë to jump off a bridge? She didn't know. She didn't know. Was the picture a clue? It might have been. She'd thought she'd known her friend but — she didn't know.

And didn't know which room Zoë had stayed in, but surely it wouldn't have been much different to this, and that thought held Sarah there a little longer, hand on the doorknob — eyeing the reds of the carpet; the creams of the bedspread; the regimented pattern on the walls — and wondering if Zoë had had such a moment, near the end of her life; a moment of hesitation on a threshold, glancing back to see if there was anything she'd forgotten. Except Zoë never forgot much. What she left behind she left deliberately, as being no longer of use.

Sarah flicked the light switch and shut the door, locking the darkness inside.

She didn't need to take the lift — she could manage a couple of flights of stairs, thanks — but with six floors to descend, she'd have made the same choice: the lift didn't inspire confidence. It had a metal grille for a door, and she suspected this might be all that was holding it together. The stairs it was then, which were wide; the landings hung with the kind of paintings that always look like they need cleaning: pairs of dead pheasants, tied at the ankle; improbably polished pieces of fruit. Sarah was compiling her own picture of the hotel's past, a brighter place than its present. Crinoline featured heavily, as did steamer trunks carted by uniformed porters, their braces showing.

The bar, too, was a hymn to faded grandeur. There was a large mirror behind the bar itself, engraved with gilt lettering she couldn't make out for the rows of bottles in front of it. The wooden counter curved like a ship's flank, and had a brass footrail. If she checked, she'd probably find the screwholes that once fixed a spittoon in place. A threadbare rug covered most of the floor. Scattered here and there were the usual round tables with small congregations of stools, but by the fireplace in the far wall was a sofa; also a couple of rattan armchairs that looked like they'd wandered in from somewhere else — possibly the dining room, whose entrance was to their left. Their backs faced the rest of the bar, as if they were engaged in private conversation.

She was the only one here, apart from the barman. Who, she guessed, was mid-thirties, which was pushing it for the look he was aiming at: head shaved to blond stubble; small gold hoop through his left nostril. But she'd be the first to admit she wasn't the best judge of what passed for edge these days; besides, his eyes were a blue so pale, they almost shaded into grey, and he smiled with genuine warmth. And when he asked her pleasure, his accent broke like a wave on a faraway beach.

"You're not local."

"Ah. You penetrated my disguise." He wiped the counter with a cloth as he spoke, as if he were method acting. He wore a collarless white shirt, its top button undone, and dark chinos. "I heard that wherever you go in the world, you'll find a Geordie and an Australian. I'm just cutting to the chase."

"So statistically, there must be a Geordie bartender in Sydney now."

"If I came from Sydney, miss, I'd never have left."

She liked the "miss". "So why not just go there instead?"

"I am. I'm taking the long way round. What can I get you?"

He chatted amiably as he poured a glass of Sauvignon: his name was Barry, he'd only worked here two weeks, and he hailed — don't laugh — from Wallaby Springs.

"Sounds like a middle-of-nowhere place."

"You wish. Wallaby's slightly left of nowhere. People heading for the middle miss it completely."

"This must feel like home from home."

"The hotel, you mean, not the city. We're not weighed down with guests, that's true." He glanced around theatrically: they were still alone. "We're not supposed to be trumpeting this — act like everything's normal, you know? — but the place is closing down. End of next month."

Sarah said, "I thought it felt deserted."

She didn't just mean of guests, either. All she'd seen of staff so far was the woman who'd checked her in, and now Barry.

Who said, "That's how come I got the job. Last guy quit soon as he heard. No barman likes to close a place down."

"But you don't mind."

He shrugged. "It's not a career. Just where I am right now. And it beats flipping burgers."

Flipping burgers, Sarah thought. Had any job summed itself up so succinctly? She took a sip of wine, which was crisp and dry and stirred an appetite: she'd not eaten since a sandwich on the train. "Speaking of which," she said, "is your restaurant open?"

"Don't worry, we're not that closed. It'll open at seven." It was ten to. "There's a party coming in."

"Party?"

"You're not the only guest." He winked, and she thought: uh-oh. There was clear blue water between friendliness and fancying your chances. She didn't want to be fending off Barry in a deserted bar. But he went on, "Some businessman, here to frighten up investors. He booked a buffet for twenty-five. Things'll get busier."

This, too, Sarah didn't need: to be sharing a restaurant with a gang of venture capitalists. "How about room service?"

He made a face. "Sorry. Must seem like a half-arsed operation, right?"

"Not your fault." The wine was going down nicely. "I'll have another of these."

"Second one's on the management," he said. "House rules."

"Thank you, Barry." When he set a fresh glass in front of her, she said, "A friend of mine stayed here a few weeks ago."

"Male or female?"

"Female."

"Dark-haired lady? Curly hair?"

She said, "That was quick. That was very quick."

"She was my first customer. Or the first not to be an overweight bloke wanting to know if I had any useful numbers. Guys who tend bar and guys who drive taxis, we're all supposed to be a sort of 18-rated *Time Out*."

"So you remember her."

"Yeah, she was here. We talked a bit. Zoë, right?"

"Zoë. Yes."

"She drank what you're drinking. Always a good basis for friendship."

"In the absence of anything else," Sarah agreed. "What did you talk about?"

Barry shrugged. He'd thrown his cloth over a shoulder, and again this struck Sarah as a little too perfect a gesture. Maybe he took his cues from that same olde-worlde sense she'd felt on walking down the stairs. Then again, what did she know about bartending? It must come with its own set of tics. "Usual stuff," he said. "She played her cards pretty close. Never did work out why she was here, or what she did for a living. But I only noticed that afterwards, you know what I mean?"

"Yes," Sarah said.

"She had a way of drawing you out without letting you in. What felt like a conversation at the time seemed more like an interrogation afterwards. I mean, she must have left here knowing all there is to know about the Springs, right? But I can't even remember where she lived. London, was it?"

"You're talking about her in the past tense."

"Occupational hazard. A lot of the people I talk to, I never see again."

There was noise behind Sarah; voices approaching from the lobby. This would be the party Barry had mentioned. "I'll leave you to it," she told him. "Thanks for the drink. And the company."

"You're very welcome." He raised his voice. "Evening, gents. It's my pleasure to be serving you tonight."

Sarah retreated to one of those rattan chairs; sat with her back to the incoming company. Businessmen. She could see it already. Loud-voiced laughter and off-colour jokes. She closed her eyes as the noise level rose, and found herself hurtling into tomorrow, when all doubts would be settled one way or the other: Zoë was dead or not dead, and Sarah would know whether she was free to mourn or not. This would be new territory. She had encountered death before, of course, but there were degrees of appropriate grief. An English attitude, but no less felt for all that. So far, there'd always been someone closer to the dead than her; she'd always been encroaching on someone else's sorrow simply by feeling less of it than them. With Zoë, that wasn't the case. With Zoë, she'd be mourning hardest.

Her wine was still dry, still crisp, but it was also rapidly disappearing.

Voices floated over from the bar.

"You can call it the Athens of the North for all I care, old boy, the clue's still in the name. North."

"It's only three hours from London by train."

"My point exactly. In three hours, I could have a good meal, asset-strip a failing charity and still get an early night."

It was the words as much as the voice, but it was also the voice — a round plump voice, which could only come from a tongue thick and fat, well used to digging the cream out of a doughnut.

20

But, of course, it was also the words.

"So you're only here to make money."

"Only God and the Treasury *make* money, old son. I'm more of a collector."

Ha ha.

"But a generous collector. As those around me can testify." The clink of a glass being set on a counter. "I don't get many complaints from those who follow where I lead."

Sarah looked at her own glass, which had become horribly empty. In her mind she was tossing a coin, but there was never any doubt which side it would fall.

"Is this all an act?"

"All? No." The pause came with stage directions: she could almost hear him tilting his head to one side. "Thirty per cent. Maybe forty. Does it matter?"

Ha ha.

She slipped out of the chair, and found her legs a little wobbly — the wine? No, not the wine. Circumstance, pure and simple.

A small circle had congregated at the bar, behind which Barry was wiping the counter again, trying a little too obviously not to listen to the entertainment. The circled characters were the usual collection of suits; were all men; teeth and eyes and hair and limbs arranged in recognizable ways. She paid them no attention. Her interest was in their focal point: the man with his back to her, making all the noise, though whatever he was actually saying now was lost in another round of laughter:

Ha ha ha ha ha.

And then the laughter died bit by bit, as the men facing her realized she wasn't about to sidestep them and make her order at the bar; that she had, in fact, come to a halt just behind their host, and wasn't going anywhere until he'd turned. Which he did, once it became apparent from their expressions that there was someone behind him.

In that first brief moment of recognition, something else flickered in his eyes: a hint of shock. Or possibly even fear.

"Good God," he said. "Sarah Trafford."

"Gerard Inchon," she said. "Fancy meeting you here."

# CHAPTER
# THREE

They'd both racked up some body miles since last meeting, but — glasses notwithstanding — Sarah was wearing hers better. It wasn't that Gerard had put on weight (though he had) or lost more hair (though he had); it was that he seemed to be carrying something extra, the strain of which tugged at his mouth, making a flat line of what had once been plump and fleshy. His face looked drawn, was her initial impression; was almost a caricature of his younger self, though that thought lasted no more than a second, and whatever reaction he'd nearly let slip was swallowed in a smile that seemed no less genuine for being hastily slapped on. "After all this time," he said.

"It's been a while," she agreed.

"You're here alone?"

He was looking over her shoulder, satisfying himself she wasn't the vanguard of a larger visitation.

"I'm on my own, yes."

He said to his gang, "Do excuse me. An old friend, an unexpected pleasure. Barry — fix drinks, good man. Introductions in half a sec."

One hand on her elbow, he drew her expertly towards the fireplace she'd just left. Which was laid but unlit: split logs criss-crossed in tepee fashion — that thing about carrying coals to Newcastle had come home to roost. Nobody was doing it, so they had to rely on wood.

"Sarah Trafford," he said again.

"Tucker," she corrected him.

"Of course." He released her arm. "You ditched the less-than-lily-white Mark, didn't you?"

She had no desire to rattle the bones of her defunct marriage. "How are you, Gerard?"

"Oh, bloody well. Not far short of fantastic, in fact. But what about you? You're not actually *staying* here, are you?"

"Yes."

"Good God. What on earth for?"

"I'm on holiday."

"In Newcastle?" Gerard Inchon could do puzzled like nobody's business. "Doncaster fully booked, was it?"

Thinner mouth or not, he could still give it some lip.

"They had a rush on," she told him. "I suspect they're having a whippet rally."

He was into his forties now: his thinning still brown hair scraped back over his head; his jowls — she rarely had recourse to "jowls", but Gerard demanded it — his jowls still wobbly, giving his face an inverted look. Still clean-shaven. Immaculately so, in fact. And, now his initial reaction had faded, still with that knack of assuming local attention as his due: for all he might resemble an extra in a forties film — a background figure at a racetrack, or remonstrating with a policeman

— Gerard would never settle for a walk-on part. Not that he'd steal scenes, precisely. He'd just acquire them at fire-sale prices, flog them to a shell company, then lease them back at rates he could claim against tax: he was, after all, a businessman — a "leading" businessman, in fact. Nor was this just his opinion. Sarah had heard him profiled on Radio 4 when Inchon Enterprises went public; she'd been impressed by how little of his private life made it on to the airwaves. His marriage to Paula had been mentioned, and that was about it. Because Gerard Inchon was a public figure, but not one anyone knew much about. She suspected that was the way he liked it.

"Now now," he said. "I'll make the slighting regional references."

He seemed quite serious about this, and perhaps was.

Sarah looked beyond him, to the crowd at the bar. "I'm interrupting your party," she said. "You'll want to be with your friends."

"Friends?"

"I'm using the term loosely," she assured him.

"I've never met most of them," he said. "But you know what it's like when you're in a new town. You want to leave your marker with the movers and shakers."

This was so far removed from Sarah's experience that she couldn't reply directly. "And what brings you here in the first place?"

"You can't guess?"

"Business?"

"You always did have my number, didn't you, Sarah?"

They both knew this wasn't so. They'd met during a troublesome upheaval in Sarah's life — the same upheaval that had brought Zoë into it — and for a while she'd thought Gerard Inchon the cause of her problems. The fact that she'd been wrong should have taught her a lesson, she supposed, about first impressions and surface values. She was never really sure, though, that life's lessons stuck.

She said, "I wouldn't have thought the Bolbec tony enough for you."

"Tony? That's New Labour speak for classy, yes? I didn't have you down as a snob."

"I mean it doesn't have wi-fi, Gerard. Or an atrium. Or a TV chef."

"Oh, I don't know. I think he used to be on *Steptoe and Son.*"

"It doesn't even have a sauna. Why aren't you at Malmaison?"

"Fully booked. Chelsea are in town. But don't worry, I'll sack my PA first thing in the morning."

"You haven't changed, have you?"

"Still the capitalist monster?"

"Exactly." But she smiled as she said it. They had an understanding, Sarah and Gerard. They'd clash broadswords, but refrain from whopping each other's limbs off. "How's Paula?"

"Fine. Fine. Fine." He glanced round. The group he'd abandoned had been augmented by half a dozen more: all male. "What are you doing now?"

"I'll just finish my drink and slip off quietly. I didn't mean to drag you from your guests, Gerard."

"Not at all. I mean, that's not what you'll do at all. You'll join us, of course. I assume you haven't eaten?"

"Well, no, but —"

"Have to have gone completely bloody native to have done that. It's not eight yet. They call it 'tea', did you know? Anyway, it's a buffet, so you'll hardly upset the placement. That's settled, then."

Sarah felt conscious that she was under-dressed; that everyone in sight, Barry excepted, was suited and tied and generally dolled to the nines. Gerard himself was tailored just short of perfection: a dark grey suit; a rich blue tie.

"Well, I'm . . ."

But she wasn't anything. All she had lined up was another attempt to contact Russ. And while meeting a bunch of strange businessmen wasn't her idea of a night out, neither was sitting in a hotel room waiting for morning, when she'd take a trip to the morgue. If she stayed in her room, she wouldn't be alone. Zoë's potential ghost would be with her, rattling memories and whispering dread.

Besides, Gerard had a deaf spot where "No" was concerned.

"Thank you. I'd enjoy that."

And besides again, what were the odds? Of Gerard Inchon being here, in the same hotel Zoë had stayed, in what might have been the last week of her life? Sarah wasn't aware they'd ever met, but she was a point of connection between the two. If time was the means by which the universe prevented everything from happening at once, coincidence was the excuse it used when things occasionally did. But as an excuse, it quickly wore thin. Zoë, dead or not, was whispering already. *What are the chances, Sarah? What's he doing here, anyway?*

Come to that, what had Zoë been doing here?

Gerard, smiling, took her by the arm once more. "Let's have another drink," he said. "And meet these no doubt charming people."

She was poured another glass by a smirking Barry, and in quick succession met two no doubt charming people whose names she immediately forgot. Gerard evidently had a Rolodex where part of his brain should be. If his story could be trusted, he'd barely met anyone here himself, but there was no hesitation in his introductions, and as soon as he'd made them he was off. The bar was filling up still, and Gerard worked the room like a politician, pressing flesh on each new arrival; producing brief barks of laughter and intakes of breath in about equal measure. It was early yet, though. She'd seen him split bigger crowds than this.

"So you know our host?"

"Not well. But yes, we're acquainted of old."

A waitress had joined the gathering throng; was cruising with a bottle of fizz, topping glasses, all bright-eyed and shiny. Sarah guessed someone had once told her her eyes were her best feature, because she was holding them open wider than natural. God, the hoops you had to jump through. It was a wonder footbinding had slipped off the agenda. She remembered Ginger Rogers' remark: that she'd made the same moves Fred did, only backwards, wearing heels. And even as the thought occurred, Sarah realized she was drifting, and that her new friends were visibly unimpressed with her sparkle . . . Perhaps this had been a mistake. Perhaps she should have sneaked off to her room after all.

"I'm sorry, excuse me a moment?"

She abandoned her glass, found the loo, then washed her hands and took a good long stare in the mirror. More and more often, this was her way of facing herself. She liked to know which Sarah she was talking to. "Are you up to this?" The Sarah in the mirror mouthed the words back at her. "Because otherwise you could hide in your room and think about your dead friend." *Not necessarily dead*, the answer came. And then, again, *What's Gerard Inchon doing here anyway?* Not a question to be answered by hiding in her room. Nor by standing like a lemon while folk talked round her.

"Party time," she told the Sarah in the mirror.

*Knock 'em dead*, Sarah replied.

She collected a glass of fizz from the circuiting girl; had barely taken a sip before a man approached her with a smile. "We haven't met, have we?"

"We have now."

"That's good. My name's Jack."

"Hello, Jack. Mine's Sarah. I don't need to ask if you're from round here."

"Holding a census?" He glanced round the room, which now held about twenty people. "I'll save you a few minutes. There's yourself, your man Inchon, and those two in the corner, there, Little and Large. My friend John. And everyone else is toon-grown."

"You know them all?"

"The ones I don't, I can tell."

She nodded in the direction of the bar. "And Barry there's from Australia."

"Oh aye?"

"A place named Wallaby Springs, would you believe."

"Now you mention it," he said, "no. I wouldn't."

He was neither little nor large himself, this man Jack; he was tall but thin, the kind of thin steel cables were. Sarah found herself remembering a soldier she'd once known. Jack, though, looked reasonably user-friendly. His dark hair, neatly styled, fell fuller than the military allowed, and the suit he wore — blue as evening fog — cost as much as everyone else's put together, Gerard's excluded. Patches of acne scarring on his cheeks were a reminder of an adolescence as far behind him as Sarah's own.

"And what is it you do, Jack?"

"I'm a career criminal."

It was so unexpected, she couldn't help but laugh. "You've fallen in good company, then."

"A regular thieves' gathering," he agreed. "No, these gentlemen are what pass for the great and good in these parts. By which I don't mean they're either great or good, just that they can be relied upon to turn up when money's in the air."

30

"Is that what I can smell? I'm surprised the room's not fuller."

"If the money was free, you'd have trouble bending your elbow," he agreed. "No, they're here to gawp at your man Inchon. Hoping some of it will rub off."

"It?"

"It's always tempting to think other people's success is based on luck."

"And what's yours based on?"

"My success?"

"You're here," she said, "aren't you?"

"Good point." He drained his glass, examined the empty vessel a moment as if surprised it wasn't larger, then said, "The family business started in haulage, but these days it's mostly storage. You know those big depots you see outside city centres? The kind trains go past when they're reaching the station?"

"Acres of dismantled cars," Sarah said.

"That's from a poem, I can tell. Well, we — the family — we own a lot of those. You wouldn't believe how much people will pay to fill them with junk."

"Nice for you."

"As you say. So there's capital to take care of, and never let anybody tell you that's not a full-time responsibility. Hence, as you've pointed out, my being here." He pointed with his empty glass to where Gerard was doing his three-ring circus act. "Your man Inchon's been scaring up local talent. I'd be failing in my duty if I didn't take an interest."

Your man Inchon. His third use of this. "What makes you think he's mine?"

"Just a turn of phrase. But you're the only lady here. And we've established you're not from these parts."

Invisible quote marks hovered over that. *These parts.*

"Fair enough. We're old friends as it happens, but I'm here by chance. I didn't know Gerard was in Newcastle. I'm on . . . other business."

He raised an eyebrow. "What were you about to say before you changed it?"

"Nothing I particularly want to elaborate on. If that's okay."

"Aye, of course." He didn't try to work it, either. "He has quite a rep, your friend."

"We haven't seen each other in some years."

"Well, he's managed all right in your absence."

Sarah didn't doubt it for a minute, but it was an interesting slant on Gerard Inchon: that people in cities he didn't frequent were keen on getting a gawp at him. Not the big beast Branson was, but he obviously punched above his weight in the marketplace. And his weight, as she'd already noted, hadn't diminished in recent years.

"And what is it you do, Sarah?" she was being asked.

"Editorial stuff. I'm a sub-editor."

"With a newspaper?"

She shook her head. "I freelance. A lot of publishing houses outsource their hands-on work. I do bits and pieces."

"But you're your own boss."

"That sounds nicer than 'spends a lot of time trolling after work'."

"Still true, isn't it? It's all down to spin. People take you at face value. You want to make a good first impression, you've five seconds to do it in. Ask your man Inchon." He put a hand on his heart. "Turn of phrase. Honest to God."

The girl with the bottle refilled their glasses. Barry, Sarah saw, was busy behind the bar too: a lot of the company had moved on to spirits. She didn't think that was a direction she'd be heading in. On the other hand, if they didn't eat soon, the fizz would be damaging enough.

As if hearing her thought, the girl said, "There'll be food in five minutes. Just through the doors, like."

"Thank you." The girl moved on. *Like*. The distance from Kensington to Tyneside could be measured in the placement of that syllable.

Jack had turned to greet a friend. Sarah sipped fizz, reminded herself to drink more slowly, then sipped again. She scanned the room as if absorbed in what she saw. Now that she was here, she was in it for the long haul. No sneaking off to commune with Zoë's ghost.

Someone materialized beside her: short man, strange hair, dark suit, orange tie.

He said something she didn't catch.

"Could you speak up? Your tie's very loud."

Her conscience would kick her for that in the morning.

"I'm sorry?"

"I said, I didn't quite hear what you said."

He was mid-to-late fifties, with a round face, its shape emphasized by a neatly trimmed beard which decorated his face cheek to cheek without bothering his upper lip. Beard; no moustache. A style choice so ill-advised, she wondered if it weren't actually a medical condition. "Wright," he said to her. She thought he'd said *right* at first, as if he were about to get down to putting her straight. "John M. Wright," he continued.

Sarah was pretty sure no one had ever introduced himself to her using his middle initial before.

"Sarah," she responded. "Em, Sarah Tucker."

"I see you're our token woman tonight."

"I'd noticed. But thank you for pointing it out."

Jack was back. "Ms Tucker's in publishing. She owns her own company."

The ghost of a wink accompanied this information, but it slipped past Wright without causing a draught.

"I also keep livestock," she said. "Ostriches."

"Ah, yes. Good money in them, is there?"

"Small change mostly. Also bracelets, watches, bottle tops. They'll eat anything, really. What do you do, Mr Wright?"

"Medical research."

"Sounds interesting."

"It's fascinating."

Why did she feel she'd just been contradicted? "Involved how?"

"I run a facility." He took a sip from his wineglass. There was something very precise about this, as if he'd calculated in advance the exact amount of liquid he cared to ingest. "A small one. Privately funded. Which is one of the reasons I'm here now."

"I'm sorry?"

34

"Funding. Wherever the moneymen gather, you see?" He laughed, as if he'd said something amusing, and stroked his ridiculous beard. "Most scientific research these days is dunning investors."

"You're here to mug Gerard, then."

"Who?"

"Gerard Inchon." She made a vague gesture in Gerard's direction. Gerard happened to be watching them at that moment, though that didn't mean he'd ceased talking to the folk around him, or indeed ceased drinking. And they said men couldn't multitask. She gave him a wave. "Our host."

"Not actually *mug* him, no."

Mr Wright didn't seem comfortable with the frivolous approach. But she couldn't stop herself saying, "But it was worth wangling an invite anyway."

Jack said, "John's here with me."

"Oh. Sorry, I didn't mean —"

"None taken," Jack said, though the offence hadn't been headed his way. "John and I have certain interests in common."

She made a stab at what they were. "You stash your equipment overflow in his storage depots?" she asked Wright.

Jack laughed, but John M. Wright said, "Mr Gannon's family are my main investors."

He wasn't local — had no particular accent she could pinpoint, but certainly wasn't a Tynesider. This was the John Jack had identified as an out-of-towner.

The girl with the bottle reappeared, this time *sans* bottle. "Would you like to move through to the restaurant?"

"We would indeed," Sarah said. "Thank you."

Word of food shimmered through the gathering like wind through a field of corn. John M. Wright was among the first to head through the restaurant doors.

"I hope I didn't offend your friend," Sarah said as they followed.

"I'm not sure personal offence figures high on John's radar."

"What sort of medical research does he do?"

"Respiratory diseases. Or conditions, whatever. You know, asthma, allergies, that sort of thing."

"And you're happy about introducing him to other backers."

Jack said, "If he finds a cure for asthma, we'll be delighted to share the profits." He caught her look. "I hope you didn't think this was a charity do, Sarah."

"God forbid."

"The kind of work John's facility does, it takes a lot of money to keep it going. And he's not happy about his current housing."

"Could you put him in one of your warehouses?"

He smiled politely. "Do you really keep ostriches?"

"A pair, yes. We rescued them when the bottom fell out of the ostrich-meat market. From a nearby farm."

"We?"

"Russ. My partner and I. Are you married, Jack?"

"I have been."

"Me too." Perhaps she'd had too much to drink. Or perhaps she just liked Jack. "Funny, isn't it? When it's over, you can't really remember what you thought you'd wanted out of it."

After a moment or two, Jack said: "I think I wanted the usual stuff. Shall we follow the food?"

The restaurant was much the same size as the bar, and similarly decorated; i.e., a while ago. Its tables had been shifted to the edges of the room, and loaded with plates of sausages and samosas; of ham and salmon; of bread rolls and tuna sandwiches and bowls of salad and rice. This was what she needed. Something to soak up the wine. Plus more wine, of course. There was no point pretending she was about to come over abstemious.

Plate filled with food, she found herself drifting towards the nucleus of the gathering, which was Gerard. It was hard to tell whether he was being viewed with fascination or horror, though she doubted he'd have minded which. For some reason, the song "Lawyers, Guns and Money" came to mind. Gerard collected guns, and it was a fair bet he had no shortage of lawyers, either. And only Gerard, she decided; only Gerard could breeze into town, get a fix on the local players, and set up an evening like this, inside what — a couple of days? He might have been lord of the manor, and these men his long-suffering tenants. No: he might have been the conqueror, entertaining brand-new subjects.

"So where's the future, then?" he was being asked. "In your field, I mean."

Inchon Enterprises was in the communications line. In that Radio 4 profile, Gerard had summed up his corporate philosophy: Money talks. *That's what communication's all about.*

But now he said, "Oh, if I'm in a field, the future's the next field along, isn't it?"

"You're looking to diversify?"

"Diversity? Can't bloody avoid it, old son." She couldn't tell whether he'd misheard deliberately or not. "I have to fill out forms, explaining how many ethnic minorities, women, wrinklies and *differently abled* people I employ. Well, I don't fill out the forms myself. An old deaf woman does that. But my impression was you had the same laws up here now."

Jack, plate in hand, was behind her. "Does this a lot, does he?"

Sarah said, "In my experience, yes, he enjoys being obnoxious."

"I suppose it sorts the wheat from the chaff."

"Meaning?"

Jack managed a sip of wine without spilling his food. "Come chucking-out time, nine-tenths of this lot'll think he's just another loud-mouthed pillock who believes the crap he's spouting."

"Well," she said. "They'll have a point."

"But the others'll remember he's a self-made multi-millionaire."

"And that'll give them pause?"

"What do you think?"

She thought she didn't much like being treated as if Gerard Inchon were her specialist subject. "So you tell me. Why does he do it then?"

"To scare away the idiots," Jack said. "He doesn't strike me as a man with much time for idiots."

That was probably a good assessment, though didn't allow for the fun Gerard derived from it. Besides, Sarah had the impression Gerard was in low gear. His attention seemed constantly on the prowl: he was forever looking her way, or maybe just in her direction.

John M. Wright had arrived on her other flank. His meal, she couldn't help noticing, consisted entirely of sausages and rice.

She felt guilty for the way she'd treated him before, so now said, "Jack tells me you're looking for new premises."

"Premises?"

"The real estate kind. For your . . ." She had to shake off the word *laboratory*, which sounded too mad-scientist. Though it wasn't her fault he had loony facial hair. "Research premises."

"I've had better," he said.

"Where was that?"

"It was a while ago now."

"But presumably still in the same place," she couldn't help saying.

Jack said, "You were in Surrey before you came here, weren't you, John?"

"Yes." He speared half a sausage into his mouth, but didn't allow that to prevent him saying, "Mr Gannon has been a friend to my work."

That would be Jack, she registered. "Asthma would be a good thing to cure."

"Children," he said, his mouth full.

"For them, especially." She could feel herself being sucked into one of those dinner party conversations, where you're compelled to have views on subjects you'd rarely considered before.

"It's to them you have to look, Ms Tucker," he said. She was surprised he'd taken hold of her name. "If you want to cure asthma, you have to look to the children. That's where the condition is at its most vulnerable."

What a bizarre way of putting it. But he was the expert. She said, "I assume cleaning the air would help too."

"We all have to live in the world as it is."

Low gear or not, Gerard was still making waves. Someone had just asked if he was interested in property.

"Well, of course I bloody am. I'm a businessman, not a Buddhist."

Sarah wouldn't have put it past him to make sure there was a Buddhist nearby before launching that line.

Jack excused himself: he'd seen someone he needed to talk to. For a frightening moment, she thought that would leave her with John M. Wright, but he was sidling off too, to fix his empty plate. Before she could get down to emptying her own, Gerard was waving her over.

"Old friend," he said to the assembled crew. "Always nice to have one around when you're surrounded by savages. Present company, etcetera."

"Gerard likes to test people's patience," she found herself explaining.

"Aye, we'd got that far."

"It's funny, like," another man offered. "If you're mad and rich, you're eccentric. But if you're a worky-ticket and rich, you're still a worky-ticket."

40

Gerard scented blood. "I knew I should have bought that phrase book."

Of the seven men listening, four laughed; two, Sarah thought, genuinely. She remembered what Jack had said, about sorting wheat from chaff. Sheep from lambs might be a better way of putting it.

"Ah sometimes think Hadrian built that bloody wall wrong side of the Tyne."

"Absolutely," Gerard agreed. "Peterborough would have been nearer the mark." He paused. "Well, just south of Peterborough."

One of the older men — one of those whose laugh Sarah had pegged as genuine — said, "Tell us, to pass this audition of yours, are we supposed to agree with you or disagree?"

And now Gerard laughed: a big honking laugh which circled the room twice before he shut it off. "Audition. Priceless. Let's have some more drinks."

There must be a line, Sarah thought — Gerard had probably mapped it a time or two — beyond which you bought more drinks or got a slap in the mouth.

Whatever instructions Barry had been given, he'd taken to heart; was already circulating with a pair of bottles with optics removed. This was the pacifier, not the drinks themselves. The pacifier was Barry: white shirt, black trousers, tea-towel over a shoulder; a reminder that this was a civilized occasion. Of course, a few more drinks, and a different set of rules would arrive. But that line wouldn't need mapping. The rise in temperature would do the trick.

As Barry refilled, Gerard went on: "I'm always keen on meeting movers and shakers. There's a lot going on in your city."

This wasn't for general consumption. The business of refuelling had fragmented the group, and Gerard was addressing the older man, though Sarah revised her adjective as she took a closer look. He was white-haired, sure, but his hair had stolen a march on the rest of him: his face was unlined, apart from the usual creases at mouth and eyes; and those eyes themselves were bright as a black-bird's. He didn't, Sarah noticed, proffer his glass for a refill.

"Movers and shakers?" he said. "I take it we're past the roughing-up stage."

And Gerard smiled a wolverine smile, and drew the man away to a quieter corner.

More drinks were poured; conversation flowed. Sarah Tucker found herself the centre of attention, which happened when you were the only woman present. It wasn't unpleasant, and the men were well behaved — perhaps because she was Gerard's particular guest; a personal friend, not a name on a list. Did they imagine Gerard would wreak awful revenge if her honour was besmirched? Or perhaps they simply didn't find her attractive. Fine by her.

As you get older, time speeds up. While you're drinking, much the same happens.

She remembered kissing Gerard on the cheek, which was almost a first; she remembered collecting a bottle of water from the bar. She didn't remember heading up to her room. But next she knew she was on her back in the darkness, alcohol fizzing in the corners of her mind. A while since she'd drunk so much. Most evenings a glass of wine or two with Russ; rarely a second cork pulled — if you could call them corks, mostly plastic now, and even Aussie wines using screwtops . . . Could there really be a place called Wallaby Springs? Jack didn't think so either. Jack's family stored people's junk for a living, but "junk" was just another way of saying "secrets", so no wonder they'd found themselves wealthy, like Gerard. Was he fatter than he used to be or just plain all-round bigger? And what were the chances, finding him in the hotel Zoë had stayed in before she died? Oh Zoë . . .

Maybe she wasn't dead. That was a possibility Sarah could hang on to until the morning, at any rate.

At some point, hanging on, she let go. Her last thought was one she'd had earlier that evening.

*If time was the means by which the universe prevented everything from happening at once, coincidence was the excuse it used when things occasionally did.*

But as an excuse, it quickly wore thin.

# CHAPTER
# FOUR

She woke with a start from a dream in which she'd piloted a bus over a cliff, still groggy enough to hope her passengers had woken too. There was a loud hissing somewhere, though luckily this turned out to be the radiator and not a snake under the bed. It wasn't light — what crawled past the blind was a grimy grey; a slight reminder of daylight — but the winking TV clock said 6.59, and flipped on to 7.00 as she watched. And as soon as she moved, she recalled she'd been drinking. This wasn't a hard, hammering reminder. It was more of a suggestion of pain to come, like a grief recalled, or one about to happen.

She'd had the sense to acquire water before hitting the bed; not quite enough to have drunk more than a swallow or two. Arranging herself into a sitting position, she poured a glassful now and drank it gratefully, ignoring the memories that threatened to intrude. Payback was the worst part of any hangover — reality's payback, when the evening's wit and glamour were revealed as alcohol's illusions. All over this strange city, she thought, grown men were waking up thinking *what was that woman like?* But this, too, was part of the payback: the mind magnifying self-inflicted embarrass-ments, and pretending anyone else cared.

There'd been a call from Russ logged on her mobile when she got back to her room. Her phone had been on silent; she hadn't heard it ring. And it had been too late to call him then and was too early now. She sent a quick text instead, using short but sincere words, then dragged herself into the shower where she washed away last night.

There wasn't water enough, though, to drown the hours ahead.

"Ms Tucker?"

"Yes?"

"The inspector's on the phone. He'll be free in a moment. Would you come with me, please?"

"You're . . .?"

"King. Detective Sergeant King."

DS King was wide in the shoulders, but his jacket looked a comfortable fit: not off-the-peg then, she thought irrelevantly. He was West Indian, and wore his hair clipped to a soft buzz, with a tidy moustache-and-goatee set completing the look. A gold stud winked in one ear. Strangely, he was wearing trainers; a worn beaten pair which in no way matched his suit.

He noticed her noticing. "It's a long story," he said. "I won't bore you with it." He was holding the door open. "This way?"

It had just gone quarter past nine. She'd been on time for the appointment, but had been asked to wait anyway: here in the police station lobby, which had a shiny tiled floor and some heavily used noticeboards. *Is there an addict in your life?* one poster asked, with small print that went on to explain how to find the answer. Another warned about alcohol abuse; a pretty raw subject where Sarah was concerned. But as her hangover's symptoms receded, she recognized them for what they were: her body's way of distracting her mind's attention from what lay ahead. *Did your best friend drown last week?* That wasn't a poster, just a noise in her head, but it was loud and getting louder. *Is Zoë dead?* She hadn't minded being kept waiting for the answer.

But now she was being dragged towards it, by a combination of time ticking past and a policeman in trainers. Down a corridor with scuff-marked walls they went, then up a flight of stairs, through whose smeary landing windows a dismal light swam. The inspector — his name was Fairfax — was kept in an office on the next floor up. His accent was not as broad as his sergeant's. He was putting the phone down as they came though his door.

"Ms Tucker?"

"That's right."

When they'd spoken the other day she'd formed a picture of what he looked like, but had clean forgotten it now, so couldn't compare the reality. Which was pretty ordinary: tall, with thin, rather elongated features. The hint of a developing paunch spoiled this effect. Like his sergeant he wore a dark suit over a white shirt; Fairfax's, though, most definitely came off a peg. "Please. Take a seat," he said.

"Thanks."

Afterwards, she couldn't remember a single thing about his office. At the time, all she noticed was the whiteboard behind him, which hadn't been wiped effectively: the ghosts of erased messages hovered tantalizingly below its surface. It was like being whispered to by a billboard.

"I understand you were a friend of Zoë Boehm's."

"Were?"

"I beg your pardon?"

"You said 'were'. That's what we're here to find out, isn't it? Not our friendship, I mean. Just what tense it's in."

From behind her, DS King said, "We don't mean to jump the gun." That "we" was taking collective responsibility a little far, she thought. "We do, though, have a dead woman. For your sake, we hope it's not Ms Boehm. But it's somebody."

"Yes. I didn't mean . . ."

What she didn't mean trailed away; joined the erased deductions on the whiteboard.

Fairfax said, "The woman had a wallet in her pocket. It contained various bits and pieces — credit cards, some business cards. All belonging to one Zoë Boehm."

"But that's not enough, is it?"

"No. Not for a firm identification."

"What else do you have?"

He had leaned his elbows on his desk after sitting, and brought his palms together in prayer. Now he drew them apart, as if releasing something invisible. "That's it, really. Your friend, she — she's a little hard to pin down."

Sarah nodded.

"Her teeth seem in good order. The dead woman's teeth, I mean. Or so the pathologist said, but we can't find that Ms Boehm's registered with a dentist anywhere. Would that come as a surprise to you?"

"Little that Zoë does or doesn't do would surprise me," Sarah said honestly. "She's too sensible not to have a dentist. But she's just — just paranoid enough to make sure nobody could trace her records."

"She's a private detective."

"Yes."

"She had reason to be paranoid?"

He was having trouble with his tenses again, but she was past picking him up on it. "I'm sure she's made enemies."

"Why might she be in Newcastle?"

"Working. That's what I assume."

"And you were aware that she was here?"

She nodded. "There was a postcard. She sent me a postcard."

"Saying?"

Sarah furrowed her brow, but was pretty sure she remembered the words. "'I'm staying in this mausoleum of a place.' The picture was of the Millennium Bridge. 'I swear at night you can hear the mice making plans.'"

DS King said, "Making plans?"

"I don't think she meant anything by it. It was just a kind of joke."

"And you're sure the postcard was from her?" Fairfax asked.

"It hadn't occurred to me it wasn't. It looked like her writing."

Now Fairfax said, "When was the last time you saw her?"

"More than a year ago."

He raised an eyebrow. "I thought you were close."

"That's as close as she lets people get." She hated this: having to explain Zoë to a stranger. Their friendship was their business. "She'd call. It's not as if we live in the same neighbourhood."

"When was the last time you heard from her?" King asked.

"That would be the postcard," she said, without turning round.

"And the last time she called?"

"I don't remember."

"But when she did, what did you talk about?"

She said, "Nothing to suggest she might head to a different city to jump in a river."

Neither man replied to that.

"That's what you're assuming, isn't it? That she's a suicide."

Fairfax said, "We're not assuming anything yet. Not until we get a firm ID."

"Well then," Sarah said. "Perhaps we'd better get on with that part."

Making her way from hotel to police station — a straightforward journey, if one that took her through what felt like three different cities, so various were the aspects it presented — Sarah hadn't been able to rid herself of the feeling of being watched: a sense not so much of eyes burning into her back as one of logged movement, as if she were leaving a trail. But then, she was in a city. Back home, her days were largely spent alone in her study; her too-frequent trips to the kitchen mitigated by a two-mile hike after lunch, during most of which she'd see nobody, unless Russ accompanied her. Human contact came at a remove: e-mail, fax, phone. So the sense of being crowded took getting used to, and didn't mean that the observation was any more than the casual once-over every citizen suffered: from passers-by, from reflecting surfaces, from the cameras fixed at junctions, which swivelled at pre-determined intervals. And they reminded her, just for a moment, of the ostriches — Mr O and Nicole — whose heads would likewise track her when she passed their pen. They were just as detached, just as unblinking. And what they did with the information was just as unknowable.

It was a cold day, and the buildings looked moist to the touch, as if the river's breath had soaked into their stone. Sarah had first been in Newcastle years ago, and had been struck then by its anonymity. She'd expected — well, she didn't know what she'd expected, but something more than she'd found, which was exhaustion wrought in concrete and scaffolding; a palpable sense of relegation that was tempered, but just barely, by the in-the-teeth-of-it humour of the locals, like the *Maggie was here* scrawled on the whitewashed window of a bankrupt business. At that time, a huge tract of the centre had recently been torn down, and a shopping precinct driven like a stake through the heart of the city. Wandering into it, Sarah had been struck by its lack of natural light, and the cheap glitz its shops afforded. It brought to mind a vision of a five-year-old in her mum's high heels and moth-chewed feather boa.

Since then, things had changed. Less of the feather boa; more of the boa constrictor, sloughing one skin to show the fresh glistening surface beneath. Down by the river was where this change was most apparent. You could stand on a bridge after nightfall and think yourself in a European capital: lights dancing on the water, and big glass buildings winking at the stars above. There was music and art and sculpture; there were the new courts buildings, with the promise they carried of justice and order and jobs for professionals, and plenty of cafés and bars and restaurants where those same professionals could satisfy their daily need for latte and Shiraz and pesto. And everywhere, new buildings were under construction: luxury apartments with urban views to rival anywhere in the country, and with immediate access to live jazz venues; to museums of storytelling; to city-farms and organic groceries.

But Sarah knew, too, that the older city remained, and you didn't have to look hard to find it. Behind the new and newly refurbished blocks on the quayside were the same small streets that had always been there; the same railway arches and lock-up garages; and hanging around them were the same people, pursuing the same lifelong objective of satisfaction bordering on happiness. There'd be untouched pubs on those old streets — untouched meaning unthemed — and in their snugs and saloons, Newcastle survived unaltered. You could doll a city up in new glad rags, but you couldn't actually change its identity. It would be like trying to forge DNA. And this was a good thing, because otherwise you could always be anywhere; the name hanging over the streets irrelevant.

As she walked, she had wondered what Zoë had made of the place. It was an oddity of their relationship that she could rarely predict what Zoë's opinion might be. That too had been a good thing. And as she contemplated this, she regretted the slippage of tenses, and recognized that all morning, she'd been preparing herself for what was almost upon her now, as the car driven by Detective Sergeant King came to a halt round the back of a large complex of buildings she guessed must be part of a hospital. Here were industrial-sized waste bins, and heating vents billowing out steamy clouds, and a pair of double doors with a horizontal Day-Glo strip painted across them; a strip which split as the doors swung to allow two boilersuited men to emerge, pushing a huge trolley laden with what looked like dirty laundry.

She'd done well, she thought, at the station. *Perhaps we'd better get on with that part*, she'd said, as if the chore ahead was just another in a long list. But now she felt her legs jellying, and had to take a grip on the door handle to assure herself she had strength in her body. That she wasn't about to collapse getting out of the car;

to choke like a Brit at Wimbledon at the enormity of the upcoming task.

"Are you all right, Ms Tucker?"

"I'm fine."

"We'll get you a cup of tea. You'll have to wait a few minutes anyway. There's hoops need jumping through first. Nothing you'll be involved in."

This was Fairfax, who managed the avuncular tone quite well. But she wasn't in the mood for being cosseted. She needed a scratching post. "Well, enjoy your boys' games. Is there anywhere special you'd like me to wait?"

Her legs worked well enough, it turned out, and slamming the car door helped. She'd folded her arms before she knew what she was doing; probably looked the archetypal angry woman, though the men hadn't emerged yet, so didn't notice. They'd be whispering a quick joke. When she unfolded her arms, her hands shook. No one had made her come here — it had been her own decision — but that initial phone call felt a long way back; felt as if it had been the first step taken on to scree, to launch a tumbling she couldn't halt. Too late now. DS King emerged from the car. Fairfax too.

"This is hard for you. We realize that."

"Yes. It is."

"The DI came on like a patronizing tosser." This was said clearly enough for Fairfax to hear. "It's just his way. He doesn't mean anything by it."

She had nothing to say. Words were sharp-edged objects, to be issued carefully, in case they caused damage. "Shall we. Get on with it?"

"This way."

Through those double doors, then, and up a stairwell: this surprised her. She'd imagined heading down; had expected a cellar, a lack of windows. King led the way. Fairfax walked beside her. Neither said anything until they reached a small room containing a glass-topped table on which a few leaflets had been scattered. There were also two plastic chairs, on one of which she was expected to sit.

"This won't take long."

She nodded.

The leaflets were on grief counselling and death registration procedures. Sarah tried to ignore them.

It was impossible, she discovered, to shake off a feeling of impending diagnosis. As if whatever was about to happen had graver implications for her own future than for anyone else's, even if its effect on the latter was a line drawn through it. Her legs felt shaky again, so she sat, but could do nothing to prevent a tremor convulsing her body. In twenty minutes she'd know if Zoë were dead. Sarah couldn't be sure what kind of hole that would leave in her own life. It was like trying to predict the injuries you'd suffer if the floor beneath you gave way.

The door opened. DS King appeared.

"If you'd like to come through, please."

The air smelled of ethanol; a still-damp aroma, as if the walls had just been hosed down, but it seemed to Sarah that it masked something earthier, something rotten, the way a teenage boy might spray on deodorant in lieu of showering. She had been wrong about there being no windows, but the windows had white plastic blinds over them, and the light was all electric. She was in a viewing area; part of a larger room, the rest of which hid behind a curtain. The curtain made it worse. It indicated that there was nothing behind it you'd be comfortable seeing.

And there was a slab in the centre of this area, with something laid dead flat upon it, covered by a sheet.

DS King and DI Fairfax stood behind her, close enough for her to feel their heat. A young man who looked vaguely Latin was present too, wearing a white coat with ID clipped to the pocket. He didn't speak, but nodded in a way that seemed kind. Sarah's lip trembled with tension as she nodded back. He withdrew the covering sheet, and stepped aside.

Sarah saw a woman, lying on a slab. She was white — so white she was faintly blue — and had black hair, and was dead. It was Zoë. Why would Sarah be here, if it wasn't Zoë?

All the air had been sucked out of the room, but leaked slowly back. Breathing was a luxury granted to visitors.

She heard Fairfax, unless it was King, clear his throat, and took a step forward to forestall words.

It felt important to be quiet, though there was nobody here to disturb.

Sarah closed her eyes, and opened them again. The body on the slab hadn't moved. It was Zoë. But it was not Zoë. It was like looking at a lamp from which the bulb had been removed, and trying to gauge how much light it once shed. The last time Sarah had seen Zoë Boehm, they'd shared a meal in an Italian place near the bus station in Oxford. There'd been photos of the owner's infant daughter plastered across the walls, and the tablecloths had been the usual red-and-white check. Almost two years ago, because Zoë had never been one for keeping in touch, but at least she'd been alive; the light she'd cast being that dark glow Sarah had grown used to: laughing and joking but holding something back — not a secret, necessarily (though Zoë kept plenty of those); more a state of mind she held at bay so as not to spoil the occasion. And now she was here, an unchecked tablecloth laid across her; more years than anyone could count waiting to be piled on top. Except it wasn't her. And then it was. And then it wasn't.

Truth was, Sarah couldn't tell. It was like Zoë, that was certain. The features were arranged the way Zoë's had been. But this woman looked both older and younger at once; this woman — this body — had been some time in the water. There was bloat to contend with, and the recoloration of death. Zoë, always pale, had never looked rinsed this way. The blue-white of the skin shaded black in the hollows of eyes and nose. The hair, a dark cap of curls, looked — well — lifeless. *Any visible marks?* was the usual question, but Sarah didn't know that either. For certain Zoë had scars, but Sarah hadn't borne witness to them. Besides, two years of living would have changed her in ways Sarah could hardly be expected to catalogue; two years of living plus one week of death would have pushed her a whole new distance away. It might be her. It looked like her. But

Sarah couldn't be sure. Corpses sink, she'd been told. Then rise to the surface three, four, five days later, when gases in the body are released. Was that how long this woman had been in the water? What would Sarah look like if this had happened to her? Would she recognize herself? Would Russ?

Again, she felt that someone was about to talk, and tensed. It was all she could do not to put her fingers in her ears.

This body had not been laid to rest. It had simply been stretched out. Under its sheet, its arms would be at its sides; its fingers thicker than fingers ought to be. Zoë had been fingerprinted, to Sarah's certain knowledge. She'd also since received notification, as Sarah had herself, that those prints had been destroyed. This had been in the aftermath of their first encounter. Sarah's copy of that letter was in a drawer somewhere. Zoë, she suspected, would have stood over its sender and watched the records fed into a shredder. There ought to be other items of equal forensic value, of course, but *we can't find that Ms Boehm's registered with a dentist anywhere*, Fairfax had said. *Would that come as a surprise to you?*

Hell, no.

Anyone might have reasons for flying under the radar. Zoë's had been better than most. A while back, she had fallen into the path of a man who killed women; murdered them so carefully they looked like unrelated accident victims, or middle-aged suicides. There'd been two Zoë had known of for sure. And these, she'd assured Sarah, had been points on a graph:

no man insinuated himself into the lives of two lonely women, and ended those lives, then decided enough was enough. It was just that he'd vanished so cleanly afterwards that Zoë was left feeling she'd been trying to nail a shadow to a wall. She referred to him by the name he'd had when he first came to her attention — Alan Talmadge — but that had been no more genuine than the accent he'd used at the time. On the few occasions Zoë had laid eyes on him, he'd borne little resemblance to the man she'd been hunting. Not that he'd been a master of disguise. He was simply anonymous; so bland that a haircut and an earring could remake him anew. All Zoë had known for sure was that he liked Motown. And even that might not have been true; might have been an overlap between identities.

Zoë had never quite stopped looking for him, and had never been sure he wasn't looking right back, waiting.

And perhaps he'd stopped waiting. Perhaps that was why Zoë was on this slab now.

If it was Zoë.

Sarah became aware she'd been holding her breath. She let it out now; a long slow sigh, involuntary but weighted. It changed the room's dynamic. Someone shifted from one foot to another behind her, his shoe scraping on the floor like wet chalk on a blackboard. Any moment now, she thought. Any moment now, she was going to be asked the question she didn't yet have an answer to.

"Ms Tucker —"

I'm not sure yet, she intended to say, but the words wouldn't come.

"There are a few other things you should look at."

She took a step back from the body. "I'm sorry?" Her voice belonged to someone else.

King nodded at the white-smocked young man, who turned to what looked like a cross between a wardrobe and a filing cabinet. When he opened it, that was pretty much what it was. On one side hung a jacket; on the other were drawers, the topmost of which he pulled open. Shallow, almost a tray, it held a scatter of objects.

"Her things," DS King explained.

Sarah recalled an ancient comedy riff, about the decline in status of possessions whose owners had died: a falling-off, from "stuff" to "rubbish". In this case, a deterioration hastened by time spent underwater. She stepped towards the drawer, and the objects acquired shape and form. Keys, watch, lipstick, pen: some other things. A tortoiseshell comb. Some jewellery. Here was the wallet she'd been told about; a wallet she didn't recognize because who would? It was just a black, fold-over wallet with a clasp, somewhat river-damaged. Its contents were splayed next to it: coins, some bedraggled notes; a soggy mass that might have been till receipts. Some of Zoë's business cards in a frothed-together clump, their lettering faint. And her credit cards, seemingly unaffected by their drenching; their holograms winking in the light, as if all they needed were a little nudge, one tiny PIN-prick, and they'd be ready to hit the shops.

Okay, all this belonged to Zoë. But the fact that this was Zoë's stuff — her rubbish — didn't mean that the body on the slab was hers too.

"Also, her clothes," King said.

Like a well-trained domestic, the morgue attendant slid the drawer shut, and pulled open a lower, deeper one, holding clothing.

Her first impression was that they'd been laundered, and for a moment she was agog at the idea that this might be standard practice; that the unclaimed dead were valeted, here in this stainless steel palace. She'd already seen how the body was sluiced and rinsed of its muddy build-up. But this impression didn't last, because the river smell hit her, and no, they hadn't been cleaned; they'd been lain flat to dry, that was all. If at first glance they looked ironed, that was simply because they'd been vacuumed — not a courtesy; just another step in the forensic process. Any evidence this clothing might have offered had been sucked up into an industrial device, though what further clues might have been needed that their owner had been pulled from a river, Sarah couldn't have said.

Black jeans, belted; a black blouse and a red top. If she'd been asked to describe what Zoë might be wearing at a given moment, that would be it: black jeans, black blouse, red top. And here they were.

Underwear too, of course: white, functional, knickers and bra. That, too, was of a piece with how she pictured Zoë.

And, on the hanger, a black leather jacket she'd seen Zoë wearing a dozen times.

Jeans, blouses, tops, underwear: you could put them on more or less anyone, and it wouldn't make much difference. Black jeans and red top wasn't an ensemble to stop you in your tracks. A leather jacket, too, was an everyday sight.

But this jacket: this was different.

"Does anything seem familiar?"

"Yes," she said.

"The jacket?"

"It's hers. It's Zoë's."

She had no doubt about this. Zoë had bought the jacket in Italy, years before Sarah met her. There was a slight tear on one sleeve, just above the cuff: Sarah had noticed it more than once; had suggested somewhere Zoë might take it for repair.

"I don't need it repaired."

"It'll just get worse."

"It's part of what the jacket is." Zoë had stroked the rip as she'd said the words. "Like keeping a diary. You know? I'm fond of this tear. But then, I remember how it got there."

Zoë, being Zoë, hadn't revealed how this was.

"You're sure?"

That was DS King again, breaking into memory.

"I'm sure."

He shared a glance with his boss. *Job done* were the words neither said.

"Ms Tucker?"

She had reached out and taken the cuff in her hand. Was stroking the tear, just half an inch long, the same way Zoë had done when they'd shared that moment: she couldn't now put even an approximate date to it.

"Ms Tucker?"

"Yes?"

"Is this the body of your friend, Zoë Boehm?"

"Yes," she said. "Yes. It is."

"Thank you."

A discreet nod and the sheet was replaced, the drawer pushed back, the locker closed, and the jacket sealed out of sight, along with the jeans, the blouse, the top, the underwear.

It felt as if the lights should be switched off too, but that didn't happen.

They spent a further ten minutes in a different room, at the end of which Sarah signed something, she wasn't sure what. It didn't matter. A signature, anyway, was just a prearranged squiggle; not proof of identity. All it meant was that you were aware of the shape of the squiggle required.

If Sarah had been asked what she was feeling during this period, she wouldn't have been able to say.

The men, Fairfax and King, stepped gently round her. They seemed decent enough, as far as that went. A little too much like a double act, sure, but if any job excused a shoulder-to-shoulder outlook, she supposed police work fitted the bill.

As they left the building, Fairfax said, "Thank you for your help, Ms Tucker. I'm sorry for your loss."

The cold air cleared her head. "You think she killed herself, don't you?"

"We'll continue tracing her movements in the days leading up to her death."

"She'd checked out of her hotel."

"I know."

"Really? The staff haven't heard the news. That she's dead, I mean."

(*She's dead.* The words struck a flat metallic note, as if someone were tolling a cracked bell.)

He said, "So you're staying there too? The Bolbec?"

"Yes."

"I hope you're not . . ."

"You hope I'm not what?"

He said, "I hope you're not causing yourself unnecessary grief."

For a moment it interested her, this apparent distinction between unnecessary grief and the other kind. She had to blink the distraction away, like a tear. "As I say, the staff aren't aware of what's happened."

"It wasn't necessary to inform them that we'd found a body to establish that Ms Boehm had checked out," Fairfax said, as if delivering a prepared statement. "What will you do now, Ms Tucker?"

"Will I be needed at the inquest?"

"Probably not. It won't be for a week or so anyway."

An unbidden image arrived: of a logjam of freshly dead corpses; too many for a coroner to deal with inside a week.

"Then I suppose I'll go home," she said.

# CHAPTER
# FIVE

At her request, they dropped her in the city centre. She wanted, she said, to do some shopping, and they saw nothing odd in this. Identify your friend's body; then a little retail therapy. But maybe — in a job entailing regular trips to a morgue — you developed a certain insight into the reactions of the bereaved, and learned there was no template to rely on. Shopping was as useful, or useless, as any other response to death. As for Sarah, she wanted to be on her own, preferably in a crowd. It didn't matter what they thought she wanted.

The air was cold, but still; the skies grey as an anvil. Sarah's mental weather, though, was storms and shattered crockery; in her mind, it rained hammers. She'd just come from a morgue, where she'd identified a body as Zoë Boehm. Her reasons for doing so didn't alter this: that a woman lay dead on a slab, her body sluiced like a disconnected drainpipe.

And Zoë's possessions had weighed her down in the water.

If Sarah tried to break down how she felt, the list would run to pages: grief for Zoë, fear of her own death, the nagging sense of tasks left unfinished, along with all the usual physical niggles: that sudden tremor in the calf; an unexpected churn in the stomach. And underlying everything, the accumulation of all she'd ever been or felt: the memories, even forgotten ones; the emotions, even those wasted. Listing them would be like trying to score a symphony by cataloguing the orchestra, instrument by instrument. And everyone was like this. Everyone carried around their own symphony of the self, with only the faintest snatch of it audible to those around them; whispered music all we hear of their real life. This was what had been snuffed out of that figure on the slab: all the music no one had ever heard.

She walked through the shoppers' streets, not paying attention. She was heading riverside.

The road sloped steeply down to the quay. Sarah passed an arts cinema and several bars that looked new, though traded on traditional names. An overhead bridge cast a damp shadow, and a building leaned over the pavement at a ridiculous angle, like an accident lawyer's daydream. The whole city was like this: the new jammed next to the old in a transplant so recent, you could see the join healing. When she crossed the road, she found herself on a paved area overlooking the Tyne. There were benches, but she didn't sit. She leaned on a rail, and gazed at the river instead.

This was the water that the body had come out of. If birth had a canal, death had its river.

The more you pondered death, she thought — if you were an intelligent, educated, well-read woman — the more you expected yourself to come up with something deep; something that, if unlikely never to have been thought before, would at least crystallize your own opinion. But Sarah had nothing to think. Death happened; would happen to her. Had happened to the woman she'd just viewed on that slab. But Sarah had nothing profound to reply to it. It was a bugger, that was all. Which was unlikely to make it into a book of quotations.

What did come, though, was the realization that it shouldn't have come as a surprise, the difficulty she'd had identifying Zoë. Alive, Zoë had never been easy to pin down. What had made Sarah think the task would be easier, Zoë dead? In a world where identity theft was rife, Zoë had kept hers close and secure; had a deliberate policy of putting anything which might have betrayed her through a shredder. Her slash-and-burn approach to friendship confirmed this.

And one of its effects was that their friendship was hard to recreate. In a film, flashbacks come with background detail: clothing, wallpaper; the quality of light as it slices through windows. The self-assembly kind has less coherence; comprises fragments pulled from a contextless soup, with no guarantee that they represent faithful reconstruction. Thinking of Zoë, Sarah saw no linear structure to their friendship. There were phrases, and moments of remembered action that always seemed to be recalled from above. Not that she had trouble recalling Zoë's face. It was just that, once you had someone's face firmly in mind, memory could put any words it wanted in their mouth. The self-assembly flashback could lie, which no self-respecting movie version could. Even Hitchcock got burned trying that.

66

Some words she was sure she recalled correctly, though. She remembered, for instance, Zoë telling her about her jacket.

And the jacket was a giveaway. Zoë had constantly worn it — her signature look. Bought in Italy. Zoë's husband Joe had picked up something similar at a street market at the same time, for a tenth of the price. Its sleeves had fallen off within six months. But Zoë had still been wearing hers years later; long after Joe died; long after Sarah had met her; right up until the time it had fallen into the possession of the killer, Alan Talmadge.

Zoë, to the best of Sarah's knowledge, hadn't worn it since.

She wasn't sure how long she stood, her thoughts clenched round her like a fist. After a while, though, it became clear that no conclusions were available yet, except for the obvious: that the body must indeed be Zoë's, and that the insubstantial Alan Talmadge had entered her life again, shortly before its end. Which cleared this much up: Zoë hadn't entered the river of her own accord. This knowledge made Sarah no warmer. When she realized that her shivering was as much due to cold as to sorrow, she began making her way back to the Bolbec.

Trusting to a sense of geography that some, Russ especially, would have doubted existed, she headed upriver towards a hotel whose tubular neon swirl of a logo was familiar, and before reaching it turned up a flight of steps between two apartment blocks still offering empty flats. At the top, she turned and looked down. On the river's far bank stood a whitewashed building, the words *Ovoline Lubricants* painted on its side. More of the old city, not fading away.

The Bolbec was up ahead of her, so geography had done its work. The other buildings in its square were abandoned. Renovation was happening from the quayside up, she supposed. A placard announced major developments: watch this space. Slouched against the wall of the building opposite the hotel — a former electrical works — was a figure which straightened at Sarah's approach. He wore dirty blue jeans, and a variety of shirts and sweaters, layered one on top of the other so their sleeves blossomed like cauliflowers at his wrists' bony junction. Topmost was a worn sheepskin jacket some sizes too small. His hair was dead straw, and his face grey from huddling in corners.

"*Big Issue*, lady?"

She didn't always, but sometimes she did. If their eyes caught hers, she was theirs. She'd fumbled a coin out before it struck her. "You don't have any."

"I can get you one."

He grinned cheekily as he spoke, and she found herself surrendering the coin anyway. "Maybe next time."

"Know where to find me."

In the hotel lobby was Gerard, who probably wasn't waiting for her, but didn't appear to be doing much else. "Exploring the boondocks?"

"Doesn't that mean swampland?"

"How the hell should I know?" He looked genuinely surprised to be asked. "See anything interesting?"

She closed her eyes briefly: a chiaroscuro nightmare unreeling on her eyelids. White flesh; black dead hair. A leather jacket with a familiar scar. "Not especially," she said. "Just stretching my legs."

"Some holiday you're having."

"Not all holidays are about being there," she said. "Some are about not being anywhere else."

"That's probably deeply clever," said Gerard. "Well done. What are you doing for lunch?"

"I hadn't thought about it."

"That was rather the point of asking, wasn't it? To put the subject at the forefront of your mind."

It occurred to Sarah, not for the first time, that conversation with many men would be a lot simpler conducted on their terms: *Yes, No, Fuck off.* It would limit the agenda, but a lot of them seemed to prefer that.

"Gerard —"

"You look like you could do with feeding." Then, presumably worried there might be a compliment in there, added, "I don't mean you're skin and bone or anything. You didn't stint yourself last night that I noticed. I just mean you look a little down. Lunch helps with that, I find."

"Why are you here, Gerard?"

"I was just on my way out."

"No, I mean, why are you *here*?"

"I already told you. Looking at investment opportunities."

"Why Newcastle?"

"Hadn't you heard? This city's one of the fastest-growing IT centres in the country. Software development, communications technologies. Thought it was about time I came and checked it out."

Sarah hadn't known, but it didn't surprise her. Everything happened somewhere. "Doesn't make it any closer to London, does it? What was it you could manage in three hours? Roast a swan, orphan a trade unionist, and still have time to fire the help?"

"Mmm, not much escapes you, does it?"

"Consistency was never your strong point."

"Consistency is the last refuge of the unimaginative."

"Sounds like Wilde."

"Everything sounds like Wilde if you declaim it rotundly enough," Gerard said. "Though in this case, I'll grant you, it's one of Oscar's. Anyway, I never claimed I was planning on living here. I'm happy to let other people do that for me."

"Big of you."

"Now now. Don't do the new North down. It's got lots of things talented young professionals want, like big glassy buildings full of rubbish modern art, and whacking great angels on the motorway."

She really didn't want this conversation. "It's too early for lunch." Where this knowledge came from, she wasn't sure, but the clock in the lobby confirmed it: it wasn't long past eleven. It was surprising how quickly big things happened.

"Well, I didn't mean *now*, did I? I've a meeting first, which is why I'm waiting for a taxi, which seems to be operating on a different timescale to the one I'm used to. And —"

"Gerard, taxis *everywhere* are *always* —"

"— and afterwards I'll be going for lunch. What's your mobile?"

Giving him her number seemed the fastest way of removing herself from this situation. A taxi pulled up outside as she did so. He was still tapping her into his Sony as he went to meet it.

There was nobody on reception. Gerard's key lay on the desk as she passed. There was something almost quaint in that: a key, not a passcard. But it was of a piece with the setting.

In her room, she lay on the bed. Her hangover had disappeared, or gone into remission, but all she'd seen since waking had filled the space it left, and her head was roaring. Lying down didn't help. She had to do something.

She should have talked to those policemen about Alan Talmadge. But Sarah knew nothing about him beyond the little Zoë had told her, which amounted, in effect, to these few facts: Talmadge killed women, Zoë had said; enjoyed Motown music, Zoë had said; wasn't really called Talmadge, Zoë had said; and some years back had walked away with the jacket Sarah had just seen in the morgue. Zoë had said. This would have involved admitting that she'd identified Zoë's jacket rather than her body, which would have made waves. Besides, Sarah had had unhappy experiences with policemen. A part of her, quite a large part, preferred their absence.

But there were things that could be done, and having so decided, she did one of them. She made a call. "Vicky? Sarah Tucker."

Vicky was Zoë's teen webhead, or that's what she'd used to be — Sarah was pretty sure she was still in her teens, but didn't know whether "webhead" remained current. Zoë had relied on her for years. No techno-slouch herself, Zoë knew her limitations, and any time she hit a firewall hotter than she could handle, turned to Vicky. Sarah had once sent her a hard drive which had crunched three weeks' work on the same day an ostrich had eaten her back-up memory stick: Vicky had returned it inside twenty-four hours, all its data unstuck. So Sarah had her listed on her mobile.

"Have you heard from Zoë lately?" she asked.

(This was cowardice. She didn't want to be breaking bad news to a teenager, over the phone.)

"I heard they pulled her out a river," Vicky said.

So much for the soft approach.

"Oh. Oh, Vicky —"

"Well, you don't think I be*lieve* it, do you? Zoë? In a river? Like that's gunna happen."

"There's a body," Sarah said.

"There's always bodies. People die all the time." But not Zoë, apparently. "Anyway, you don't believe it any more'n me. Else you wouldn't be asking if I'd heard from her."

It was no time to start deconstructing how much she'd been prepared to divulge. Besides, the kid probably had a polygraph wired to her phone. "Either way, she hasn't been in touch," Sarah said. "Don't you think, if she was able to, she'd have let us know she was okay?"

Teenagers have a gift: they can shrug audibly, over a mobile. "I said she wasn't dead, that's all. I dunno what's happened to her."

"You want to help me find out?"

Vicky said, "Like for a job?"

"Like for a friend."

To give her her due, Vicky didn't think about it long. "Okay."

"You're sure?"

"Yeah. I'll just bump up the fee next time she needs me, that's all."

"That would be my approach." Sarah shifted the phone from one hand to the other. "Can you access her computer?"

"Nothing easier. You got her door key?"

"Door key?"

Theatrical sigh. "Zoë wouldn't go anywhere, least of all a river, and leave her computer live. You want to know what's on it, you need to go and plug it in."

"Maybe she —"

"Trust me."

"Okay. So short of breaking into her flat, what can you tell me?"

"Anything that's out there. Anything in the air. I can fetch you her e-mails. I can tell you anything she's ordered online, and I can tell you her bank account details. Actually, I can do that quite quickly, because she's always trying to plead poverty when she wants a job done. So I keep her records handy so I know when she's fibbing."

Sarah reminded herself never to piss Vicky off.

"But anything on her desktop, forget it. And you want to know what I think, I don't think Zoë's gunna leave anything lying around for others to read. And when I say lying around, I mean out there in the air. She knows about this stuff, you get?"

"I get."

"But I'll do what I can."

"That would be great."

For a moment they shared a silence. Silence is louder over a phone.

". . . Sarah?"

"Still here."

"You don't believe it either, do you? About Zoë, I mean?"

She closed her eyes briefly: saw a white body on an overused slab; a black leather jacket on a wire coat hanger. The river at night lapped darkly beneath any number of dangerous bridges. "No, Vicky. Not for a moment."

"Good. 'Cause I don't, either."

"That's why I want to find her, actually. To ask her who she thinks she's kidding."

"Yeah. And tell her what I said, won't you? That I'm like, *that's* gunna happen."

"Oh, I'll tell her."

They promised to talk later, then Sarah put her phone away.

74

The roaring in her head had subsided, as if action had reduced the pressure. That Vicky could do what she'd said, Sarah had no doubt. That her efforts would reveal what Zoë had been up to was less certain. On the other hand, Sarah already had a pretty clear picture of what that had been — Zoë had been looking for Alan Talmadge. Though even as the thought occurred, Sarah picked it up, turned it round, and set it down again. Perhaps Alan Talmadge had been looking for Zoë. Perhaps Zoë hadn't known he was here until it had been too late.

After a while, Sarah dozed. The body was capable of making its own decisions whatever the mind was up to. It wasn't a refreshing nap, more a bumpy ride through the outer borders of sleep, and when she came fully awake twenty minutes later she was in desperate need of coffee, but also in possession of an idea.

Coffee could wait. The idea needed to be acted on immediately.

In the lobby, Barry was back on reception, door keys hanging neatly on the board behind him.

"Good morning, Ms Tucker. Afternoon, I should say."

"Hi, Barry. Barry, is that man still outside?"

"Man?"

"Some homeless guy. Selling *Big Issues*, except he didn't have any to sell."

"Was he bothering you?"

"He wanted change. Was pretty insistent."

She felt dreadful, saying this. Made a mental note to make amends.

"I'll take a look, shall I?"

The time it took him to cross the lobby and look outside was all she needed. Gerard's key was in her pocket before he'd turned.

"Over the road?"

"Yes."

"He's still there. I'll move him on."

"Oh — no. No, don't do that."

"No worries. If he's been upsetting you —"

"Not really. Just startled me. No, leave him be. I'll avoid him, that's all."

"Well, if you're sure."

"Thanks, Barry."

"And I'd put a coat on, I was you. If you're going out, I mean."

"I am. In a bit. And I will. Thanks, Barry."

On the landing she paused, before getting paranoid about being caught on camera, pausing. Except the hotel didn't have CCTV, did it? Though there were mirrors everywhere — one on this landing, even — and it was possible they were placed to allow whoever was on reception a reflected view of every staircase, every corridor; a Wizard-of-Oz perspective of every floor at once. But *Get real*, she told herself, resuming her ascent. That wouldn't be a security system, it would be an art installation.

On Gerard's floor, she checked the number on the key fob: 37. There was nobody in the corridor. The key felt fiddly in her hand, and wouldn't fit the lock on its first attempt. Too late it occurred to her that she should have knocked, in case Gerard had come back while she was napping, but — get a grip. The door opened. If Gerard had returned, his key wouldn't have been hanging on the board. She slipped inside, closing the door softly behind her.

The first thing that struck her was the smell; not an unpleasant smell; not even, especially, a masculine smell, and Sarah wondered if Gerard used his wife's soap when he was away from her. The thought struck her with guilt. Gerard was a friend, or at any rate, not a stranger. What was she doing? Looking for clues, she answered. What was Gerard doing, that was the question, at the same hotel Zoë had stayed in before winding up in the river? If this was coincidence, Sarah could live with it, because strange things happened. But to believe it coincidence, she had to lean on it first, to see if it broke.

Gerard wasn't Alan Talmadge, and maybe Talmadge had followed Zoë here rather than the other way around. But Sarah had to be sure there was nothing else happening. If Gerard was hiding a connection to Zoë, his reasons couldn't be good.

It was early afternoon now, but gloomy out, and the window was a murky oblong. There seemed no reason not to turn the light on. Once she'd done so, Sarah could see that the room mirrored hers, but with enough of Gerard's stuff in it that it might have beamed down from a different time zone. His laptop sat on the chest of drawers, next to a snake's nest of recharging cables: for a mobile phone, a BlackBerry, and God knew what else — an electric wine cooler, she wouldn't be surprised. A sandwich-thin, moneymaker's briefcase lay on the bed, but it would be locked: nobody with a case like that left it unlocked, the same way no one with a Merc forgot to set the alarm. His suitcase sat on a deckchair-arrangement in the corner. On the dresser was a scatter of loose change, along with a pocket-sized packet of tissues, a set of house keys, and a small deck of business cards secured by a rubber band. A pile of shirts, socks and boxer shorts lay on an armchair, on whose back hung a bag named Laundry Service — this gave Sarah pause. It was one thing eyeing up a locked briefcase. That had a professional anonymity to it. Gerard's dirty laundry was a different story.

But burglars aren't distracted by guilt pangs. Burglars switch laptops on instead. While it hummed to life she tried the briefcase, just to prove it was locked, then turned to the suitcase, which opened. It didn't hold much — some more recharging cables: for God's sake, Gerard, are you powered by the grid? Along with an M&S four-pack of red-and-white striped boxers, and an HMV bag containing, still wrapped in cellophane, a DVD boxed-set of *Buffy the Vampire Slayer*, Series 5 . . . Okay. Probably not germane. In the case's side pocket was a buff folder, the kind that came in ten-packs from Rymans, but a quick flip through it revealed nothing relating to Zoë: just printoffs of Internet downloads from newspapers, stories about orphanages. Gerard's wife Paula had been orphanage-raised, she remembered. The Arimathea Home. Gerard was a donor. She replaced the folder, and closed the suitcase.

The laptop, meanwhile, had swum into life, and was asking for a password. Sarah hit the return key, on the offchance Gerard didn't actually use one, but the screen blinked, then asked again. She closed it down. With any luck, it wouldn't register the attempted intrusion.

Getting nowhere fast. There was a burglar's rule, she thought, about spending time on invaded premises: Zoë would have been able to quote it. A few more minutes, though. She turned to the dresser, where — behind the loose change, the packet of tissues, the keys, the business cards — lay a letter, still in its envelope. The address — to Gerard, here at the hotel — was handwritten, in what didn't look like Zoë's writing, but Sarah picked the envelope up anyway; aware as she did so that this was a line she wasn't sure she was ready to cross. She turned it over. On the back flap was the sender's name: Paula. Gerard's wife wrote him letters when he was away. Definitely not a line to cross, then. But the envelope had been lying on a folded-over sheet of paper, and this she did read. It was a computer-generated list of names, headed by Jack Gannon's, and including a couple of others she recognized from last night. Invitees to Gerard's soirée. She refolded it, replaced it, laid the envelope on top. Whatever that rule was, it was time to obey it.

But first she looked around again, ignoring the contents and absorbing the room; same wallpaper, same paint on the ceiling; a one-storey-higher view from the same sash window. Just like her room, only not. We could all sit in identical boxes and we'd all make a different mess, she supposed. Then came a footfall outside the room, and the doorknob rattled.

Sarah didn't know she could move so fast. Wasn't really sure why — there'd be no hiding from this — but moved anyway; stepped into the bathroom, closed the door gently. Slid the bolt across. The door to Gerard's room opened, and someone stepped inside just as Sarah sank to the tiled floor and put an eye to the keyhole.

Already she knew it wasn't Gerard, though didn't know why she knew. Whoever it was had a key, or something that worked as well as a key.

Silence. The somebody remained out of Sarah's eyeshot. In the bathroom, what she was mostly conscious of was the aftermath of a morning's ablutions: the towels piled on the floor were damp; the shower curtain still dripped. The smell of toothpaste lingered. So whoever had just come in was the maid, right? The maid or whatever the male equivalent was: this was no time for PC semantics. He, she, it: they had a right to be here, and Sarah hadn't. And they knew Gerard had left — except they couldn't, could they, because his key was in her pocket. If it wasn't hanging on the board at reception, the maid would assume he was in his room.

The somebody moved. His hip — it was a he — passed into her eyeline, then out again. Grey or black trousers: the keyhole's dimness didn't allow for subtle variation. A hand flashed into view. And then she might have been alone, crouching by a bolted bathroom door; there was no noise for almost a minute, as if whoever it was was simply standing, taking in all the Gerard-junk — the nests of cables; the laundry; the leather case.

And what if it's a sneak thief? she thought. What if Gerard's about to be ripped off, while I hide here doing nothing?

There was something amusing about two people breaking into the same hotel room at the same time, but pardon me, pardon *me*, if I don't appreciate the humour just yet. Movement happened; the bed sighed as a weight descended on it; there was the snick of a clasp as something, probably Gerard's laptop, surrendered its lid. Of the man himself, nothing . . . Not a sneak thief. A thief would carry off the laptop without pausing to review its contents. But someone versed in silent invasion all the same; someone who could adjust to another's surroundings, and move comfortably within their space: calibrate their possessions, breathe their air, all without leaving any telltale scratches on the atmosphere; no coughs or sighs; no rustle of clothing. A ghost, playing with a machine. Sarah's mobile trilled into life.

*Da-da da-dah da-da-da-dah-dah*

She snatched it from her pocket, hitting buttons as she did; a meaningless string of numbers threaded across its screen and already a voice was barking tinny queries into the damp air — she'd hit the wrong bloody button; answered the call instead of killing its ring. Not that it would have made a difference; the noise was out; had slipped through the keyhole to dance round

Gerard's room. Any moment, whoever it was would batter the bathroom door. An unfamiliar terror grabbed Sarah's throat — she was in the wrong, caught where she shouldn't be; it was the inverse of those nights you woke at a sudden sound, wondering who was creeping about downstairs. Wide-eyed she looked round, as if a disguise, or a way of escape, or a cast-iron reason for being there would present itself, but found only damp air and a dripping shower curtain and a tinny voice repeating *Sarah?* until she turned the phone off. From the bedroom, footsteps approached the bathroom door, and then whoever it was paused, as if listening intently, waiting for a password to be called out: proof of friendship, or membership of the same burglars' club. She held her breath. There were too many films where this happened, and she had seen too many of them; films where a woman cowered on one side of a flimsy wooden door, while a man with a wolfish grin crouched on the other, nostrils flaring. Axes were sometimes involved. She heard a crack — a strangely organic, splintery noise — and understood half a second later what it was; not the first assault on the door, but the noise a man's knees could make when he was straightening up from a crouch . . . There were no footsteps. But a moment later came the faint sound of a door opening, then closing. She was alone. She was almost certain she was alone.

The curtain dripped. The damp air waited. The loudest noise was her own heartbeat; a percussive lollop slowing to a canter. She closed her eyes, and let her head fall into her hands. Her brow was wet. Truth to

82

tell, she felt clammy all over. And what she really needed to do was get out of here, and back to her own room.

Before she could move, her phone rang again.

*Da-da da-dah da-da da-dah-dah*

*I want you back.* A ringtone Russ had downloaded for her after a minor row.

Her hand shook badly as she pressed the button to receive the call.

"Sarah?"

"Gerard?"

"What just happened, you drop the phone or something? Where are you?"

She allowed that question a moment or two to be forgotten about, but his silence forced an answer. "I'm at the hotel, Gerard. Having a rest."

"Yes, well, it's lunchtime. How long'll it take you to get to the city centre?"

"Gerard —"

"Only we're famished. So you really ought to get a move on."

He gave her a street name, a restaurant, and was gone, leaving her sitting on his bathroom floor, looking at the damp heap of towels he'd abandoned earlier.

She stood. If she allowed her nerves to have their way, she'd remain rooted to the spot, unable to open the door in case the exiting noises had been a ruse, and he — whoever he was — was still out there, waiting. Paralysis, though, wasn't a sensible choice, so she threw back the bolt and emerged like a legitimate tenant, to find the room empty. She released the breath she'd not been aware of holding. Nothing looked different. The prowler had left everything the way he'd found it.

While she herself, of course, was empty-handed.

It seemed a paltry return. There must be something she could salvage, to convince herself this hadn't been a pointless breach of trust . . . "Well, all right, then," she said out loud. Sheer bravado. But all right, then. One last look.

The laptop remained tempting, but was hopeless; the suitcase, she'd already searched. On the dresser was the same scatter of loose change, tissues, house keys, and business cards — she picked these up, and slipped them from their elastic band. Topmost was one Brian Harper: a name and two numbers; landline and mobile. The name was vaguely familiar, but too ordinary for her to be sure. She thrummed the deck as if it were one of those flickbooks, with little stickmen dancing under her thumb, and surveyed the room. The wardrobe — she hadn't checked the wardrobe. This didn't take long to rectify, but it held nothing to grab her attention: shirts and suits on hangers, a spare blanket on a shelf. Sarah dropped to peer under the bed. Nothing there either, bar a flock of dust bunnies. She rose slowly, brushed her knees with her free hand, used the other to steady herself on the bed, and dropped the business cards, which hit the floor and fanned out wide: *bugger*, she thought, stooping to gather them up. He wouldn't have memorized their order, surely? Brian Harper was topmost; the rest she stacked as they came to hand. One or two had landed face down. She turned them over. The first was Zoë's.

Sarah rewrapped the cards in their elastic band and put them back where she found them. Then turned the light off and left the room.

# CHAPTER
## SIX

The restaurant, tucked off one of the main shopping arteries, had mirrors lining the walls on which the day's specials had been scrawled in red crayon. This rendered them illegible, but the effect was nice. Half a dozen pairs of lunchers provided ambient chatter, while over in a corner two tables had been pushed together. She could see Gerard, his back to her. With him were three others. "*We're* famished," he'd said. She hadn't noticed at the time.

She faltered at the doorway, and might have turned and slipped away if one of Gerard's companions hadn't spotted her first.

Jack Gannon waved; mimed *over here*.

There was no turning back. As she approached the table Jack stood, and pulled a chair out.

"Thank you."

"Fruitful morning?"

"I did what needed doing. I'm sorry, I didn't realize you were having a business lunch. Gerard, you should have said."

He really should have.

"All done and dusted," he replied. "I've been wandering round. Taking in the sights." He put invisible quote marks round the word.

"By yourself?"

"These chaps had better things to do. We've just reconvened. Did you meet Harper last night? Brian Harper, Sarah Tucker."

Harper was the white-haired man from the party. "We weren't introduced." He shook Sarah's hand. "But I saw you of course. Brightening the room."

"Token woman," John M. Wright offered. A beat or two after the other men, he too had made it to his feet.

"Does that charm school do refunds?" Gerard asked Jack. Then said to Sarah, "You met Mr Wright, I think. And Jack Gannon."

They sat. Harper poured Sarah a glass of wine. Jack handed her a menu. Wright stared, lips pursed. Perhaps he was worried she'd eat his share of lunch.

Eat? Drink wine? After the morning she'd had? It would be like picnicking over a grave. But she was hungry.

She glanced at Gerard, who was studying his menu. He had Zoë's business card among his collection, and coincidence's lease had just expired.

"So," she said. "Successful meeting?"

"Could be," Gerard said.

"Mr Inchon is very interested in my research," Wright said.

Jack said, "I'm sure Ms Tucker doesn't want to hear about a business meeting."

Ms Tucker was pretty sure she did. Anything that might cast light on what Gerard was up to.

Brian Harper asked her, "Have you visited the Baltic yet?"

Small talk. It was like hitting a sharp curve in a road. "The gallery? Not yet, no. Not this time, I mean. I've been before."

"How about the Laing?"

"The Laing?"

"More art. Less modern."

Jack Gannon leaned across. "They have a number of John Martins. Do you know his work?"

"The name rings a bell. I might be thinking of someone else."

A waiter came, took their orders, collected menus.

"Local artist," Jack went on. "Nineteenth century. He painted these big biblical extravaganzas, full of sound and fury. Very popular in his day, but he's fallen from favour since."

"Story goes, they used to need crowd control when he exhibited new work," Harper said. "He was the Hollywood blockbuster of his time."

"I don't see the point of art," Wright said.

"Well," Gerard said after the moment of silence that followed this. "That's admirably focused of you."

"I just don't see its use."

"Which doesn't mean it has nothing to teach us," Gerard said smoothly. He picked up his glass; revolved it by rolling the stem between finger and thumb. Light splintered off its contents. "This Martin chap. Didn't he paint the destruction of Sodom and Gomorrah?"

Harper nodded. "Yes. He did."

"There you go," Gerard told Wright. "The terrible vengeance of a righteous God. We can all learn something from that."

**88**

Gerard, Sarah decided, would only surprise her when he stopped being surprising. It didn't look like their current encounter was going to include that development.

When the waiter brought their starters, she had to be reminded what she'd ordered.

All of this had a surreal quality, as if she'd wandered from one story into another. If she looked at her watch, she'd know to the minute how long it had been since she'd borne witness to that body on the slab; how long since she'd cowered in Gerard's bathroom, listening to breathing on the other side of a locked door. And now there was duck salad, and conversation in a well-lit restaurant with three men she didn't know and a fourth who was hiding something. The impulse came to heave cutlery to the floor. But she couldn't. Partly, of course, this was social training. But underneath was the awareness that both stories were part of a whole; that whatever had brought Zoë to Newcastle was bound up with what Gerard was doing here . . . There'd been a soggy clump of business cards in Zoë's drowned wallet; a single pristine example in Gerard's collection. It would be difficult to ask him about this without revealing that she'd been in among his things.

Conversation had slipped back Gerard's way.

"First advice I give about taking over a company," Gerard said, "is sack the HR and PR departments."

"How very broad-minded of you," she said.

"Not really." Sarcasm bothered him the way kittens bother tanks. "It's like buying a second-hand car. Before you do anything else, you knock the rust off."

"You've never bought a second-hand car in your life."

"But I'm capable of making that imaginative leap."

"I thought we were staying off business?" Brian Harper reminded them.

John M. Wright's knife scraped against his plate, making everyone else jump.

Jack Gannon said, "Well, we'd better steer clear of religion and politics too. How about family. You got a son and heir waiting to take up the reins, Gerard?"

He seemed to lose focus. "I'm sorry?"

"You have children?"

"Never been blessed, old man." He picked up the wine bottle and waggled it in the air, indicating its emptiness to the waiter. "How about you?"

"A daughter. She lives with her mother."

Harper had two children: one of each, both grown. Wright offered no information.

The waiter delivered another bottle, sparing Sarah's contribution to the topic.

"Aye, thanks," Brian Harper said. His accent was thicker addressing the waiter than it was when talking to her or Gerard.

But there was nothing unusual about that. Most people adjusted their social face depending on who they were talking to. And she liked the Geordie voice; was collecting specimens of it. *How, man, woman, man*, she'd heard an exasperated male address a female companion: Sarah hadn't parsed that yet, but "man" was obviously doing two jobs. She'd also divined that "wuh" meant both "us" and "our", and also "me" and "mine". And possibly other things too.

Harper asked Gerard, "How long are you here?"

"Plan to be back in civilization day after tomorrow at the latest."

"Well, we'd hate to keep you longer than you're comfortable."

"No danger of that, old man." He'd finished his first glass from the new bottle already. Sarah, who'd never dream of tallying anyone else's drinks, wondered if she'd seen him quaffing at this rate before. "So if you want me to look at this place of yours, this afternoon might be the time."

"Works for me."

"Mind if we tag along?" Jack Gannon asked.

The we presumably covered John M. Wright, who'd finished eating, and whose abstracted expression suggested he was remembering something more interesting that happened to him once somewhere else.

"What place is this?" she asked.

"A property," Gerard said abruptly.

"It's a cinema," Harper told her.

"You own a cinema?"

"Not quite. But I have an interest in a concern that owns a building that used to be a cinema. On a pretty prime site, in fact, but legal wrangles have kept it in development limbo for some time."

"But it's still a cinema?"

"A fleapit," Jack said. "One of your actual local picture houses, exactly like you don't get any more. Only it hasn't shown a film in, what, ten years?"

"More than," Harper said. "But if you mean, does it still have an auditorium and all the rest, then yes, it does. Bit dilapidated, mind."

"I saw *The Italian Job* there," Jack offered. "And *The Magnificent Seven*."

"Ah, sweet bird of youth," Gerard said.

He's drunk, Sarah thought. Maybe I am, too. She'd had just one glass, but added to what she'd put away last night, it had probably tipped her back into the ditch.

She said, "Moving into the entertainment biz, Gerard?"

He looked aghast, as if she'd suggested he was planning a chain of brothels. "It's a *property*," he repeated, slowly. "It *used* to be a cinema."

Wright said, "It might be just the place I've been looking for."

"For a research lab?" She couldn't see it, somehow.

"We're a long way off that," Gerard said. "A very long way."

This, too, was said slowly.

Wright's eyes turned flinty, but he didn't reply.

Harper said, "Well, like I say, I'm free this afternoon. We could go and have a look now."

"Let's finish eating, first."

"Of course. I didn't —"

Gerard grinned evilly.

Sarah looked at Harper, and decided it was quite an effort for him to swallow a response.

They ate, and another bottle of wine was drunk. Sarah switched to fizzy water. But whenever the

92

conversation stalled, whenever the ring of cutlery echoed round the restaurant, she was dragged back to her morning's viewing: a white body, with curly black hair, stretched out on a slab like cold meat.

"Are you all right?" Jack asked her.

"I'm — yes, I'm fine. Thanks. I'm all right."

"You look a bit out of it."

"Probably train lag."

Over coffee, Gerard regaled them with tales of business triumph. She suspected there were various hidden messages here, not least of which was that he wanted them to think him the kind of bore who would blather on about his business triumphs; while at the same time letting them know about some of his business triumphs. The suspicion forced her to revise her opinion of how drunk he was.

When the last refill had been seen off, and Gerard had settled the bill without even pretending there was any chance he wouldn't, they gathered outside on the pavement. It had grown colder, and the wind had picked up. A lost seagull swam across the sky.

"So how do we get to this place of yours?"

It seemed Sarah was part of this excursion. That was okay. She wanted to stick to Gerard for the moment.

"We can take the Metro."

"The *Metro*?"

"It's a good service."

But Gerard was looking puzzled. "Is there a taxi strike?"

"When was the last time you took the tube?" Sarah asked.

"Can't recall. It was full of Bay City Rollers fans, if that helps."

"Seriously, Inchon, it'll take half the time."

"Oh, well. If we must."

Sarah suspected that all he'd wanted was the Lady Bracknell moment.

The nearest station was round the corner, and Brian Harper took charge: bought tickets, ushered them down the escalator, positioned them at the optimum point on the clean and tidy platform. "It's not so much like the tube, is it?" he asked.

"More like Barcelona," Sarah offered.

Harper liked that, she could tell. "Feels like it, some days," he said. "Number of foreign students we get."

Probably not the way to impress Gerard, Sarah thought but didn't say. Then an emerging wind from the tunnel heralded the arrival of the train.

She was delighted to find that you could sit at the front of a Metro and look out of the window. She'd never seen a train tunnel unwind in front of her before; didn't get much of a chance to do that now, because the train pulled overground all too soon. And then they were in the northern suburbs; the train riding through a small valley whose edges were lined by scrabbly bushes. The next stop was theirs.

"Told you it wouldn't take long," Harper said.

"Probably full of drunks in the evening," Gerard said.

"And some lunchtimes too," Sarah suggested.

They crossed the tracks on the pedestrian bridge, and already they could see it. The cinema — it called

**94**

itself a picture house; the words painted across its upper storey in large letters — sat on a corner diagonally opposite the station entrance, and had evidently been closed for years. Bare brick oblongs on its whitewashed walls indicated where posters for future attractions had hung, but that future seemed used up. No windows were visible, barring a row of blackened, book-sized panes at attic-level. The shelter covering its doorway might once have kept rain off the queues, but now resembled the lowered eyelid of a building just barely conscious.

"You called it a fleapit," she said to Jack.

"And I don't think I can be accused of talking it up."

John M. Wright said, as if answering a question, "Lack of natural light is actually an advantage when you're trying to maintain a controlled environment."

Harper and Gerard reached the foot of the steps and crossed the road first. There were parked cars, but few people in sight. The shape of the junction suggested that there'd once been a station car park, perhaps occupying the space where a housing development now stood. Undramatic residential streets fed away somewhere more central, that lay out of sight. The whole place seemed to be holding its breath.

The cinema, on the other hand, seemed to have breathed its last.

Flanked by Gannon and Wright, she joined Gerard and Harper on the opposite pavement. Heavy metal security panels were bolted in place across the doors. From one hung a padlock the size of Sarah's hand. Even as she noticed this Brian Harper was approaching it, taking from his pocket a key twice the size of Sarah's finger.

"I can't help feeling there'll be spiders," Sarah said.

"There'll be no spiders," Gerard promised.

"What makes you so sure? There's bound to be spiders." The word *spiders* had dropped from a web in Sarah's mind and was scuttling round, enjoying a sticky purchase on her imagination. Spiders.

"Sarah." Gerald looked at her, all seriousness. "This place has been closed for years. Any spiders will have been eaten by the rats long ago."

The creak of the door as Harper pushed it open might have been an escaping sound effect.

"Ladies first?" Gerard offered.

Die screaming, she conveyed with a glance.

Harper said, "Allow me," and produced a pencil-thin torch.

Did he always carry that? she wondered. And the keys — had he known they'd be coming here? And then thought: well, he was always going to suggest it. Given which, he'd have been foolish not to bring key and torch.

Gannon stepped inside on Harper's heels and said, "Careful. There's steps, and some broken glass."

He was talking to her, she thought.

Gerard waved her ahead, and she went with the flow. Better than being stranded outside with John M. Wright. As she stepped inside, Harper's torch beam played on the floor in front of her like a spotlight. It took a moment for her eyes to adjust to the gloom.

96

In the centre of the lobby sat what had presumably been the ticket booth and was now half a shell, in whose lee a slew of broken glass and plaster crumbs sheltered. The surrounding walls remained upright, if tatty and peeling, with empty poster frames at intervals — she was imagining Hollywood heyday fare, *Gone with the Wind* and *Road to Morocco*, but this place had functioned up until the mid-nineties; had probably sold its last box of popcorn to a Tarantino fan.

The booth's remains sat at the top of a flight of shallow steps, beyond which, from one corner, steeper stairs led up to the circle. Access to the stalls was to Sarah's right. A pair of doors used to hang there, and the empty space now beckoned them into an even darker arena where the air smelt fungally damp. Was this anywhere Sarah wanted to be, after a trip to the morgue?

Gerard, at her back, was breathing heavily, as if he'd walked here. Wright hung behind, silhouetted in the doorway. The world outside felt years away, as if all the time that had gone to waste in here had swallowed them once they'd entered. Her throat was dry. She tried to swallow, but couldn't.

"You might want to wait a moment," Harper said.

His torch beam skittered across the wall and located a row of switches. When he threw them, a watery light filtered down; just enough, it seemed to Sarah, to frighten the smaller shadows away.

Gerard leaned in close. "Did you hear that?" he asked.

"What? Did I hear what?"

"Oh," he said. "It was probably nothing."

If I kill him now, and these others don't tell, his body might never be found, Sarah thought.

It was on the tip of her tongue to say she'd wait outside — that she really didn't like this — when something in what Gerard had said struck her. Not the words, but a slight quaver. Was he frightened? It might have been fear; might have been excitement. Excitement at knowing she was afraid? There'd been a time when she'd have believed that of him, but now she was less confident. He'd make jokes about spiders and unseen beasties, sure, but she was pretty sure he'd stamp on either if it came too close to her. But a frightened Gerard was a new thing. She'd have to stay.

Jack Gannon took her arm as she walked up the steps. "There've been exterminators here a time or two. Besides, any rats'll have disappeared under the floorboards the moment we opened the door."

She lived in the country. She knew about rats. They'd disappear under the floorboards when it damn well suited them and not a moment sooner. But she didn't want to worry him, so kept this to herself.

Besides, it wasn't rats that bothered her. It was spiders. They had them in the country too, which was the single worst thing about it. Including the hunting lobby.

Harper threw more switches. "The auditorium's through here. Well, you'd probably guessed that." Lights went on in the big arena. "It's a bit musty, but really nothing to worry about."

Gerard said, "Well, I want to see it. Damn waste of time otherwise."

Sarah mentally added a *What!* to that.

Jack said, "Sarah? We can wait outside if you'd rather."

"I've always liked going to the pictures," she said.

Behind them, Wright moved away from the doorway, and closed it.

Harper led the way into the auditorium.

The first thing Sarah noticed was the way the floor felt under her feet; then she forgot about that and took in the view. It was a cinema, yes: the floor sloped towards the front, and there was a stage, atop of which a screen used to hang, though there was no screen any more — just a dark space whose depth she couldn't gauge, on one side of which a red curtain still hung. A dim pile on the other suggested that its partner had collapsed some while ago. But the screen, or its absence, wasn't what grabbed her attention; it was everything else — it was the rest of the place.

Again, she tried to swallow. Again, she couldn't.

Maybe half of the seats had been ripped out, with no apparent logic dictating which, and over the remaining rows bridal veils had been laid, or that was how it appeared at first — grand thick lacy veils had been dropped over the cinema furniture, forming silvery-grey canopies between the armrests of adjoining seats; making sheiks' tents in the gaps between rows. And hammocks of it were slung from one broken sconce to the next; there were traces of it hanging from the balcony, drifting in the draught that blew through the

**99**

missing doors behind her. All of it spider-web. It was as if she'd had a nightmare, and here it was: upholstered. It was everywhere, or everywhere except on this aisle that led towards the stage, like a path through a jungle. To her left, to her right; above her — if there were light enough to penetrate the upper darkness, she knew she'd see more of it up there, hanging over this huge space like a marquee over a crypt, its sticky canvas studded with the raisin-like corpses of spiders, and the well-wrapped parcels of their prey. Hidden in the corners would be nests of shiny eggs, pulsing to an arachnid beat. A high-pitched spider music that crawled through your hair, and made your scalp itch.

The floor was sticky. That was the first thing she'd noticed, and she noticed it again now.

Harper said, "As you can see, it's a bit of a mess."

Gerard laughed a big booming laugh, which went shivering round the empty space. "You have a gift for understatement," he said.

Nothing about his demeanour suggested he'd ever heard the word *fear*. She wondered what it was she'd noticed thrill through him earlier, then had to suppress a shudder of her own. "Are you sure this place is safe?" Her voice didn't ring true to her own ears. If it had been a glass, she'd have held it to the light to check for cracks.

Brian Harper said, "The structure's sound, don't worry. The furnishings aren't, though. I wouldn't sit down."

"That's not going to be a problem," she assured him tightly.

Jack Gannon was right behind her. He said again, "We can wait outside, if you'd rather."

"I'm okay. Thanks."

"It's not you I'm worried about."

She glanced at him, but he smiled: joke. It was okay for men to make such jokes, provided everyone knew it was a joke, and they weren't actually afraid of, say, spiders.

Gerard said, "Square footage?"

Harper started talking numbers; mentioned the graded floor, which levelling off wouldn't be a problem. The building would take three storeys. Wright had stepped past Sarah to listen to this, or at least to be quite near it while it was being delivered. She wasn't sure he listened to much, unless it lay precisely within the sphere of his interest. Though perhaps he was hoping this would turn out that way.

Gerard didn't look at him, she noticed. Gerard didn't appear to like him, which was understandable. But if Gerard decided that John M. Wright was a blue-chip investment, he'd probably find a way to get over his dislike.

Sarah felt something crawl across her cheek.

She yelped, slapped at herself, and everyone turned to look. Gannon reached out and put a hand on her shoulder.

"Sarah —?"

"It's nothing, it's okay." The draught had brushed her cheek, that was all. "I thought —"

She didn't need to tell them what she'd thought. It was screamingly obvious.

"You thought what?" Wright asked.

"Oh, for God's sake," Gannon said.

There were no spiders: not on her cheek, nor anywhere near. That was what she told herself.

Gerard said, "What's the stage area like? I can't see it from here."

"You go on and look," Gannon said. "Sarah and I'll wait outside."

All of this she was hearing as if through a bottle held to her ear.

. . . Once, she'd been prone to panics; wild moments at which reason threatened to escape her, and she'd have to bite down on reality — clench her nails into her palms — to prevent her mind revisiting an appalling episode: the step she'd taken, armed only with gravity, from the roof of a four-storey dwelling. This had happened when she was little more than an adolescent, and she'd had waking visitations for years afterwards, with the capacity to reduce her to a whispering wreck. There were any number of triggers, most of which occurred in public — sudden loud noises; sudden fast movement: these could conjure up those brief moments which had taught her she'd never fly. And here was another: in this dim-lit spidery palace, she was having that waking nightmare all over again, in which she skydived from the roof of a high terraced house, city lights cartwheeling in her head as she turned over and over, and never hit the ground.

". . . You okay yet?"

They were outside. She had no memory of the last minute.

102

"Sarah?"

Deep breath. "Jack. Thank you. Yes, I'm okay now."

And she was — she more or less was.

They were on the wide apron of pavement on the cinema's doorstep. Gerard, Harper and Wright were still inside. Part of her curdled with embarrassment at the thought that she hadn't been able to hack it — already, she was starting to find her own fears ridiculous — but they'd been real at the time, and would be again, if she set foot in that place once more. A warmth at her elbow suggested that Jack's hand had guided her out. She shut her eyes; made herself as aware as she could be of her body. And there was nothing there. She was nearly positive about this. No eight-legged passengers had smuggled themselves out in her folds or crevices — or if they had, they were keeping very still — NO! No. There was nothing there. She was spider-free, and staying that way. She opened her eyes and Jack quickly looked away, as if he'd just seen someone he knew crossing the bridge over the railway line.

"Really," she said. "I'm fine."

"Not much of a place for a post-prandial wander."

"I'm not big on spiders."

Gerard, she thought, would have jumped on that; twisted it round to place *big* and *spiders* next to each other.

"Who is?" He produced a packet of cigarettes. "Want one of these?"

She was tempted, but shook her head.

He said, "I shouldn't either, you know? But once in a blue moon, what harm can it do?"

A small man-made cloud drifted down the road.

She looked behind her, at the door into the dark they'd just come through, and said, "A research facility?"

He said, "You're seeing the cinema. The auditorium, the tapered floor. The rows of seats."

"I'm seeing the spiders."

"We'll come to an arrangement with the spiders. What Gerard's looking at, what Brian's showing him, is square footage. Lots of space in there."

"The right kind of space?"

"I'm not an expert. I think Brian's got a few other places."

Sarah nodded absently. A Metro was pulling up at the station. She said, "Your Mr Wright's a strange one."

"Because he's a scientist?"

"Because he's a strange one."

"He's very focused."

"That's one way of putting it."

Jack smiled and blew out smoke. "He's worked for years on his research. I think he tends to see things in terms of, will this help the project or not?"

"Things?"

"Okay. People."

The Metro pulled away.

"And he doesn't go anywhere without you holding his hand?"

"I'm not his keeper. But if Inchon's going to invest in Wright's research, then we'll be partners, more or less. I'm just keeping an eye on what develops."

"But he's only one plum in your pie."

"Ha! If you want to put it like that."

*Da-da da-dah da-da da-dah-dah*

He blinked.

"My phone. Excuse me."

Sarah took a step away from him to answer it, in line with the developing etiquette. It was Vicky, Zoë's web-wizard — *web*: she shuddered. "Vicky. Hi."

"I got into her e-mails."

"Ah."

"You want to start with the earliest?"

She glanced at Jack. "Now's not a great moment. Can I call you back?"

"I suppose."

"It won't be long. Thanks."

Jack said, "Nice ringtone. The Jacksons?"

"'I Want You Back'."

"Innocent days."

For the world, or just for Michael, she wondered. "Motown fan?"

"Used to be. Don't listen to music much any more."

Her hand had tightened round her mobile phone, and she deliberately relaxed it, so the whitening of her knuckles didn't betray her tension.

Harper, Gerard and John M. Wright emerged from the cinema, and stood blinking for a moment in the cold air.

Gerard said, "Makes it feel like you've got them in your hair, doesn't it? Place like that."

Sarah said, "Those of us who've got hair, sure."

Everyone laughed, and she pretended to join in. But she was thinking *Motown fan*.

Alan Talmadge was a Motown fan.

# CHAPTER
# SEVEN

They took the Metro back into the city centre, and went their separate ways at Monument. *Al-an Tal-madge* had been the rattling of the rails all the way. *Al-an Tal-madge Al-an Tal-madge*. It rang so clearly through the carriage, Sarah was surprised no one remarked on it; she kept waiting for Jack Gannon's reaction — except he couldn't be Talmadge, could he? Talmadge had come from nowhere, and was no one. Zoë had said so: trying to get a handle on Talmadge had been like making a fist around smoke. He'd simply passed through various women's lives, taking those lives with him when he left. If he'd come from anywhere real, Zoë would have tracked him down — if Talmadge hadn't been smoke, she'd have had him. And Gannon wasn't smoke. He had family. Roots. And lots of people liked Motown.

This was the point, and this calmed her down. Lots of people liked Motown. Once you removed that from the equation, there was nothing to link Gannon to Talmadge or to Zoë. Sarah had met him in the hotel Zoë had stayed in, and that was all. The Motown ringtone hadn't even been his: it had been Sarah's own, loaded by Russell. It made more sense to think Russ was Talmadge.

"You weren't really attacked by a spider, were you?" Gerard asked her once they were alone.

"No. But thanks for your concern."

"I think Gannon would have come to your rescue."

That wasn't a line she wanted him pursuing. "So long as I wasn't depending on Wright."

If Gerard had been drunk before, he was over it now. "Shall we walk down through town?" he asked.

"If you like. Where are we, exactly?"

He gave her a long-suffering look. "Don't worry. We're not lost."

There were plenty of people around. There was no reason for this to surprise her — it was a big city — but her day had long passed normal: bodies, burglary, spiders . . . It would have felt fitting if the streets were deserted, in the aftermath of something namelessly huge. Also, it was cold. She checked her coat's buttons. She loved its cut and its length, but today would be a good day for it to be longer, thicker, warmer.

She also hoped there was no spiderweb stuck to it.

She said, "A research facility?", aware that it was the second time she'd framed that question.

Gerard said, "Time will tell."

"Bit out of your usual line, isn't it?"

"The usual lines in business," he told her, "come to sudden ends." He put a hand out to stop her crossing a road just as a car flashed past. "Nobody stays ahead without changing their game when it's needed."

"It's like listening to a motivational tape," she said. "What are your rules for success?"

"Number one would be, don't step into the road without looking."

"Are you really planning on investing in that man? Wright?"

"Do I get the impression you don't like him?"

"It's like he's just visiting earth," Sarah said. "And hasn't got the hang of it yet."

"I'm sure people said the same of Einstein."

"You don't seriously put him in that league?"

"No," said Gerard. "I just couldn't think of any non-famous scientists."

They'd walked down an impressive street: elegantly curved, with tall graceful buildings, but left it now for a side road. Gerard seemed to know where he was going. She wondered how much of this was natural sense of direction, and how much sitting down with a map beforehand. That was the kind of preparation successful businessmen did, she supposed, although she couldn't remember seeing a map in his room — a thought that struck her like a cartoon anvil, leaving a guilt-shaped dent in her head. She had been in Gerard's room without his knowledge, and now was pretending to be his friend. Or not exactly pretending, perhaps, but this fact remained: he had one of Zoë's business cards. There might be an innocent reason for this, but none sprang immediately to mind.

Gerard had spoken again, but she'd missed whatever it was, and made a non-committal noise. He looked at her strangely, but didn't pursue it.

She should make an effort. Stay within the moment. They passed a cosmetics shop; then a clothes store with various brand names stencilled on its plate glass: Christian Dior all the way down to Diesel. A good example of bets being hedged, Sarah thought.

It caught Gerard's attention too. "Clothing to die for," he said. "*Dolce et Gabbana est pro mori*."

"That's not the first time you've said that, is it?"

"It's the first time anyone's got it."

There was a compliment in there, but it was aimed as much at himself as at her. "Does Paula take you shopping?"

"From designer labels to my wife. What a seamless shift. You think she's shallow, don't you?"

That stung, largely because the answer was yes. "It was the Latin made me think of her. She has such classically good looks."

"Nice try."

Sarah said, "I don't feel I got to know her well."

"I don't feel you made much of an effort."

The shops dwindled into office blocks. They walked past the cathedral, then under a metal railway bridge and on to a cobbled square where the city keep stood. From there, Gerard led her down into a minor labyrinth of alleyways and stone steps and chunks of Hadrian's Wall.

"Is this a shortcut?"

"It's the scenic route."

On a terrace overlooking the Tyne, in the shadow of the High Level, he stopped to gaze upriver at a bunch

**110**

of grubby seagulls, fighting over scraps on the oil-flecked water.

"Perhaps you're right," she said. "About Paula. I'm sorry."

He shrugged. "Nothing to be sorry about. It's not like she craved your friendship."

Sarah deserved that. She watched the seagulls for a while, wondering if their abrupt clattering had a personal aspect, born of gull-on-gull enmity rather than a straight-forward tussling over food. Though if one bird didn't like another, it could simply fly away . . . "The Trophy Wife" was how she'd characterized Paula. Who was a decade younger than Gerard, and had been blonde when Sarah met her, with a figure loaded with natural advantage, but doubtless maintained in an expensive gym. And always draped, whenever Sarah had met her, in seriously costly threads. Even now, picturing her, it was with a copy of *Hello!* under one arm. I am woman, see me shop. What was that joke about a lifestyle being what the rich had, instead of a life?

But there she went again. Paula had a life. It was just that Sarah wasn't privy to it.

Guilt, probably, led her to say, "She was adopted, wasn't she?"

That hit a nerve. "Who on earth told you that?"

"You did." He must have done. How else would she know?

"Yes." The word came out grudgingly. "You paid some attention, then."

Oh, for God's sake. It wasn't like he'd asked about her own life; her own partner. It made her wonder what was wrong. Touchiness suggested bruising. "You're different when you're with her, I noticed that much. You'd do anything for her, wouldn't you?"

He said, "I'd kill for her, if that's what you mean. Quite happily, as a matter of fact."

She didn't doubt it. When lists were compiled of motives for violence, love and money topped the list. Not hatred and money. "Did you ever think about children?"

"There's really no need, Sarah."

"I'm not sure I —"

"All these questions. This interest. You're feeling guilty about what I said earlier. About not making an effort. Well, I absolve you." He made a clumsy hand movement, and she remembered he was Catholic. "Let's not talk about it any more."

"Okay."

"And she doesn't, by the way. Take me shopping, I mean."

"No. That doesn't surprise me, somehow."

"Men only shop twice a year," he said. "During sales."

"If women did the same, we'd have a migrant retail industry."

He laughed, a short sharp bark. "I might borrow that."

They moved on. She wasn't sure where they were, exactly, but they were presumably closing in on the hotel. Where they might, for all she knew, be swept up

**112**

into more impromptu networking, perhaps culminating in an expedition to — what — a deconsecrated church? A dried-out aquarium? If she wanted to tackle him on Zoë, now was the time.

Sometimes, the direct approach was best.

"You never met Zoë, did you?" she asked.

"Your friend? The one who helped you that time?"

"She saved my life," Sarah said.

"Then it was a very good thing she did," Gerard said. He paused for a moment, perhaps unused to making such statements. Certainly unused to making them in Sarah's hearing. "No. I never met her."

A body on a slab: white face, dark hair. Bloated beyond recognition, unless you knew what you were looking for. Or expected to find it.

She said, "She was here."

"Newcastle?"

"Yes. She stayed in the Bolbec."

"Ah. Is that why you chose it? Personal recommendation? Hmph." He produced a cigar from an inner pocket, and unwrapped it. "I applaud her feats of derring-do, obviously. But I don't think much of her taste in accommodation."

"Do you mind not smoking?"

"Not especially. I prefer smoking, though." He lit up. "For God's sake, Sarah, we're in the open air. I'll bend to the legislation where it's necessary, but . . ."

"They'll never take your freedom?"

"Precisely."

A waft of smoke drifted into Sarah's face, here in the open air.

He said, "Wait one moment. What was her surname?"

"Boehm."

"Boehm? Good lord!"

"Gerard?"

"I found her business card. On the mantelpiece in the bar. First night I was here."

"Zoë's card?"

"I put it in my pocket. Force of habit. Never made the connection, though. Don't think I knew her surname. Did it say private eye on it? That's what she is, yes? A consulting detective?"

"That's what she is, yes," Sarah said slowly, trying to slot this new information into what she already knew. Or subtract it, rather. Subtract this new information from what she'd thought she'd known. Which was like trying to remove an ingredient from a blender, once she'd flipped its switch.

"Doesn't say a lot for the staff, does it?" Gerard mused. "Leaving former guests' cards lying around the place. Still, makes you think, doesn't it? Weird coincidence. Of all the gin-joints in all the cities in all the world. That sort of thing."

She looked at him.

"*Casablanca*," he said. "Sorry. Not Jane Austen."

"I got the reference," she said tightly.

He blew smoke. "So, what was she doing here?"

"I don't know," Sarah said.

"I suppose we can rule out pleasure. On a case, was she?"

"I don't know," Sarah said again.

**114**

"I thought you were friends."

"We weren't in each other's pockets."

"Has something happened to her?"

"Why do you ask?"

"Because you're here," Gerard said. "I assume *that's* not coincidence."

Coincidence, she thought. She might have to revise her opinion on that subject.

They'd reached the railway arch, and turned left into it. Cars were parked along its length, in metered spaces. At the far end was the *Big Issue* seller, this time with an armful of his wares. Sarah recalled the use she'd made of him earlier, to distract Barry while she took Gerard's key, and felt the need to make amends. Or make Gerard make them for her, which would suit her mood.

"Buy your *Big Issue*, sir, lady? Yunno you wannoo."

"I already have," Sarah reminded him, though she appeared to ring none of his bells. "But my friend will take one."

Gerard looked at her. "You're referring to me?"

"It's cold, Gerard. And it's already dark. Buy the magazine."

"I fail to see what the weather's got to do with it."

The homeless man looked at him, then at Sarah. He seemed about to say something, but thought better of it.

"Because this man's here until he's sold all these copies."

"Lady's correck." He obviously couldn't help himself. "Need to sell the ress."

"Do you mind? This is a private discussion."

**115**

"Gerard! You can't —"

"Sarah. Do you understand the *economics* of homelessness? The cash-drink-drugs cycle? Now, I write cheques to various —"

It came on suddenly, born of everything the day had shovelled her way so far, and she couldn't remember the last time she'd been this angry. "Gerard. Stop talking right now. Buy the magazine. That's not a suggestion."

Gerard flashed his evil smile, the one that showed the points of his teeth. She was used to him getting a rise out of her — would maintain that it was water off a duck's — but it was unforgivable to use this man for effect. "Oh, I see. We're doing things your way, are we?" He handed over a fiver, took a magazine, and waved away the change. "Don't want to spoil the lady's day." He gave Sarah the *Big Issue*.

"Don't drink, guvnor," the man said.

"You really should give it a bash," Gerard assured him.

Magazine tucked under her arm, Sarah strode towards the hotel, not waiting to see if he was following.

Though if she'd heard him struck by a lorry, she'd have turned to watch.

In her room she flung the *Big Issue* at the wall, where it made a comforting *splat!* before hitting the floor like a concussed moth. If she'd been holding a bottle she'd have flung that instead, she told herself, half believing it. Then, as long she was throwing things, she threw herself on the bed, where she lay for a moment seething before getting up and taking her coat off in case it creased. She put it on a hanger, then occupied the bed again. Seethed more.

It occurred to her that he'd done that on purpose: lit her blue touch paper just to watch her shoot sparks. There were men who'd try that on for sexual reasons, obviously, but with Gerard you could never overlook the profit motive. There'd been something in it for him. Maybe it was just that she'd ceased asking questions he didn't want to answer. Except she hadn't got around to asking questions, had she? Before she'd raised the issue of Zoë's business card, he'd addressed it himself, and that pretty much left her all out of questions. Or at the very least, left her unsure it was Gerard she should be putting them to.

So think about that for a moment, Sarah. Think about Gerard taking the wind from your sails. Had he simply been trying to distract her attention?

She arranged herself into a more comfortable thinking position. The distraction theory was a possibility, but it would need working through. If Gerard had made up his story about finding Zoë's business card, it had to be because he knew Sarah had been in his room; had guessed she'd seen the card; and figured he needed a reason for having it. Except he couldn't *know* she'd been in his room — could only speculate — and why would he do that? Straightforward paranoia?

Well. You couldn't rule it out.

Because there was an aspect to their both being at the Bolbec that only dawned on Sarah now: if it wasn't a coincidence, then it must bother Gerard as much as it bothered her. She remembered his reaction on first seeing her: that flicker in his eyes. A hint of shock, or possibly fear. If it wasn't a coincidence, then Zoë must be the point of connection, because Sarah had no other reason for being here.

So maybe that was it: she'd brought up Zoë, and he'd just headed her off at the pass. He was a businessman, after all. They invented the contingency plan. And didn't have to be sure a bad thing might happen before working out ways of avoiding it.

A chain of reasoning which suggested one big shiny link: that Gerard having Zoë's card in his possession was a bad thing. Was something he needed an alibi for.

And then something else struck her. Gerard might have known she'd been in his room because he'd been there too.

Sarah sat very still after having that thought, as if movement would make her lose her mental footing. She became aware of sounds she hadn't noticed until then — that not far away, there was music playing; that the street outside was not deserted; that hotel rooms always *ticked*, as if her very presence were subject to a timer — but through all that, she clung to the thread she'd just cast through the day's maze. What if it had been Gerard himself who'd returned to his room while she was inside it? One of those possibilities which made you see the picture differently: now it was a vase; now it was a cat on a pogo-stick.

First things first, she thought. Was it even possible? She cast her mind back, and the timing worked. Gerard had been in a meeting, that much was true. He'd left the hotel when that taxi picked him up, and had headed off to join, as it turned out, Gannon, Harper and Wright. After which, they'd gone their separate ways. *I've been wandering round, taking in the sights. These chaps had better things to do. We've just reconvened.*

So he could have come back to the hotel.

Sarah shook her head; not because she was denying the train of thought she'd just boarded, but because it was too horribly plausible. Gerard had phoned her while she'd been cowering in his bathroom, yes, but could easily have done that from the other side of the door . . . She'd talked to him, but not until after the man in the room had left. He might have wandered no further than the floor below before calling again. It could have happened. It could have happened. She closed her eyes. The phone rang.

*Jesus* —

It was the room phone, on her bedside table. She stared at it a moment or two, as if it were an entirely unfamiliar object, before picking up.

"Ms Tucker?"

That twang. She knew who that was. "Barry?"

"Ah . . . You've not checked out."

"Oh, lord . . ."

"Don't worry, no biggie —"

Hotel rooms always *ticked*, as if your very presence were subject to a timer. Which, of course, it was.

"I should have been gone by noon, shouldn't I?"

**119**

"We have a twelve o'clock punch-out, but you weren't around. It's okay, Ms Tucker. Like I said, we're not exactly choking for space. Do I take it you want to stay another night?"

"Yes. Yes, I'd better. Look, I'll come down and —"

"No need. I'll change your booking. No one's gonna turf you out, don't worry."

"Thank you, Barry. That's really kind."

"No problem, miss."

"What time is it, anyway?"

It was dark outside — she'd drawn the curtain — but it was February, it was Newcastle. It had been dark for ages.

"Just gone seven thirty."

"Thanks, Barry."

She hung up. His voice had brought her back to reality, but she wasn't ready for great chunks of it yet. She didn't want to think any more about Gerard, about Talmadge, about Gannon, about spiders; she didn't want to eat again; didn't want to drink. Didn't know what she wanted, except maybe to sleep, but it was too early for that. She plucked the *Big Issue* from the floor, and collapsed back on the bed. Half-read an interview with a Hollywood star, whose hobo-chic rendered him plausibly homeless himself, then had to put it away when a *have you seen this woman?* box brought Zoë too painfully to mind. She thought of the river: how cold and black and heartless it ran; and how hard it must feel, approached from a height. Being in there for any length of time wouldn't do anyone good. The long-term effects would be dreadful, if the short-term effects hadn't killed you.

It was no good. She had to do something. There was no point being here otherwise.

Doing something without going anywhere meant her mobile phone, of course. Vicky had called earlier: she'd forgotten that. She dug her phone from her coat pocket. "Vicky? It's me. Sorry about earlier."

"I thought you were going to call straight back."

"Well, like I say, I wasn't able to talk."

"Only it's not like I'm not busy."

Sarah was about to apologize again, in standard Sarah fashion, then recalled that Vicky was used to dealing with Zoë. "Vicky? I couldn't talk, okay? Get over it. Now, what did you have for me?"

There was a pause, and she wondered if she'd hurt the girl's feelings. But then Vicky laughed. "You kind of sound like her."

"That's the effect I was aiming at," she admitted.

"Okay," Vicky said. "Well, I've got Zoë's e-mails. She kept her inbox pretty clean."

Sarah could believe it. Paranoiacs make good housekeepers.

"And she emptied her deleted folder regularly too. Not much in there. I can retrieve it for you, of course, but it'll take a little longer."

Of course. "What did you find?"

"What are you looking for?"

"Anything to do with a Gerard Inchon. G. Inchon. Or anything like that."

"Sec."

Sarah waited. *Zoë Boehm — what an extraordinary thing. I found her card, on the mantelpiece in the bar. So he said. So he said. What are the chances?* Billion to one.

"No. Nothing."

". . . Nothing at all?"

"Unless he's calling himself Mervyn Cleate. Nope, that's viagra. Or Douglas Button. Nope, that's viagra."

"I get the picture. Is that her inbox or her deleted stuff?"

"Both. I'm flipping between the two. The new mail in her inbox, the last two weeks' worth, is mostly spam, plus a couple that look like work offers. There's one from somewhere called Roleseeker Services, saying they've invoiced her for the names, whatever that means."

Probably headhunters. Zoë did background checks for headhunters, to weed out chancers with credentials downloaded from the web. "But nothing from Inchon."

"There's an odd one, though. Just from at."

"Just from at? What's that mean?"

"You know. At. The a with a little circle round it you get in e-mail addresses."

@, Sarah realized. "What's it say?"

"'Missing you'."

"That's all?"

"That's all. No return address or anything. So it's not been replied to."

"I didn't know you could do that. Send an e-mail without an address."

"Yeah, well. You can."

"When did it arrive?"

Vicky told her. It was the day after Zoë had checked out of the hotel.

"And she'd read it?"

"Opened it, certainly. Didn't delete it, either."

"But no reply."

"Nope."

"You're sure?"

"You get this little arrow icon when —"

"Right. Got you."

"So she didn't, no. But hang on. I haven't checked her sent items."

Sarah could hear Vicky clicking the mouse, talking to her computer. It didn't talk back. "No, that's wiped too. I can retrieve it from the server, but —"

"It'll take time, I know. Thanks, Vicky."

"No problem. I'll get back to you."

Sarah stood once the call was over. There wasn't a lot of room for pacing, but she needed to be on her feet. She walked to the window, pulled the curtain back. The street below was lamplit, with not a soul in sight.

@, she thought. At. A.T. Alan Talmadge.

# CHAPTER
# EIGHT

Down on that same street twenty minutes later Sarah felt insubstantial herself, as if, in peering into the ether Zoë had left behind her, she'd caused that ether to peer back into her. It had hollowed her out. A walking shadow, she made for the railway station; crossed the road upon reaching it, then headed up a slantwise street flanked by a hideous-looking club and a kebab shop. A board outside a newsagent's indicated that all was not well with the local football team, and she couldn't help absorbing this information even while more important things clamoured for her attention. Because this was what your head did, when it wasn't playing tricks. It stored information for later retrieval, when it might be just what you needed to ace the pub quiz.

Concentrate.

Of Talmadge's involvement, there could be no doubt. First the jacket; then the e-mail. He was not merely leaving his fingerprints at the scene, he was setting up flares around it, to mark his location to passing aircraft. And Zoë had known this; had either followed him here, or known she was being followed.

If she had been following, it was because Alan Talmadge had been leaving a trail. And the trail Alan Talmadge left was dead women.

Without breaking stride, Sarah pinched the bridge of her nose between finger and thumb. It was no simple task, deconstructing Zoë's motives. What she needed was Zoë's input. *You kind of sound like her*, Vicky had said . . . So, where would Zoë start? She'd start with Gerard. Gerard was involved somehow; was Zoë-connected, but denying it. And had acquired a list of names, at the top of which was Gannon's. Whatever Sarah had thought earlier about Gannon's roots — his substance; his family ties; all those things that made him definitely not Alan Talmadge — he still needed looking at. Which was why she was now headed straight for the brightly lit Asian grocery looming up on her left. Lots of cards taped to its windows, offering cheap foreign phone calls and Bollywood DVDs. Secondhand furniture for sale. And Internet connections, at 75p an hour.

The man at the counter was sweet, thanking her profusely for paying for the service he was providing, and pointing out the vending machine, which offered too much choice to tempt Sarah. Anything that produced coffee, cocoa, tea and cola from one nozzle was for emergencies only. But she sat on a stool next to a young Chinese woman and opened a browser. Instantly, she could have been anywhere. A browser was a portal, sucking the user inside. There were those who never emerged.

She Googled "Jack Gannon", added "Newcastle" to narrow it down, then had a rethink when all she hit were genealogical sites. Jack was a popular name, but wasn't it short for something else? Jackson? James? She reduced it to "J Gannon", which didn't help, then keyed "storage", and started getting hits on the family company. First up was its website, which didn't mention Jack, but whose "About us" page named one Michael Gannon as the firm's founder, originally Gannon Haulage of Walker. ReGoogling, she skipped through a page or two and found her attention snagged on a gobbet of text: *acquitted on charges of kidnapping and assault.*

Sarah clicked the link.

It opened a page on the local newspaper's archive which told her that Michael Gannon had been acquitted on charges of kidnapping and assault. These related to dealings he'd had with business rivals — rivals who'd since gone out of business. Quotes from Michael Gannon's solicitor indicated that all concerned were glad this ludicrous matter had been dismissed out of hand, and that any further suggestion that his client had been involved in the unfortunate events would be rigorously dealt with. The date was November '87. A photograph showed a man much heavier than Jack, moustached, and with a look in his eyes somewhere between triumph and contempt. It had been taken as he emerged from the court building. If he'd worn that expression during the trial, he'd probably have come up guilty.

She had no notebook. The shop sold them, but she wasn't sure there was any point. Jack Gannon's father had once stood trial for assault. With the snap judgement everyone's prey to, based on one photo, Sarah had decided he'd probably been guilty, but what difference did that make? So Jack's father was a local gangster: that didn't make Jack a psychopath. She returned to the search engine. With new terms to throw in the mix, she found more references to Gannon senior, but nothing on Jack. She sat back. Bit her lip. Thought hard. Got her phone out.

"Vicky?"

"Again?"

"Sorry. Are you in bed?"

"Course not. I'm imming with friends in LA. What's up?"

Instant messaging? She'd ask another time. "Sorry. It's just something you said — Roleseeker Services?"

"They e-mailed Zoë, yes."

"Did they say they'd received Zoë's invoice? Or invoiced her?"

"Invoiced her, I think. Sec." She was tapping away: imming fellow webheads? But no: she went on, "Yep. Please find attached invoices, terms and conditions, yada yada." More clicks. "Hundred and twenty quid. No details, just an invoice number. You want it?"

"No, that's okay."

"Plus their address. Eldon Square, Newcastle."

". . . Right," said Sarah.

"That means something, yeah? Zoë was in Newcastle, and she wanted something from these people. Hang on." She was clicking away again: she must have a hands-free phone. A teenage girl, in her bedroom on a school night, and so wired into the world she needed a hands-free set, in case anyone called while she was imming LA. Round a dinner table, Sarah might have found that food for a state-of-the-nation address. As it was, it was kind of useful. "Placements and opportunities, their site says. You want the url?"

"I'll Google it. Thanks, Vicky. Sorry to disturb you."

Ending the call, she found the firm's site: it offered, as Vicky had said, *placements and opportunities*. She thought about Gerard's list of names, Jack Gannon's at the top. The rest, she was sure, made up the crowd Gerard had invited to his soirée. What had he said? That she'd know what it was like, being in a new town. *You want to leave your marker with the movers and the shakers*. To do which, he'd needed to know his target group, so he'd acquired a list of the city's worthies from a local headhunter's. Except, of course, he hadn't. Zoë had. So Zoë had been working for Gerard, and everything Gerard had told Sarah was a lie. Why didn't that surprise her?

She wondered what the job had been. It wasn't as if Gerard needed a private eye to conjure a list of names; he must have legions of PAs and office-bodies for jobs like that. And this dropped into a growing list of other questions: why was Gerard staying in, let's face it, a dump like the Bolbec Hotel? *Malmaison's full*, he'd told her. *Chelsea are in town*. Nice line, but it didn't ring true. No, Gerard was staying at the Bolbec for the same reason he hadn't used his staff to do his research:

he didn't want them to know what he was doing, or where he was. Which meant he was up to something dodgy, Sarah decided; then had to revise that a moment later. Would Zoë have involved herself in something dodgy?

Well. You couldn't rule it out.

The screen-timer hit sixty minutes, and her browser died. She considered buying another session, but decided she had enough to think about, not that any of it had drawn her closer to Alan Talmadge. Another thought struck, and she closed her eyes, trying to visualize the list of names she'd found in Gerard's room. Jack Gannon's had been at the top, and it was unlikely that alphabetical sorting would have left him there. Were the names ranked in order of importance? John M. Wright's hadn't featured at all. *John's here with me*, Gannon had told her. But maybe Gannon was at the top because he'd been the reason for the list in the first place. *Find me some people to go with this man*, the instruction might have run. Whatever Gerard was up to, Gannon was at the heart of it, and Gannon came from a family of crooks.

*I'm a career criminal*, he'd told her.

Sarah had thought he'd been joking.

Leaving, she wandered aimlessly for five minutes before finding an alternative-looking restaurant and deciding she was hungry. One bowl of chunky lentil soup and a slab of black bread later she was back on the street, trying to work out what she'd forgotten to do, other than forgetting to let the hotel know she was staying another day — oh Christ: she was staying another day, and hadn't told Russ, who must be crawling walls. Her hand was reaching for her phone even as the thought formed.

People brushed past, their voices thick with beer. It wasn't far off ten o'clock, and was cold, damp and dark, but boys in short-sleeved shirts were just warming up.

Her home landline switched to voicemail, so she left a quick message then tried Russ's mobile. When he answered there was background noise: jukebox, voices, drink being taken. "Sarah?"

"You're in the pub."

"I'm in the pub. Where are you?"

"Not in a pub. I'm still in Newcastle, though."

"You're still what?"

"Still at the hotel."

"Still? Why haven't you checked out? Jesus, sorry, I should have — what happened? Was it her?"

"I don't know, Russ."

"Sarah? What do you mean — you couldn't tell? Oh fuck, I'm saying this wrong. I've had a few pints. Was it awful? I'm so sorry, darling."

She could feel tears starting, and didn't want to cry, not here on the street. She swallowed. "It was awful, yes. Horrible. The woman — she'd been in the water, Russ. I couldn't tell if it was Zoë or not."

"But didn't they — wasn't there evidence? I mean, she wasn't naked or anything, was she?"

"She was wearing Zoë's clothes. Or clothes that could have been Zoë's. And she had Zoë's wallet and stuff. I told them it was Zoë."

**130**

"You told them that? But you're still not sure? Oh fuck, look, give me a moment, I'll go outside where I can hear you properly."

"No. No, don't. I'm all right, Russ. Don't worry. But I'm going to stay another night, okay?"

"You're going to *what*?"

She couldn't tell if he hadn't heard, or just not liked what he'd heard. "I'm staying another night. I'll be back tomorrow evening, Russ. Very soon. But I can't leave yet. Not until I know what happened."

There was a sudden squirt of noise: a collision of some sort, a squawked apology.

"Russ?"

"Jesus, look, I've just spilled this gentleman's drink, I'd better — yes, yes, sorry, I'll get you another. Sarah? Call me back, okay?"

"I'll call you tomorrow, Russ. I love you."

"Sarah. Love you. Look, I'm really sorry, I'll just —"

The apology wasn't for her. The phone cut off, and she was still here, still in the cold damp night, still alone, though surrounded by happy strangers.

Someone said, "Grab a granny night, is it?"

She realized she was heading away from the hotel — into clubland, by the look of it — so abruptly switched direction. And it wasn't dark after all, she registered. There were lights all around; the beautiful blurred runniness of city neon, splashing reflections in windows and puddles. She'd forgotten what this was like. Even when her eyes cleared — the tears not falling, but soaking back into her — the colours remained a liquid rainbow in the air. She wished Zoë were with her. She wished she could point these lights out to Zoë, and dare her to find them less than beautiful.

In the dark the Bolbec resembled a trailer for one of those films in which misguided travellers check into their last night on earth. It was hard to dispel such thoughts once they've occurred, but Sarah did her best. The lobby was empty. It was after ten, and she was tired but not sleepy. She decided to have a drink.

Two men were at the bar when she entered, and both gave her appraising looks without bothering to pretend they weren't. She almost turned and walked back out — in some situations, too few men was as bad as too many — but Barry was already reaching for the Sauvignon. She was beginning to wonder how long his shifts were.

It wasn't clear how she scored on these men's charts, but a drink was a drink. And the fire, she noted, was lit.

"Long day?" Barry asked. Then: "I'm assuming you want a white?"

"I'll get that for the lady," one of the men said.

"Thank you. But I'd rather get my own."

"Rubbish," he said. A pile of change sat next to his whisky glass, and he began fingering coins Barry's way. "What's the damage on a large white, Baz?"

"Behave, Derek," Barry told him, pouring the wine. "It's on your room, Ms Tucker." He slid the glass across.

"Thanks, Barry."

Derek's mate snorted, and Derek said, "Now then, pet. No need to burn your bra."

Sarah opened her mouth to retort, but Barry got there first.

"That TV series where the guy falls asleep and wakes up in '73? They got your life backwards, Derek. You should write and complain."

Derek's mate snorted again, and nearly fell off his stool.

Derek looked sheepish. "No offence meant, pet."

"None taken, lamb," she assured him.

Barry was pretty good, though. Wringing a laugh and an apology from a situation which might have turned nasty.

She told him, "Put the next round on my room too, Barry. Excuse me, gentlemen, I need a comfy seat."

"Mind the dragon," she thought she heard as she headed for the sofa by the fireplace. Didn't get the reference, but understood it once she arrived.

Slumped in one of the rattan chairs, hunkered so low he couldn't be seen from behind, was Gerard. On the table was a bottle of Macallan; its level below the label, its optic plonked next to it like an amputated digit. At lunchtime, she remembered, she'd wondered if he'd been drunk. There was no doubting it now.

"Thought I told you to fuck off," he said without looking round.

"Told you the same once, I remember," she said, lowering herself on to the sofa. "Didn't fucking work."

"Sarah. Christ." He nearly attempted to stand, but sensibly gave up the idea. "Thought you were somebody else."

"Pleased to hear it."

"No, really, I — oh, hell." He swallowed what was left in his glass. "Those buggers by the bar still there?"

She didn't look round. "Yes. Been making a nuisance of themselves?"

"Seem to think I must want to join them. Seem to think I'd rather listen to them than sit by myself."

"I'm sure you put them wise."

"Where are you going?"

Sarah had regained her feet. Now she laughed. "Gerard? You're definitely giving the vibe of someone who doesn't want company."

"That's for their benefit. Stay a bit. Finish your drink."

She sat, glad she hadn't needed to find her own reason for doing so.

He said, "Can't get over that coincidence. Picking up your friend's card."

"It's a biggie, all right."

"What are the odds?"

He wasn't slurring, but was woollier than she'd known him. She wondered if the bottle had been full when he'd started. Then added what he'd drunk at lunchtime, multiplied it by how much he'd put away last night, and decided it didn't matter.

She said, "Higher than I'm comfortable with."

"You think there's something funny going on?"

She was about to reply, but had a sudden flashback to the body on the slab, the leather jacket, the tray of possessions that didn't matter any more. Her mouth filled, and she had to swallow. She lifted her glass to disguise the moment, but it didn't work.

Gerard said, "What's the matter? Lost touch with her?"

She hadn't told Gerard that Zoë was dead. Events had intervened when they'd discussed her. So he didn't know . . . unless he did.

Either way, she wasn't about to tell him.

"You might say that," she said.

She felt like she'd just made a dirty joke on her friend's grave.

"What was she doing here?"

"I don't know."

"And where is she now?"

Sarah shrugged.

"There's a lot you're not telling me, isn't there?"

"I think she stumbled over some of her own history."

"How very fascinating. Can you repeat that in English?"

"Would you like a refill?"

And this was Barry, who'd arrived so quietly he might have been a butler. He had wine bottle in hand, and was tilting it towards Sarah's glass; was pouring it before she had the chance to reply.

"Sorry about the guys back there. They mean well."

Gerard said, "Was there ever a phrase so geared to have you run away screaming?"

"But you know what I mean."

"Thanks, Barry," Sarah said. "We do."

"Shall I leave the bottle?" Sarah shook her head at the same moment Gerard nodded, so he gave a rueful grin and set it next to the whisky. "You don't have to drink it all," he said.

"That ever happen?"

But he was heading back to the bar.

"He seems a nice bloke," Sarah said.

"Naturally," Gerard said. "That's his job." He leaned forward heavily, and replenished his glass with the precise movements of the visually impaired. "'Stumbled over her own history.' Meaning what?"

"Something came out of her past. I think."

"What kind of something?"

"There was a man. A couple of years ago."

"Oh God. Not one of *those* stories, is it?"

"Gerard —"

"Unmarried woman hitting the change. Then up rips some young heartbreaker and —"

"Gerard? Shut up."

"Sorry," he said, without really saying it. "Floor's yours."

"His name was Alan Talmadge. Some of the time anyway. And he wasn't a heartbreaker, Gerard, he was a killer. He killed two women Zoë knew of."

Sarah reached for her glass, hand shaking. Zoë had never adequately described Talmadge. Had referred to him, instead, through the effect he'd had on other people; on those women, not a million miles from Gerard's brutal summing up, who'd allowed him to slip into their lives, and fill a space previously reserved for their own desperation. Lives he'd then ended.

Her wine felt colder, as if the temperature in the bar had dropped.

Gerard said, "Are you sure about this?"

"Zoë was."

"His name doesn't ring a bell."

"Should it?"

"Killed two women? That's as good as *Big Brother* for getting your name in the papers. And if it was only a couple of years —"

"He was never caught."

Gerard said, "Ah."

"Never even looked for, far as I know. The two women — they were thought to be accident victims. Zoë was sure they were murdered. But they both looked like accidents."

Gerard said "Ah" again, at a different pitch.

"I believed her."

"Well, of course you did. You're her friend."

And oh joy, there it was: the male battle cry in all its naked vigour. Not *What would you know, bitch?*; nor even *Don't worry your pretty head about it*. Just *Well, of course you did*. Words to accompany a pat on the head.

"You'd have believed her too."

"I dare say," Gerard said. "It doesn't take much to convince me. Just hard, incontrovertible evidence."

He made to drink, and looked down in surprise on finding his glass empty.

She emptied her own. "Did you really find her card?"

He looked left, then right, demonstrably wondering where this was coming from. Then at her. "I can show you if you like. 'Supstairs. In my room."

"Really."

"It's upstairs," he said more clearly.

"In your room, I heard you. That's not what I meant. Did you really find it? Or did Zoë give it to you?"

"You think I've met your friend?"

"I'm asking if you did."

"No, Sarah. I didn't meet her."

Drunk or not, he gave her a solid, straight-eyed look saying that. He was, of course, a very rich businessman, not one of whom on this sweet earth ever got where he was without lying. But she didn't think he lied.

She shook her head. Reached for the bottle, and splashed more wine into her glass. Then excused herself, and headed to the loo.

When she got back, Derek and his friend had gone. It was past eleven. Barry was emptying the till. "I'm supposed to close. But if you want anything —"

"I don't, thanks. And he shouldn't."

"Well, if you need a hand . . ." He did something with his eyebrows that conveyed the difficulty of steering heavy objects upstairs without help.

"If it comes to that, he can sleep where he lands."

Barry smiled a goodnight, and she returned to the fireplace.

The fire was dying, but still radiating a steady glow. It made the rest of the room feel darker, even more so when Barry turned the light over the bar off before leaving. Sarah picked up her glass. The wine stung her taste buds, as if she'd eaten a strawberry since her last sip. She looked at Gerard, who sat immobile, staring into the low flame. She couldn't tell whether he'd drunk more in her absence.

"Are you all right?"

His gaze left the fire and locked on her. It held no recognition.

"Gerard?"

Somewhere, a door closed with a bang. She started. He didn't.

"Gerard?"

He said, "I have a son."

She couldn't have heard that right. She stared.

"*We* have a son. He's eight months old."

"Gerard." Even as she spoke, she knew her words would be wrong; that she was heading down a cul-de-sac it wouldn't be easy to back out of. "That's wonderful. That's —"

"He's called Zachary." She might have been background static. Gerard wasn't talking to her; he was talking to his glass, whose half-inch golden pool threw back images she couldn't guess at. "Sometimes when I stand over his . . . his incubator, I imagine him smiling at me. Eight months, you'd expect a smile, wouldn't you?"

The fire flickered, and shadows scampered into corners.

"Something bad happened," Sarah said flatly.

"He has no arms," Gerard said. "But then, he has no legs, either. You know what he looks like? He looks like a ping-pong ball balanced on a boiled egg. And I look at him, and I know I'm supposed to love him. And I do. I love him. But I want him to die. Because he's not living a life, not in any sense you or I would recognize. He'll never know what it's like to . . . be ordinary. To walk by a river, or have a job, or drink brandy, or . . . or

**139**

anything. Even stay in a crappy hotel like this. Anything can seem like a pleasure, if you compare it to a life utterly bereft of possibility."

He put his glass down, and emptied the bottle into it. It was a measure beyond healthy. It was a measure on steroids.

She said, "Do they know . . ."

"Do they know what?"

She'd never heard this from Gerard before: genuine aggression. He lived his life — that part she'd witnessed him living — wrongfooting the foolish and charming his targets, but aggression was new. "Why," she said. "Do they know why?"

"It happens."

"Yes, but —"

"It happens."

The male wall. Tell her about it. Beyond this point, we don't discuss.

"I'm sorry," she said again.

"If I thought you were responsible, that wouldn't be enough."

For some reason, she found herself recalling what he'd said at lunchtime. *There you go,* he'd told John M. Wright. *The terrible vengeance of a righteous God. We can all learn something from that.*

She looked for more words she already knew wouldn't help. "There are —"

"Don't. Don't tell me there are . . . *benefits.* Or procedures. Or no way of knowing about quality of life. Don't tell me any of that self-serving platitudinous bullshit."

**140**

"I wasn't going to."

"My son would be better off dead. That's not self-pitying rationalization. He would be better. Off. Dead."

His voice had risen, and for a moment afterwards an echo ricocheted around the bar, stirring ghosts of ancient conversations and long-forgotten sorrows.

Then he said, "I was a practising Catholic, did you know that?"

She nodded, but he wasn't looking at her. "Yes," she said.

"Paula still is. That's the funny thing."

"You've lost your faith?"

And now he looked at her, with eyes that were dark absences. "Lose it? No, I didn't lose it, Sarah. I nailed it to a tree and set fire to it."

"Gerard —"

"I'd like to be alone now."

She wanted to ask if he was sure, but he was sure. If she was Gerard, she'd be sure too.

He raised his glass to his lips. Shadows from the dying fire danced on the walls as she left.

# CHAPTER
# NINE

Next morning she knocked on Gerard's door, quietly, so as not to disturb him — why do we do that? She knocked again loudly, but there was no reply. Perhaps his hangover had woken him early, and he'd gone for a walk to shake it off. Or he was still in the bar. Or he'd hanged himself in his bathroom.

She'd never seen Gerard like he'd been last night. But then, she had lots of friends she'd never seen in that state. With Gerard, it was more a case of: she'd never imagined him as other than full-on Gerard. Annoyed, irritated, condescending: he could be all those things and still be Gerard of Oz, larger than life and louder than loud. But heartbreak turned out to be the man behind the curtain. She'd never imagined anything so ordinary pulling Gerard's levers. Not that his heartbreak took an ordinary shape — his poor child, poor Zachary. Poor Paula. Poor all of them. But she had to remember, too, that none of this meant there wasn't something else going on. Gerard could be crippled by sorrow, but that didn't wipe out the Zoë connection.

*You* think *I've met your friend? No, Sarah. I didn't meet her.*

But there was the list of names in his room; there was the Roleseekers e-mail in Zoë's inbox. It was true Sarah had no proof the two lists were the same, but how many coincidences could one hotel hold?

*I didn't meet your friend.* But that didn't mean they'd not been in contact.

She wondered how long it would take Vicky to unearth Zoë's deleted correspondence.

She wondered other things too, as she made her way downstairs.

The woman who'd checked her in was on reception. Sarah still didn't know her name, and it felt too late to ask. She said something about Barry instead. About how rare it was not to see him here.

"He'll be in later. Did you want him for something?"

There might have been, Sarah thought, a touch of a leer in that.

"I'm sure you can manage," she said. "I'll be staying another night."

There were three others having breakfast, at different tables, so there was no conversation. Sarah ate a croissant, drank a cup of coffee, then another while texting Russ. She'd have called, but it would have felt like public speaking. In the end, the text mostly became a promise to speak to him later: there were too many words, too few abbreviations, for all she needed to tell him.

If she had to break it down to words of one syllable, though, it would be: *I can't leave yet.* That would be to ring down the curtain before the stage business was over. It would mean turning her back on whatever Zoë had been caught up in, and while Zoë might have been elusive when it came to the common currency of friendship — birthday cards, phone calls; casual droppings-in — she'd have been first on the scene when Sarah needed help. It had happened before. Guns had been involved.

She hoped Russ would understand — she wasn't sure he had last night, with beer under his belt. And there'd been that moment back home, when he'd worried she'd be *drawn into* whatever Zoë had been involved in. She'd feigned misunderstanding: what did *drawn into* mean? But it meant this. This was what it had always meant. That she'd be having breakfast alone in a last-chance hotel; texting Russ to tell him she'd not be returning yet.

There were grounds in the bottom of her coffee cup, but that was okay. That meant it was real. You couldn't argue with proof like that.

Sarah put her phone away, returned to her room, and took it out again. The thread she'd started tugging at last night could do with another pull. She made the call quickly, before she could change her mind.

It took a few minutes to get through.

"Ms Tucker? I thought you'd gone home."

"I decided to stay on a while, Inspector."

"So what can I do for you?"

Encouraging words, delivered in a guarded tone. This wasn't an offer of help. It was an enquiry as to what she was up to.

144

She said, "Do you know anything about a family named Gannon?"

"Do I *what*?"

"A family named Gannon. They run a storage firm, used to be a haulage —"

"Yes, I know what they run."

She waited.

"Ms Tucker? What's this about, exactly?"

"It's just that I've met a man named Jack Gannon, and I . . ." She paused. I what? "I heard he had some dodgy connections."

Fairfax said, "You're aware I'm a police officer?"

"That's why I rang."

"We get 999 calls from idiots whose TVs aren't working. I don't remember being asked to check out a prospective date before."

"He's not —"

"You've been of assistance, Ms Tucker, but that doesn't put me at your beck and call. We'll be in touch if there are developments in, in the other matter. Now excuse me, but I'm busy." He disconnected.

She sat stunned for a moment, and then guilt and shame flushed through her. Did he really think she'd called just to check on a new acquaintance's standing, criminal or otherwise? That she was some, Christ, some *flibbertigibbet* who thought she had a hotline to the cops because she'd sat in a police car?

Blood pounding in her ears, Sarah wanted something to throw. But there was no big outdoors here; she couldn't storm out and romp across the hillsides, kicking stones. She made do with viciously turning her phone off: one pointy stab of the finger. Then turned it on again, in case anyone called. Then went back up another flight of stairs, to knock on Gerard's door.

Which was ajar.

Someone was moving inside, but she could tell it wasn't Gerard. No one who'd drunk the quantity Gerard had put away last night would be capable of movement without lumbering. They wouldn't be humming, either. Sarah pushed the door gently. The humming stopped.

"Miss?"

"I'm sorry," Sarah said.

A young Indian woman was stripping the bed.

"Ah . . . Did you want me to see to your room?"

"No. No, I was looking for —"

But it was clear that the man she was looking for was no longer there. Yesterday's clutter: those nests of charging cables; the briefcase, suitcase, laundry bag — all of it had gone. A vacuum cleaner stood by the bathroom door. The maid held a pillow; had paused in the act of coaxing it from its cotton slip.

"It doesn't matter," Sarah said. "I have the wrong room."

She returned to reception, where she rang the bell, because the woman was nowhere to be seen. Ten seconds later, she rang it again. She'd have rung it a third time, but the woman appeared: a little flustered; a bit pissed off, too, as if she didn't appreciate the summons. Sarah would care about that later. Round about the time it occurred to her she was taking out Fairfax's rebuff on an innocent party.

146

"Has Mr Inchon checked out?" she asked.

"I'm sorry?"

"Inchon. You haven't got that many guests. Has he checked out?"

"Oh. Yes. Yes, he left early this morning."

"How early?"

"Before I came on. I mean, pretty much the middle of the night. I suppose he had a flight to catch."

"A flight?"

"I can't think why else he'd leave at three thirty in the morning."

The woman had recovered some poise. Her tone suggested she could actually think of a few good reasons, most of them standing in front of her.

"Did he leave a message?"

"A message for you?"

"A message of any kind," Sarah said through gritted teeth.

The woman took her time. Looked through the few papers scattered on the desk; checked the pigeonholes behind her. She all but whistled while doing so. "I'm sorry, Ms Tucker. There doesn't seem to be anything."

"I see."

"He didn't push a note beneath your door?"

"Well, if he had," Sarah began, but could see it wasn't worth it. "No. Thanks."

She left the desk, heading for the front door; realized almost immediately she had no special need to be heading that way, but couldn't face pulling a U-turn under the receptionist's scornful gaze. I've given her quite enough merriment for the moment, Sarah

147

thought, and stepped on to the street coatless, into the path of a withering wind.

*This really is not my best morning . . .*

Gerard had gone home, she supposed. Last night's conversation had brought that about; Gerard, in the cold light of morning, couldn't face seeing her with pity in her eyes. Which was fair enough. Sarah was reasonably sure she'd have been able to regard him without a trace of visible concern, but it would have been there; the memory of a fireside conversation in which he'd opened his heart, and showed it in splinters. There were friendships which such a moment would have strengthened, but not the kind she and Gerard shared. She wasn't even sure "friendship" was the word. And while she was questioning terminology, "cold light of morning" didn't work either: there'd have been precious little light at three thirty. She was surprised Gerard had been able to stand, let alone pack.

Cold, though. There'd have been cold enough to go round. And plenty of it yet, come to that.

The *Big Issue* man was nowhere to be seen. Office hours, though, didn't apply. As she stood there, a detail occurred to her: Gerard had checked out before the woman had come on duty. So who checked him out? It must have been Barry. Poor guy. He'd closed the bar; probably hoped to see his shift out having a nap in the office. But instead had to deal with a drunken Gerard, who would no doubt have had a complicated bill to deconstruct, and probably wasn't in the best of moods.

What was it Barry had said about his job? *It beats flipping burgers*. Probably he'd reconsidered that, back in the early hours.

As she re-entered the hotel, her phone rang.

She answered it climbing the stairs.

"Ms Tucker?"

"Yes."

"It's DS King. From yesterday morning."

"Yes." She felt her vocal cords tighten: what now? An official reprimand for misuse of police time?

"The boss said you'd rung."

"It's not important."

"I doubt you'd have called if it wasn't. He goes off the deep end sometimes, but, well, you know. It's a stressful job."

"Give him my commiserations."

"So he mentioned it to me. That's his way of making sure he wasn't too hasty."

"So why didn't he call back himself?"

"Now that, that's not his way. So. Jack Gannon. How'd you come across him?"

She took a breath.

"Ms Tucker?"

"I met him at the hotel. In the bar."

"That's the same hotel Ms Boehm was staying?"

"Yes."

"And you don't think that's a coincidence."

"You're aware that Zoë — that Ms Boehm was a private detective?"

"We'd established that, yes."

"Good for you. I think she was up here on a job of some kind. I think that job involved Mr Gannon."

"Who was her client?"

"I don't know."

She could have given him Gerard — if Gannon was involved, so was Gerard. But something held her back. Call it loyalty; that plus the knowledge that she'd misjudged Gerard in the past. He deserved a hearing before she threw him to a wolf.

"She was investigating criminal activity?"

"I don't know what she was investigating."

"Because the reason we have a police force in this country —"

"I know why we have a police force, Sergeant. I don't know what Zoë was doing. But it seems likely that whatever it was, it had something to do with Jack Gannon."

"And you thought we should know."

"I thought Inspector Fairfax might be interested. It turned out he wasn't."

"He gets a little uptight when he thinks people are trying to do his job."

"If I was interested in impersonating a police officer, I'd wait till I was needed, then make myself scarce."

He said, quite mildly, "I suspect your stereotype's out of date."

Sarah took a breath. She'd reached the landing, down the corridor from her room. "Whatever. The point is, I found out what little I know inside five minutes on the web. It's not as if I blundered into a top secret investigation."

His silence sounded like a point conceded.

"Tell your boss I'm sorry I bothered him."

He said, "The Gannons are a well-known Walker firm. I'm not talking about haulage. Back in the seventies and eighties, when Michael Gannon was ruling the roost, they were basically your North Tyneside crimelords. Mostly robbery, mostly big delivery — if a lorryload of fags or booze got knocked over, it was the Gannons behind it. They also supplied fruit machines to local clubs, along with door security and working girls. You didn't get involved in after-hours entertainment from Wallsend to Benton without rendering unto the Gannons, if you catch my drift. One or two tried, and found out what the blunt end of a closed shop feels like."

"Gannon was tried for kidnapping and assault."

"Among other things."

"So that was then. What about now?"

"Michael G's still among the living, but he had a series of strokes in the early nineties. The eldest son, Tony, tried his shoes on, but was hampered by being a stupid dickhead, pardon my Dutch, and spent five years contemplating his misdeeds in Durham. By the time he came out, the other brothers had, ah, diversified their interests. Gangstering's not the prospect it used to be. I like to pretend that's not because I've joined the force since, but you can't argue with the facts."

"Your modesty does you credit. And Jack Gannon's behind their shift into legitimate business?"

King said, "He's never broken any laws we've found out about. But the way I look at it, the money he's investing, the business he's helping run — all that capital came out of crime. Doesn't matter how often it's been washed, it's dirty money."

"Have you met him?"

"I have, as a matter of fact. At a charity auction, raising funds for a police cadets' gym. He bid large for a painting my three-year-old nephew could have done. Only he'd have called it colouring, not art."

"What did you think of him?"

"I thought he was a charming man."

"And?"

"And I don't like charming men. I always wonder what they've got to hide."

"That makes your boss an open book."

He said, "I think that theme's run its course. Anyway, the Gannons. Like I say, Jack's never broken any laws we've heard about." He paused, giving himself room for a shrug. "If Ms Boehm was investigating him, she knew something we didn't."

"Thanks for calling."

"I'd like to know what you're planning."

"I'm not planning anything. I just don't want . . . I don't want things to fade away. I guess."

"They won't."

"I got the impression you were regarding this as a suicide."

He didn't reply.

"Sergeant?" It sounded odd, saying that. But she could hardly just call him King. "Isn't that so?"

"Ms Tucker —"

"Or an accident. But you didn't know Zoë. She didn't have accidents."

"This wasn't an accident," he said at last.

"You're sure about that?"

"We're sure."

He'd come this far, she thought. She only had to wait. He'd give her the rest.

"She drowned," he said.

"I know."

"But it wasn't river water in her lungs."

Sarah closed her eyes; tried to shut out the image this information provided.

"Ms Tucker?"

"I see. I see." She saw. She saw Zoë being held down in a bath; strong hands forcing her head underwater.

DS King fell silent.

Sarah had to say something — she couldn't just hang up. So she said, "Thank you," though it came out more quietly than she'd intended. She cleared her throat. "Thank you for telling me," she said again. Then she ended the call, walked down the corridor to her room, let herself in, and lay on the bed.

Closing her eyes did not help. Sarah opened them, and stared straight up. Thin cracks threaded outward from the corners, forming a faint road map on the ceiling. It didn't direct her anywhere she wanted to go.

But when she closed her eyes again, the view was worse: was of Zoë, forcibly held underwater.

Zoë had always struck Sarah as the strongest person she'd met, but strength wasn't necessarily a factor. Not

153

for a woman. A woman could be strong, and still be no match for the wrong kind of man. Sarah hadn't allowed herself to wonder about how Zoë had ended up in that river, but the thought had sneaked up on her a time or two; catching her off guard, like an unexpected car rounding a corner. What she'd seen had been swift, and shrouded in darkness. Zoë on a quayside or towpath; looking down towards water on which starlight trembled. And something coming out of nowhere behind her: a glancing blow on the head, then more darkness.

In this version, Zoë entered the water without a ripple. It happened swiftly, and the first Zoë would have known about it was the last thing she'd ever know. But it hadn't happened like that. Sarah closed her eyes again. And this time it was all struggle and violence, with Zoë well aware of what was happening, and doing her damnedest to make it stop. And it happening anyway.

She'd have tried to shout; tried to fight. And she'd lost. It happened anyway.

The road map to nowhere dissolved as Sarah's eyes filled. For a moment she was teetering on a brink, and if she let herself fall now, the landing would shatter her. She had to pull back: a willed enaction of that involuntary spasm found on the edge of sleep. Going to pieces was not an option. Going to pieces would let Zoë down. She had to be strong. If their roles were reversed, Zoë would have grieved, might even have wept, but she would not have fallen apart. Not before discovering what had happened.

I'll do my best, Sarah thought, as if Zoë were in the room with her. Then she said it aloud. "I'll do my best."

She sat up. Dried her eyes. Planned her next move.

Of the fragments of information she'd gathered — she supposed you could call them clues — none cast special light. What she'd learned about Jack Gannon made it clearer than ever that he couldn't be Talmadge: he couldn't float around the country, assuming different guises, at the same time as steering his criminal family into the legitimate world. That Gannon was part of what happened to Zoë, Sarah had no doubt. But she couldn't see where he fitted. It was as if she'd been given something to glue back together without having been told what it was. She had to keep choosing pieces, testing their shape. Propelled into action by the thought, she moved from the bed. In the bathroom, she splashed water on her face.

Gerard had vanished for the time being, but he couldn't simply disappear. She'd find him when she needed to. For the moment, there were other threads to follow through the maze.

There was Gannon, and then there was John M. Wright.

Wright might not matter in himself — he hadn't been on Gerard's list; the one Zoë had produced — but he was a close associate of Jack Gannon's; seemed to dog his footsteps. On the other hand, he was so wrapped up in himself, that might not count for much. It might be simpler to tackle Gannon directly. But *tackling* implied Sarah knew what she was after, when the truth was, she was adrift. She didn't know what she needed to know. She just knew she didn't know enough. And she doubted she could pump Gannon for information without him noticing.

They got on, though. There was something of a spark, there — not attraction, exactly, but you couldn't rule it out.

There was a phone book in the dressing-table drawer, and she flicked through its Business section. Wright's company had been mentioned at lunch yesterday: ResearchWorks. One word. She made a note of the address then riffled through the pages again, looking for Gannon. There were three separate entries, along with a box trumpeting a storage facility. She made a note of those too.

Wright or Gannon? Gannon or Wright?

A storage depot would be a big warehouse full of walk-in containers, and the man in charge would be jacketless, biros lined up in his shirt's pocket protector. As soon as Sarah had gone, he'd be on the phone, tipping Jack off. Where Wright worked, on the other hand, would be a neat square building where studious people worked in clean white coats. A receptionist would offer coffee while chatting about Nice Mr Gannon, who often dropped in . . .

It was the mental equivalent of whatever-you-called-it; the practice of opening the Bible at random, and taking the verse your eyes lit on as God-mail. It didn't matter what it said because your brain would twist it so it read the way you wanted. She had no idea what storage depots looked like, but sometimes it was safest to go with the stereotypes. And bearding Wright would at least have this advantage: Sarah already knew she didn't like him. People you didn't like could be easier to deal with. It wasn't necessary to make space for them.

Sarah put her coat on, then checked in the mirror. The coat looked good, but Sarah was not at her best. Her cheeks lacked colour, and her eyes seemed different. Flintier. Suicide, she had heard, left the bereft feeling grief with the anger turned up. Murder had much the same effect.

She found her spectacles and put them on. Maybe they'd soften the anger. Maybe not.

# CHAPTER
## TEN

The map from the rack in the hotel lobby was for the city centre only, so at the Central Station Sarah bought an A-Z, then caught a Metro towards the coast. The train ran mostly overland, but the outside world seemed painted grey. Or maybe that was the natural colouring of Palmersville, Shiremoor, West Monkseaton; names that fell agreeably strangely on her ears, but would no doubt disappoint if she ever walked their streets. A line from a half-forgotten poem stirred: *People live here. You'd be amazed.* And there was that whispered music again; a snatch of the soundtrack to which unknown others spent their lives.

When her stop came, the station seemed awfully grand for a two-track service. Once, it dispatched steam-trains hither and yon, while mutton-chopped guards blew whistles. Outside, the houses were large and imposing — three-storey Victorian villas — and the streetlamps vintage Narnian. The air had a salty sting. Sarah was only a mile or so inland, if she read her map aright.

And if she was doing that, she had a walk ahead of her. She set off briskly, compulsively checking the A-Z at each junction; confirmation that she hadn't gone astray. Twenty minutes took her clear of the town; deposited her on the fringe of an industrial estate where maps were no use, but God or something sent a postman cycling past, and she flagged him down.

"After a bakkie, pet?"

"Just directions, thanks."

Research Works — one word — aye, he knew it.

"Gan past all them yellow vans, and it's next building along. ResearchWork's on the upstairs. The stairs are on the outside, like."

Sometimes, events conspire to place you in a fairytale. She thanked the nice postman, and set off on her way.

"Gan canny, pet."

She mentally filed that. "Thanks." I think.

The yellow vans belonged to a courier service. The next building looked like a warehouse, and so much for her vision of a research facility: it was an old construction with an iron-sheeting roof, its grimly stuccoed walls shadowed by damp. The stairs indeed were on the outside, like a fire escape, but made of wood. The sign on the door, *ResearchWorks*, was a laminated card drawing-pinned in place.

She knocked, and there was no answer.

A minute or so later she knocked again, and this time the door was flung open, as if someone had just happened to be passing, and couldn't believe their ears. Student. Young, anyway, with a shiny bald head and thick framed spectacles: and if he hadn't been able to believe his ears, it wasn't because they weren't big enough. They emerged horizontally, like a giraffe's. He

**159**

wasn't wearing a white coat, but a big T-shirt and paint-spattered jeans, and was waggling something between the fingers of his right hand so quickly, it took her a moment to identify it as a pencil.

"I'm looking for Mr Wright?" she said.

The young man's failure to cash in on this opening pretty much proved him a virgin.

"The doc?" he said.

She agreed that was possibly the same man.

"He's on the 'puter."

"Could I disturb him?"

"He'll be another five minutes."

That probably meant no. "Well, is it all right if I wait?"

He shrugged. "S'pose."

Half a dozen heartbeats later she was being shown into a tiny room with a sink in one corner, and a few plastic chairs, and a formica-topped table on which a coffee machine sat. Its jug was empty, but an open packet of coffee was spilled next to it, and she was given to understand that it would be acceptable for her to make a fresh brew. She decided she'd be equally happy not doing so. The student returned to whatever task he was busy with, and she was left to contemplate the wisdom or otherwise of her current course of action.

Perhaps not so wise. But being in a different city made this easier. What they called the visiting-fireman approach: it didn't matter what kind of idiot you made of yourself among people you'd never meet again. What goes on tour stays on tour. She didn't have long to

**160**

dwell on it anyway, because John M. Wright came in three minutes later.

"Oh, it's, ah — you."

It was difficult to tell whether he was disappointed or just not very interested.

"Sarah," she reminded him. "Sarah Tucker."

"What are you doing here?"

*I was just passing* was a tempting response. A ride on the Metro, a twenty-minute walk, directions from a postie — she might just get away with it. But settled, instead, for, "I wanted to see where you worked."

"Why?"

"What you've been telling me, about your research — it's interesting stuff." *Ms Tucker's in publishing. She owns her own company*, was how Jack Gannon had introduced her to Wright. "My company produces soft-science books. There might be something in this."

"A book?"

"A chapter," she said, freewheeling like mad. "Not so much about the results of your research. More how you go about doing it."

"Did Inchon send you?"

Well, that might work too. "I know Gerard will be interested in anything you have to say."

He scratched his beard. Marvellous, Sarah thought. Not only does it look ridiculous, it feels uncomfortable too. It's a wonder suspender belts aren't part of male formal dress.

"Well," he said at last. "I've time for a chat, I suppose."

It was the first thing he'd said that wasn't a question.

**161**

"Is there anywhere we can go?" Sarah asked. "For lunch or whatever?"

"There's a sort of canteen."

She had visions of a room like this, but with ketchup stains. "You don't want to drive into town? I'm sure I passed a Thai. My treat."

"I don't eat that sort of food," he said, as if she were offering him the first apple. "The canteen's for the whole estate," he added. "It's quite good."

He led her down the stairs and round the back of the building, through a gap in a scruffy hedge, across a small car park, and through a door in the side of a building similar to the one they'd just left, and which turned out to house the canteen. This was cleaner than Sarah had been expecting, and brightly lit. Wright, mind, looked like he'd successfully navigate it in the dark. From the self-service area, he loaded a plate: steak, chips; five green beans. Sarah chose a pre-wrapped Caesar salad, and followed him. At the till she was about to offer to pay, when he saved her the bother by telling the woman, "She's got these."

"Treating your boyfriend, pet?" Sarah was asked.

Wright was already off to a table.

"He's not my boyfriend," Sarah said. "I'm his probation officer."

He'd started eating by the time she sat. She peeled the cellophane from her salad, and said, "How long have you been here?"

"At RW?"

ResearchWorks. "Yes."

"I set it up, you know."

162

"So I gather."

"In these premises, four years."

"Right. And the Gannon family fund you, do they?"

"They're among my backers."

"Because your research might one day be worth a lot of money."

"There's no 'might' about it. It'll be worth millions. If I'm allowed the resources to proceed with my work."

"What kind of resources might they be?"

He sawed a wedge from his steak and delivered it to his mouth. While he chewed he regarded her. Not so much as he might a person, Sarah thought, as he might an unimportant problem. A Sudoku, say. When he'd finished chewing he swallowed, then said, "Is this for your book?"

"Chapter," she said. "Yes. It's all background."

"I need a more powerful computer system," he said. "I get to use the University's StarWheel once in a while. I really need one of my own."

"Starwheel . . .?"

He sighed. "It operates some rather complicated software." Like someone explaining to a three-year-old what it was that watches did. "Which models gene behaviour. I use it to replicate potential reactions in the respiratory system to various stimuli. When I'm allowed near it."

"That sounds . . . interesting."

"Yes. Well. It's a tool, but a useful one. And if you don't want the animal rights brigade on your case, you need some fairly sophisticated alternatives to . . ." He speared a chip with his fork. "Animals."

**163**

"You don't use animals in your research?"

"You need a licence."

She was pleased to hear it. "So what about the new premises? Why do you need those?"

Now she was really being moronic. "Because it's a large system. The StarWheel. And needs a purpose-built environment."

"It's a virtual reality device?" she guessed.

He directed his attention back to his plate. "There are VR elements involved, yes. Should I be getting paid for this?"

"For eating lunch?"

"For sharing my knowledge. A royalty."

"Royalties generally go to the writers," Sarah explained. "There might be a consultation fee. If the book goes ahead."

"Chapter. You said."

"In a book, yes. Tell me how you met Jack."

"Why do you want to know?"

"Could be an interesting story."

"Don't see how."

"He's a rich man, endowing a science project. You don't think other scientists will be interested in hearing how that came about?"

"It's not that big an endowment," Wright said.

Somewhere on the Internet, there was a joke to which that was the punchline.

"Did you ever hear him mention Gerard Inchon before the other night?"

"I don't know."

"The name didn't ring a bell?"

"I'm not very interested in other people," he said, dividing the last of his steak into two equal pieces.

That was a compliment other people were no doubt happy to repay. "But you get on with Jack."

"I suppose so."

"Do you know his family at all?"

"His family?"

"Yes. You know — parents, brothers, that sort of thing."

Wright said, without taking his eyes off his lunch, "Why on earth would I want to meet his parents?"

"I don't know. Because they're endowing your work?"

He shook his head. "I've never met Mr Lloyds TSB either," he told her. "But he gives me an overdraft."

Her salad was limp and uninspired. She had a good idea how it felt. She ate a few forkfuls, though, before returning to the fray. "How far along are you with your research?"

Now he looked at her, but with detached irritation. "Do you know much about asthma — I've forgotten your name?"

"Sophie," she said. "No, not much. Apart from the obvious stuff, which everyone knows."

"Well, it affects over five million people in this country alone. And nobody knows what causes it. So you can probably work out that it's not a problem that's about to be solved overnight."

She said, "I don't remember suggesting it was. But Jack described it as your life's work. So I presume you're further along than just counting who's got it."

"People think of it as just being short of breath."

(She'd been starting to think it didn't matter what she said, but a penny dropped now. He wasn't interested in other people: okay. But he was interested in asthma. Interested in it for what it was, not for how it made those other people suffer.)

"But it has an interesting array of side-effects. Weight gain. Osteoporosis. Cataracts."

"From *asthma*?"

"From common forms of asthma treatment. Steroids."

"They prescribe steroids for asthma?"

"You don't know anything about it at all, do you?"

"No," she said. "I'm a publisher, not a scientist."

She was quite proud of herself, for remembering she was a publisher.

"Well, trust me. It's not a small subject."

And one she was getting interested in, despite herself. Or despite John M. Wright, rather. Something he'd said about his magic computer swam back into her mind. Intelligence was largely careful listening. "And what's your approach? Gene treatment?"

"Not exactly."

"You don't think that's the way to go?"

"Ultimately. But gene treatment's way in the future, whatever you read in the papers. Oh, it'll be available for the rich within our lifetime. But not for anyone else."

"So you think a safer form of steroid treatment is what's needed?"

He laid down his knife and fork. "I'm not sure I want to announce my aims through your book."

"Chapter. But I take your point."

A sudden draught announced the arrival of a crowd of local workers, who came in laughing and chattering, and generally feeling at home. A look of distaste curled Wright's lip. "I'm going back to work now."

He stood.

Sarah hadn't got anywhere, she thought. She'd come all this way, but learned nothing.

She said, "How close are you to finishing?"

"That's not an easy question to answer."

"But Jack Gannon's prepared to fund you until you are?"

"You'd have to ask him that. But you can tell Mr Inchon that I'd be very happy to discuss how he can help. He won't regret the investment."

"And you don't think Jack would object to that?"

Wright said, "Do you have any idea how much money will result, once my research is successfully concluded?"

"None at all, no."

"Jack Gannon won't be out of pocket."

She said, "Why aren't you working for big pharma? Then you wouldn't have to scrub around for private backing."

"That's not your concern."

There was clatter, and more laughter, as tables were colonized and plates deposited. Sarah's salad was only half-finished, but it was clear that Wright's work here was done. She stood, collected her bag from the back of her chair, and followed him into the cold.

He surprised her then. He said, "Were you wearing those glasses last time we met?"

"Yesterday. No. No, I wasn't."

"I thought not. When will this chapter be written?"

She said, "I haven't commissioned the book yet. But there's a lot of promising material here."

He pursed his lips. "I'll need a consultation fee. When I speak to your writer."

"Oh, it's all above board. Don't worry about that."

He turned abruptly, and walked back the way they'd come: across the small car park, through the gap in the scruffy hedge. He didn't look back.

Sarah had the distinct feeling she'd been forgotten about the moment she'd left his sight.

She took the Metro back into town; spent the journey staring out of the window, weighing up the morning. She'd learned something about John M. Wright, in whom she was not interested, and nothing about Jack Gannon, in whom she was. And meanwhile, time was passing. She was no nearer finding out what had happened to Zoë, and had let Gerard, who might have had answers, slip through her fingers. And she remained miles from home, and Russ must be thinking she'd vanished down a rabbit hole. With that thought she fished out her mobile, but couldn't get a signal. She wrote a quick text anyway, stored it for later, then resumed her window-watching. Heavy skies stretched into the distance. Well, she thought. Obviously the distance. Where else was the sky going to go?

It wasn't raining when the train dipped underground on its way to the city centre, but it couldn't be long in coming. Perhaps she should buy an umbrella. Accessorize before the event.

Emerging at the Haymarket, she paused at an ATM, feeling as she did so that little hint of validation — as if her PIN were giving her a good reference — along with an equally familiar resentment that life was now dependent on an ability to remember bloody numbers. And as she tucked the banknotes into her purse, she remembered Zoë's wallet, fished out of the river, Zoë's plastic still tucked in its pockets. All of whose numbers cried out that this was Zoë.

But before she could pursue that thought, she heard music coming to meet her; a distant whisper, but growing in volume. There was always music in city centres, most of it unwelcome. This was different. As she approached the cavernous entrance to the city's monstrous mall she saw the musicians responsible: two young men and a woman, playing fiddles and a guitar. The males were twins by the look of them, and shared a joke as they played, while the woman, surely their sister, began a solo. The music, a reel of some sort, went swirling over the heads of the gathered crowd, and despite the February chill and the heavy grey sky, brought a touch of sunlight to the city street. The tune was as much the sound of an English summer as a lawn sprinkler, or Jonathan Agnew being more disappointed than angry.

Sarah stood there, drinking it in. One tune finished and another began: this one slower and haunting, conjuring a cold and windswarmed beach on a northern coast. She could have listened all day, but supposed she shouldn't. At last she left, but not before finding out that they were called XYZ. It wasn't a name she'd forget.

The rain was still holding off but she headed into the mall anyway, and looked at micro-umbrellas in the first clothing shop she came to. She'd scoffed, yesterday, at the idea that shopping could ease pain, but the guilty truth was that it could, a little. Force the mind to focus on making a choice, and it eased its grip on other subjects. She decided, at last, on a black design with a red pattern, then browsed the rest of the floor, looking at shoes she didn't need and jackets she couldn't afford. As if to rub it in that it was winter, there were summer tops on display too, and she fingered her way through a rack of them, their factory-fresh cotton a kiss on her fingertips.

A shop assistant approached. "Can I be of any help at all?"

"Just looking. Thanks."

"It's a very popular line, this. Especially in black. It's dead slimming, the black."

There were plenty of shops where such advice was a challenge: you withdrew or got your plastic out. But this girl offered it as if it were new information, the slimming properties of black having lately been uncovered by the sisterhood. For a moment, Sarah

**170**

thought this was some kind of northern innocence, then realized it was simply that the girl was very young.

"It is," she agreed. "Very. It doesn't perform miracles, though."

And they laughed, and the girl left her to her devices, but as Sarah went to pay for the umbrella she mentally kicked herself for making that moment happen: the one in which women surrender to an image they were taught to have. Sarah wasn't overweight. As for the girl in the shop, you could stick a stamp on her and post her home. So why did they do it?

Zoë wouldn't have joined in. Zoë wore black a lot — wore a famous black jacket — but that had nothing to do with wanting to appear slimmer. It was simply what she wore. Red tops, too. Black and red, like Sarah's new umbrella.

And there was that thought again, the one that had pricked her as she'd entered her PIN on the money machine. Identity wasn't just the numbers you carried, and clothes are not the woman. The body on the slab had Zoë's possessions and Zoë's jacket, but did that mean it was Zoë? It had looked enough like her for those things to seem conclusive. But the convincer had been the jacket, not the body — the jacket which long ago had been taken by Alan Talmadge. Its presence proved Talmadge's involvement. But had Sarah allowed that to cloud her identification?

Taking her change, she wandered from the shop. This route into the heart of the mall was on a gradient, and she walked up it. She seemed to have done a lot of walking these past few days: less than she'd have done back home, perhaps, but city walking was more of an effort. You had to be wary of all the other people. There were always far too many people.

An exit took her on to a walkway, which she followed until it left her looking down on the square that gave the mall its name, and was currently being developed. The railing was spangled with moisture. She stood, still thinking about Zoë's jacket. Okay, so it didn't prove Zoë was dead. But in that case, why hadn't Zoë showed up, demonstrably undead? She must have known she was thought to have drowned. Apart from anything else, she'd be missing her wallet. So if she was still alive, she had good reason for staying hidden.

Or was being kept hidden, of course. That was another possibility. That Zoë was still alive, but had no way of letting the world know.

Sarah shivered. She'd ragged on Gerard yesterday for smoking, but the truth was, she'd been known to take the odd cigarette herself. She could do with one now.

Down below, on the far side of the square, a woman rushed to catch a bus. It had started pulling away, but slowed for her, opened its doors, let her on. Then it shunted off on its journey. A happy ending, Sarah thought. Except, of course, that it was only an ending from Sarah's point of view. On that moving bus, the story continued.

But for someone else, it was well past over. Zoë or not, there'd been a woman on that slab; perhaps murdered in Zoë's place. Fresh water in her lungs, and a river for a grave. Somewhere, a woman was missing. And Sarah thought of the *Big Issue* Gerard had paid for, with its columns of absent faces, and its enquiries hurled into the dark: *Have you seen this woman? Have you seen this man?* If the body wasn't Zoë's, there was a void somewhere else; a life that had been lived, and now wasn't. There must surely be people with questions. Though Alan Talmadge, of course, had preyed on those least likely to be missed.

If anything could chill the heart, it was this: that there were those who wouldn't be missed.

It was something else to tug on. Another loose thread. What she needed now was a session on the web.

As Sarah made her way towards the stairs that would take her to the street below, she thought she caught a snatch of that music again; of the young band on the far side of the shopping centre. But she couldn't have done. There were too many buildings in the way. She must be carrying the music in her head, she decided. But that was a good place to carry it.

The rain was holding off as she made her way river-wards once more, new umbrella tightly folded in her hand.

# CHAPTER
# ELEVEN

Last night's Internet café seemed the right destination, though Sarah had second thoughts before she'd gone a hundred yards. What were her chances of Googling a likely candidate for the body on the slab? Wouldn't the police have found the woman first? What made Sarah think she could do better?

Only that the police hadn't been looking. The body had been carrying Zoë Boehm's ID, and Sarah had identified it — *her* — as Zoë. So why would the police have looked elsewhere? All the evidence pointed in the same direction. And it wasn't like Zoë had appeared anywhere else.

Put that bluntly, what made Sarah think it wasn't Zoë?

She found herself at a junction she didn't remember, and had to rustle through her bag for her A — Z. Being in a city was taking a toll; living in a room was fraying too. Her guide told her the hotel wasn't far: drab, unwelcoming, cold and poorly lit. It would be easy to give up.

Sarah allowed the thought to roost. If she left now, she could be home by supper: a brightly lit fire, a bottle of wine; Russ on the sofa. The knowledge that her own roof was over her head; that her office contained all she needed for her working life; that the two ostriches were outside, roaming their pen. Everything she'd made into a life, these past years. But the thought didn't last. Russ would want to know what happened in the end, and there wasn't an end yet. And while he would willingly trade that for her safe return, Sarah couldn't.

But still — that drab hotel room. Its unsatisfactory bathroom. Its paltry array of toiletries.

She would stay, but would treat herself to a pampering. After a stint on the web she'd have a long warm soak in that unsatisfactory bath, and first she'd acquire the wherewithal to make that soak worthwhile.

It must have been a memory that prompted that decision, because here was the cosmetics shop she'd noticed yesterday with Gerard. It was one of those animal-friendly franchises with Technicolor packaging, and prices scrawled in chalk on blackboards; the sort of place you wouldn't be surprised to find had morphed into a female-friendly sex shop since your last visit. Returning the smile of the blonde in the smock at the till, Sarah went to browse the soaps, which enjoyed a back room to themselves: down two steps and through a bead curtain, like entering Ayesha's cave. More soaps than you could wave a loofah at. All shapes and sizes, including a huge block for shaving slices off, like a cheese. And any colour you liked, so long as it glowed in the dark.

Heaven.

There was an ethic to this. There were two kinds of shopping. You came in armed and dangerous and bought everything in sight, or you restricted yourself to a single item, which took longer, but was peculiarly rewarding. This was one of the latter trips. A clock on the wall said 2.45. Okay, thought Sarah. Fifteen minutes. Let's forget everything for fifteen minutes and choose ourselves some soap.

She was absorbed in this task when the bell jangled in the outer half of the shop: someone coming in. She heard the smocked blonde's bright greeting, and a man's reply: "I'm after some moisturizer." Pause. "Not for me, like. For me girlfriend."

It was an odd thing about the Geordie lilt: lots of folk could imitate it, but almost no one faking it could catch its genuine warmth. Smiling, Sarah returned to her task. She'd almost decided on tangerine. It wasn't exactly an out-there choice — not when guava-jelly soap was available — but she only had herself to please. One last scout round and, failing a message from on high, she'd go with what she was holding. Passing the bead curtain, she looked through it at the new customer. He had his back to her, examining something the assistant had produced. Moisturizer. He spoke again: she didn't catch the words. Then he half turned, pulling his wallet from a pocket and he was Barry, from the hotel.

Barry, who'd told her that everywhere you went, you found a Geordie and an Australian. And who appeared to be both himself.

Sarah dropped her umbrella, dropped the soap, and Barry looked round as they hit the floor. She sank to her knees, retrieved the oblong block with her back to

**176**

the curtain, and the blonde called out, "Everything all right in there?"

"Oh, yeah, no, I was just —" What did her voice sound like? To herself, it sounded strained: but would he recognize it? "I just dropped — it's okay. I'm fine."

Another pause, followed by the mumble of a transaction being completed. The bell above the shop door jangled again, and then the blonde was there, professional concern on her face. "Can I help, like?"

Numbly, Sarah showed her the dropped soap. It had a flattened edge where one curve should be.

"Oh, put it back on the stand, man. Pick another one."

"This is fine," Sarah said. "It'll be fine."

Somehow she paid; somehow she left. Out on the pavement, her new suspicions hit her like a headwind, and kicked the breath out of her. She had to lean against a wall. Alan Talmadge, Zoë had told her, wasn't an easy man to build a picture of. A man who smuggled himself into the lives of older women; bringing them love, Zoë had speculated. And because love doesn't last forever, or perhaps simply because there were other lonely women waiting, he had to move on after a while, and rather than leave broken hearts behind him, Alan Talmadge had ended lives.

"If he can't make a happy ending, he can at least make an ending."

This had happened twice that Zoë had known of, and nothing about those events suggested they were his first adventures. A woman had fallen from a crowded underground platform. Another had slipped into a ditch on a stormy night. It was pure accident, Zoë had told her, that she'd found a connection between the two deaths; the connection being Alan Talmadge, though he'd been using different names. And Zoë had encountered him in the flesh eventually, though she hadn't known it at the time. She'd been looking for a fastidious man with longish hair, who would twist it round his finger when lost in thought. She'd encountered a buzz-cut matey type instead, who'd been following her for longer than she'd been looking for him.

Not long after, Alan Talmadge had slipped off the map. Or so Zoë had thought at the time.

Sarah was gripping her left hand in her right; digging her nails in as if that was all that was keeping her from falling over some unseen edge. And she had dropped the bag holding her soap.

She scooped it up. Opened it briefly, and took a deep breath. The scent of tangerine whipped her away from a Tyneside street for a moment, then dumped her back. Escape wasn't that simple.

Barry was Alan Talmadge. It didn't matter which side you looked at it from, that was the only answer.

Slowly, Sarah started walking; barely aware she was doing so, much less conscious of where she was headed.

Talmadge had slipped off everyone's map but his own. Meanwhile, Zoë had always been on his. He'd followed her here; had taken a job at the Bolbec Hotel . . . *She was my first customer,* he'd told Sarah. Well, of course she was.

**178**

So why hadn't Zoë recognized him?

Her steps faltered, stopped. Picked up.

Of course Zoë had recognized him . . .

He was — what was he? He wasn't a master of disguise; that gave the wrong impression, Zoë had said. No, he was anonymous. The kind of man you looked through.

But Zoë had encountered him before, Sarah thought. There was no way she could have looked him in the eye and not known him. No one was that anonymous.

*We talked a bit. She drank what you're drinking.*

No, Zoë would have pegged him before he'd poured a drop. She'd have known who he was, word one.

He'd wiped the counter as if he were method acting, Sarah remembered. Had been full of gestures a little too perfect; a little too studied.

Except they hadn't worried Sarah, had they? She'd noticed them, but they hadn't worried her.

And he spoke like an Australian — *Wallaby Springs?* — except when he was buying moisturizer with only a Geordie girl in earshot. Then he was northern too; so much so, Sarah had found herself thinking about the Geordie lilt's genuine warmth.

He was good, there was no denying it. But not good enough to fool Zoë twice.

No: whatever had happened to Zoë — whether she was the woman in the water or not — she'd known what she'd got herself into. And it was more important to her than what she was doing for Gerard, or with Gerard, or despite Gerard . . . Here was a knot Sarah hadn't yet untied. But for Zoë, it had been sliced

**179**

through. Whatever had brought her here had faded into insignificance once Alan Talmadge reared his head. He was her unfinished business. He was the one who'd got away.

And here was Sarah, turning under the railway arch; and there was the hotel up ahead.

When she stepped into the lobby Barry was on reception, not the woman she'd been expecting, and this caused her heart to lose a beat — she stumbled, but caught her balance in time. *Steady*, she warned herself. *Steady.*

"Afternoon there, Ms Tucker."

That antipodean twang again, which seemed to take a bite out of *Tucker*.

"Barry."

"Been taking a wander?"

"Yes. Just — here and there."

*How about you?* she almost asked. *Popped out to do a little shopping?*

"Having a nice holiday?"

"Could I have my key?"

"But sure." He'd already plucked it from the rack. "You know, when you came in there, it was like a breath of spring."

"I don't —"

"Tangerines," he said. "I distinctly smelt tangerines." He nodded at her bag. It was plain brown paper, and could have come from anywhere. "Pick up some fruit on your wanderings?"

"No," she said. "No. Not really."

And this must be what it was like when you were a mouse, and the cat had a paw either side of you. Big bright smile on its face, as if it intended you nothing but pleasure.

"Oh," he said. "I meant to ask."

She'd already taken the key, and was measuring the distance between here and the stairs. "Ask what?"

"About your friend. Zoë, right?"

Something cold shifted position between Sarah's shoulder blades. "What about her?"

"The other night. You were wondering what we were discussing."

Sarah said, "It's not important. It was just something to say, that's all."

"Well, I was wondering, why don't you ask her?"

She stared.

He shrugged. "Women have better memories for that sort of thing."

"You've seen her?"

"Why? Is she still around?"

"I — I'm not sure. Have you seen her?"

"Not since she checked out," Barry said. "Not since that evening we chatted." He picked up a pen, and rolled it between finger and thumb, but didn't take his eyes from Sarah. "But I presume you're in touch with her. Friends, right?"

"Yes," Sarah said.

"So give her a call." He winked. "Send her my regards, yeah?" The phone rang then, as if it had heard its name mentioned. "Bolbec Hotel, can I help you?"

The stairs welcomed Sarah like an old friend.

In her room, she dropped the keys on the bed; put the bag of soap on the dresser. Barry hadn't been wrong. Just carrying it in had charged the atmosphere: it was a small zesty bomb. But he must have known it wasn't fruit. Real fruit didn't smell like that: not in this half of the world.

*Give her a call. Send her my regards, yeah?*

Had he known it was Sarah in the shop?

He hadn't come through the bead curtain, and hadn't been in sight when she'd left. But he'd heard her voice, even if she'd tried to sound different. And she was carrying this brown bag, which must have been like the one he'd been given for his moisturizer.

*Not for me, like. For me girlfriend.*

That Geordie lilt, with its genuine warmth.

But had he known it was Sarah in the shop?

It would be foolish to assume he hadn't. Isn't that what Zoë would tell her? It would be exceedingly unwise to imagine that everything was okay.

But more than that, there was something in what he'd said.

*Give her a call. Send her my regards, yeah?*

Yes: if a cat could talk with a mouse between its paws, that's the kind of thing it would say.

*You've got a friend? Give her a call.*

It would then lick its lips.

*Send her my regards. Yeah?*

And there it was: the something hidden in his words.

**182**

Sarah sat on the bed and closed her eyes. Screwed them tightly at first, in the effort of memory, then loosened up as the images flowed.

There was a game she'd played as a child: Kim's Game. She had a vague notion its name came from Kipling. Eyes shut, she played it now; imagined a tray hovering in front of her and then, one by one, placed these objects neatly upon it.

Keys. A watch. A lipstick. Zoë's hairbrush. A wallet. Things that were in the wallet — a clump of till receipts and credit card slips. The credit cards themselves, of course, and some coins and notes . . . Some other things. But she couldn't bring them to mind.

She opened her eyes. The room remained as it had been; same dull pattern marching up and down its walls; same dusty lamp in the corner. There was no tray hovering in front of her. But when she closed her eyes again, it came back:

Keys, a watch, a lipstick, a hairbrush, a wallet, till receipts, credit card slips, credit cards, coins, notes. A pen. That was one of the other things, but there was more, too — the jewellery. A silver chain she couldn't remember Zoë wearing, but had no difficulty picturing her doing so, and a ring, a plain gold band, which was probably her wedding ring but which she now wore on a different finger.

What else?

The clothing, the jacket, the belt. But this wasn't about what Zoë had been wearing; it was about what she'd been carrying.

What else?

Keys, watch, lipstick, hairbrush, wallet, till receipts, credit card slips, credit cards, coins, notes, pen, chain, ring — she thought that was all. She was sure of it.

In her mind, she went through them again: laid these objects out on the tray she'd conjured up, which left no more room upon it. The tray was as full as the slab the body had lain upon.

So she sat up, opened her eyes, and turned on the bedside lamp. Immediately the room took on a different configuration. Shadows rearranged themselves. Fresh ones sprang to life.

Sarah reached for her mobile, and pressed a familiar sequence of buttons; waited while the numbers negotiated with the ether, and made bells ring.

Rang once, twice, three times. And then the recorded voice kicked in:

*You've reached Zoë Boehm. Leave a message.*

She couldn't stay. The room had grown smaller; the whole hotel had, as if bowing to the inevitability of its coming closure. If she remained, she'd be trapped inside an ever-shrinking space; a box she was forced to share with Alan Talmadge.

When she replayed his words, they came out the same:

*Why don't you call her? Give her my regards.*

Which meant what? That he knew Zoë was dead? Or knew she was alive?

Or maybe he was just telling her that he knew that the body pulled from the water was missing a mobile phone. And that Zoë never went anywhere without her mobile.

Sarah grabbed her purse, opened the door and paused on the threshold. The corridor was empty. The only sound came from downstairs; a coughing, chugging noise it took her a while to identify as a vacuum cleaner. The other night she'd wondered if the mirrors were arranged so you could sit at reception and spy on every floor. But that couldn't be possible, could it? Not outside a creepy film.

She wished Gerard hadn't checked out. His viewpoint might have been useful right now. *This is nonsense. You're in a large hotel in a big city. Alan Talmadge? If he ever existed, he doesn't now.*

But too many details were conspiring to suggest that he did. And Gerard wasn't here.

Though only Barry had seen him check out, of course.

It was just another detail, but it led down a corridor as empty as this one. What if Gerard had never checked out at all? What if Barry had lied about that too? Gerard might still be around; strapped up in one of the utility cupboards, or —

"No," she said aloud. No. That was seriously outside the realm of possibility.

Except that, now the thought had formed, there was no dismissing it.

Closing the door behind her, she moved towards the staircase just as the asthmatic vacuuming choked into silence. The air continued humming for a beat, as if it missed the company. Sarah paused again, then caught herself in the mirror on the landing, and moved in a hurry. One flight. Another landing. Another flight.

Reception was unattended, but any moment, he'd be back. Pop his head out from the office: *Did you speak to your friend yet? Zoë, right?*

His accent breaking like a wave on a faraway beach . . .

Sarah got as far as the front door before she heard the voice behind her —

"Ms Tucker?"

— but it was the woman. The one whose name she'd never got hold of.

"Will you be here for supper?"

"I — no. I mean yes."

"That's a yes, right?"

"That's a yes."

"Thank you."

"Is, ah — I thought Barry was on duty?"

"He's taking a break. Another break."

"Oh."

"He's already been out this afternoon. But I owe him a favour."

Words accompanied by a hint of smirk.

Sarah left. The skies had darkened further; already, it felt like evening. And Barry could be yards away, watching from round a corner. He'd known she'd been in the shop: she'd convinced herself of that now. He'd known she'd been there from the moment she'd walked up to the reception desk, carrying the brown bag with its scent of tangerines.

But the only watching man she could see was the *Big Issue* seller at his post by the parking meters.

It made no difference. Alan Talmadge was a watcher, a hider. If he didn't want to be seen, she wouldn't see him.

The *Big Issue* man gave her a wave. But she didn't have time, she didn't have time. She began hurrying towards the railway station.

A crowd, she had decided. She needed to be near a crowd. At the Central Station, there would be a crowd. She'd feel safer there. And that would give her the chance to work out what to say when she rang DS King. She had to be able to explain it so he'd understand: the things she hadn't told him about Zoë — about Zoë's jacket — about the man who'd taken it from her. About why she was frightened now.

The other one, Fairfax, she didn't want to speak to. The best she could expect from him would be another outburst. Why was she wasting his time?

The sky grumbled, and she walked faster.

But before she'd got as far as the Lit & Phil, she found herself reaching for her mobile, and then reaching again, checking one pocket after the other, in confirmation of what she already knew: that she'd left her phone in the hotel. She should go back. But that would be like the fly returning to the spider's web because — . . . But she couldn't think of anything a fly might leave behind. Which didn't change the situation. Barry — Talmadge — might be following her even now, and if he wasn't, it would be stupid to give him the chance. She didn't have King's number, but she knew where the damn police station was.

With the thought came another rumble from above, and this time it wasn't kidding. The skies grew darker still. And then brightened suddenly, as if they'd been ripped apart to reveal the light behind.

The first spats hit the pavement like footballs, bouncing.

Along with her mobile phone, she'd abandoned her new umbrella. She had no idea where.

"That'll be the rain starting up," someone behind her said, as if it were always the same rain, and generally began about now. It fell hard, from long practice, and among a crowd of others Sarah rushed for the station portico. Within seconds, the rain was lashing the road, turning traffic amphibious. An overhead gutter became a tap, directing a thick stream on to the pavement.

A wheeled suitcase overturned on the nearby zebra crossing. Its owner struggled to right it in the downpour, while waiting cars were carpet-bombed by rain.

"It can't last."

"It'll never last."

Voices off.

She'd have called this idle chatter, were it not for the effort needed to make it. At high volume, to be heard above the rain, a consensus formed: this will never last. But the skies didn't brighten, and the rain didn't stop.

Sarah stood among a crowd of strangers, in this large porch, and felt afraid.

People were anonymous in the rain. Hoods came up; umbrellas unfolded; disguises were unpacked and artfully donned. Barry had gone AWOL just as she'd left the hotel, and could be anywhere. Could be one of those soaked rats trying to crush themselves against the wall over there, as if the slim ledge above might shelter them. Could be one of those sinners still striding the pavements; faces obscured by the melting newspapers they used for hats.

And the rain fell like a curtain. This area Sarah had fetched up in, a place for taxis to pull into, was like the secret space behind a waterfall, but more crowded. People streamed in and out of the station, catching trains or just released from them; heading for the Metro or one of the concourse bars, to wait the weather out with a cup of coffee. She thought about joining them, but wouldn't be able to sit still. And couldn't face the Metro, with its escalators and subterranean platforms. But knew she wanted to be on the move.

Barry was not among these close-at-hand strangers. But he could be close, veiled by rain. Could be in the newsagent's over the road, watching through a steamed-up window.

Her hand curled into a fist. Her nails dug into her palm.

A bus was arriving at a stop over the road. Without consciously deciding to do so, Sarah moved; sprinted from her shelter and across the zebra, earning an angry squonk from a car, but making it over in one piece; making it to the bus stop too, just in time.

"In a hurry, pet?" the driver asked as Sarah fumbled for her fare.

Sarah said something. She wasn't sure what.

"Sooner get there in one piece, myself. There's another bus just after."

As she sat, she saw it pulling up behind: another yellow double-decker, monstrous in the rain. Its screen-wiper slashing to and fro like a blade. A man was jumping aboard. He had his collar turned up, and his head averted.

Wet city traffic was a fractious thing. Tyres slapped the tarmac, and horns blared disgust. Raindrops smacked like bullets off car roofs. Outside, pedestrians waded from one doorway to the next. And then, with a jerk, the bus arrived at an unclogged channel and forged ahead, carrying Sarah into unknown country: a land of wet streets and fogged-up shop windows.

The bus behind splashed along in their wake.

She became aware of conversation around her: strangers exchanging bulletins on how their day was going. *Owa' wet* was the general verdict.

All of these people, and were any of them who they appeared to be?

Sarah's palm ached.

Barry was the barman at the Bolbec Hotel: he doubled as receptionist, and goodness knows what else. She didn't even know his surname. He was from "Wallaby Springs". But he wasn't from Wallaby Springs, and he hadn't been anything at the Bolbec Hotel for more than two weeks. All those tricks of his trade — the tea-towel over the shoulder; the counter-wiping while he talked — sang *Look at me. I'm a barman*. But in the soap shop, his accent had been northern.

Details that bounced around her head again, faster than the first time.

Barry was Alan Talmadge. And he knew she knew.

*You want to talk to Zoë? Why don't you give her a ring?*

The bus pulled up: people got on, people got off. The air cleared when the doors opened, but fogged again immediately they closed. The bus behind also stopped to disgorge passengers. Through the runny windows she could make out furry shapes, the blooming of umbrellas. There was nobody following her. It was not possible for anyone to be following her. Least of all was it possible for that person to be Alan Talmadge. But still she looked, in case a shape took form, and boarded this bus.

If he does, I'll know him, she thought. If it's Barry. He might be able to shift his shape — might be different things to different people — but he couldn't be different things to the same person, could he? Geordie Barry was also Barry from Oz. She'd not have known him otherwise.

And he was not, she told herself, he was not he was not he was not on this bus.

Stop. Calm down. Take deep breaths.

The voice in her head was not her own.

It was Zoë's. For just one moment, she thought it was Zoë on the bus, but it was only Zoë in her head: *Calm down. Take deep breaths.* She didn't remember

Zoë ever saying those things, but it was possible. They'd shared tense moments.

Tears stung her, and her vision fogged like the bus's windows.

She wished she'd spoken to Russ today.

She wished she had her phone.

Through the window to her right the land fell away, perhaps down to the river. Sarah could make out what might be the roofs of allotment huts, but it was raining too hard to be sure. And then the gap was filled by a row of terraced housing, with each and every door and window covered by metal sheeting.

At the end of this row was a Metro sign.

The bus stopped a hundred yards further on. Sarah slipped out the middle door, where the weather hit her like a dustbin lid, and hurried back down the road. The second bus splashed her as it passed.

But the sign was for an off-licence, not the Metro.

She turned in time to see the second bus disappearing. There was no telling if anyone had emerged from it. A man — collar up; indistinct in the rain and the gathering dark — waited to cross the road, twenty yards away. A couple of lads were gaining ground, but split round her like water on a rock. Their voices blurred in passing, as if she'd spun the dial on a radio. She looked for a street sign, but couldn't see one.

Rain continued to fall.

# CHAPTER
# TWELVE

It had been a while since smoking was legal in pubs, but here was a temple to its memory: the walls still nicotine-tinged; the tin sheet screwed into the door advising *Senior Service Satisfy*.

Sarah dripped in the doorway. Everyone in the room had turned to look at her, or that's what it felt like.

A sofa ran round the wall, hemmed in place by tables and wooden stools, most of them occupied. It seemed early for a bar to be full, but if the alternative was being outside, she could see the argument. There was drink being taken, and enough noise to go round. Some of it poured from a wall-mounted TV, tuned to sports coverage.

A gas fire banged out heat so hard, Sarah could almost see it warp. The air was heavy with damp from drying clothes. It was like attending a wet-dog conference.

She headed for the bar. She was the only woman there, she thought, then realized that no, there was another; an old woman on a stool at the counter, the shape and approximate colour of a postbox.

The barman asked, "What can I get you?"

Sarah had no idea. Didn't seem like a good moment to say so, though.

She'd come through that door because it was the first she'd found which looked like it would open when pushed. There were no shops, or none that were functioning. Even that off-licence had been locked. If another bus had come she'd have been on it in a flash, but none appeared. The pub offered shelter, at least.

"Just a water. Thanks. Mineral water. If you have it."

He stared, and she wondered if she'd mortally offended him. Then his face broke into a smear she took for a grin.

"You've not had enough of that yet?"

"Maybe you're right. Make it a whisky."

"Bells?"

She nodded. Whatever.

In a western, there'd have been a general release of tension with that.

The nearest stool was free, so she sat. There was nowhere to drape her coat. She wondered if it was ruined. What a stupid thing to do: buy an umbrella then immediately lose it. But not the worst thing that had happened today. Elbow on the bar, she rested her head on her hand. That man who'd hopped off the bus behind her. That couldn't have been Talmadge, could it? She couldn't be positive. She was starting to think of Talmadge as a phantom; able to move at will through obstacles. Mostly unseen. Only ever glimpsed. When she wrenched her mind back to his other identity, Barry the barman, she was unable to summon up his features.

194

It was as if her new knowledge of him had obscured his previous self.

Her drink was placed in front of her, and she raised her head. "Thanks." She almost knocked the glass over, reaching for her purse.

"When you're ready, pet."

She flushed. But before she could retrieve her money, someone spoke. "Ah'll buy the lady's drink."

A clatter of coins accompanied this.

Sarah said, "No. Really."

"It's done, love."

The barman scooped the payment up, and it was indeed done.

"See?"

Looking at her gallant, Sarah saw a fiftyish-looking man with a well-lined face and greying curls that fizzed into sideburns. He wore damp denims over a T-shirt that did nothing to hide his paunch. If you had to itemize a stranger you didn't want buying you a drink, this one ticked all the boxes.

She placed three pound coins in front of him. "Thank you. But there's no need. I'll pay for my own drinks."

"Now that's not polite. Turning down an honest gift."

He pushed the money back her way.

Something similar had happened the other evening, in the hotel bar. A drunk had tried to buy a piece of her attention. And even if Barry — *Talmadge!* — hadn't smoothed him away, Sarah wouldn't have been worried. You took this sort of thing in your stride.

Accepted the drink or refused it, and tried not to give offence. Not because you didn't want to give offence, but because you didn't want a scene. It wasn't like you didn't get the practice.

But that had been somewhere else; somewhere similar to places she knew and felt comfortable in. Here, she was on foreign ground. She'd known pubs like this in her youth, but only as part of a crowd. Force of numbers, plus teenage invulnerability, had rendered her oblivious to threat. Now, though, she was alone, off balance, and — she was beginning to suspect — down the wrong end of the city.

"You're kind. But I'm fine. Really."

He stared, as though she were speaking a different language.

The barman had retreated to the far end of the counter. He knew damn well what was happening: he just didn't care. There was a sly awareness to his posture; a trapped laugh he wasn't releasing yet.

Her unwelcome benefactor said, "Ye divvent want to be perched on a stool like a parrot, pet. Come away and sit on the sofa, like."

"I'm fine where I am."

"Just being friendly." His fist was wrapped round a gassy pint, its rim laced with froth. He smiled at Sarah as he raised it to his lips. The two events — the smile, the swallow — merged into a single ugly act.

From where she sat, Sarah could see the door. The afternoon accordioned in her memory, its events squeezing into a single long mistake: from buying her lost umbrella to shopping for soap to taking that bus

**196**

ride through the dark rain, whose every shadow belonged to Alan Talmadge. Somehow, all this had brought her through that door and dumped her on this stool. Somehow she'd wound up at the mercy of an export-swilling Lothario.

She should get up and walk back out, but where would that leave her? In the rain again, lost among those shadows.

As if to underscore her thoughts the weather made an assault on the pub's windows, and the sound of rattling frames joined the clinking of drinks, the sharing of jokes, the TV's mutterings; all the communal noise surrounding her, but which Sarah wasn't part of. She felt trapped behind a pane of glass herself. Something preventing her from raising her voice to say: *Take this man away. I came in here for shelter.* Something whispering that even if she did so, nobody would hear, or take action.

This man clearly wasn't Alan Talmadge. But he was from the same tribe, even if he didn't know it. He was further down the chain, that was all.

"So what brings ye doon here?"

"I got caught in the rain."

"Aye, it's fockin' brutal out."

She hadn't tasted her drink yet. She picked it up now; mentally formed the words *Please. Go away* but didn't say them. The whisky bit her throat. She didn't drink spirits often. It wasn't a pub, though, where you asked for a Sauvignon.

*She drank what you're drinking,* Barry had said. *Always a good basis for friendship.*

In the absence of anything else . . .

Zoë, she thought. What were you doing?

"Come on, then. See that off, and wuh'll have another."

"Please," she said. "No offence. I just don't want company right now."

"But Ah've paid for your drink, like."

The coins were still on the counter in front of her. Wordlessly, she slid them his way.

"Ah divvent want your money, pet." This with an air of irritated explanation: a teacher faced with a dunce. "Just a smile and a chat. Is that too much to ask, like?"

She closed her eyes briefly. When she opened them again, he was still there.

"Or are ye too fockin' posh to smile?"

He pushed the money back towards her — pushed it deliberately roughly. A coin dropped to the floor and rolled under a table. Sarah bit her lip.

"Ye want it, ye'd better pick it up. Hadn't ye?"

She looked at him. That was a mistake. It didn't matter how much you wanted to pacify, the straight look could be a threat to some men. Especially grey and frazzled men, stuck in a pub before the working day was out.

"Gan on. Ah divvent mind watching ye crawl roond the floor."

There was a noise behind Sarah; a throaty rattle. Half a cough. Followed by words. "Trev? You've had your fun. Off you fuck, now. There's a good lad."

It was the old woman on the next stool along, and she wasn't even looking Trev's way. Didn't have to.

He said, "Ah was just —"

"The lady's not interested. She stopped in out the rain. Pick her pound up and go sit down. I won't ask twice."

And it was his turn to look at Sarah, and now he was the one hoping for understanding — *Can you believe these old women get away with this?* She didn't alter her expression. But she looked away before he did, and took a sip of her drink.

He slipped from his stool, and went foraging for the runaway pound.

Sarah turned to the old woman, who hadn't raised her head during the exchange. With a folded-over tabloid in front of her, she was stuck into Sudoku. Before Sarah could speak, a coin was pressed down into the space between them. The thumb doing the pressing wanted to drill it through the counter.

"Thank you," she said.

"Don't . . . mention it."

Don't *fockin'* mention it, he meant.

He removed himself to the corner he'd emerged from. Slunk back, Sarah wanted to say, but he didn't; he swaggered, rather, as if he'd won on points in a romantic encounter.

She guessed a man like that did a lot of rewriting of immediate history.

"He meant no harm," the woman said.

"I'm sure he didn't."

Rain still beat the windows, but she thought she'd be leaving here regardless, just as soon as she'd finished her drink.

"And it's not like he imagined you were going to fall for him." The woman still didn't look up from her paper. "The gap's as visible from his side as yours."

Sarah put her glass down. "You think I'm a tourist?"

"I think you came in out the rain."

"Well, then."

"Just not sure what brought you here in the first place."

Sarah said, "I must have wandered across a checkpoint. When I got on the bus, I was in the twenty-first century."

"There's your error. Walker's still suffering through the twentieth."

At last she looked up, and Sarah saw her eyes for the first time: bright robin's eyes in a face that might have been modelled from papier mâché. Not well modelled, either. Saggy lumps at her jaw and below her eyes looked like mistakes. Sarah tried not to stare at her moustache.

She said, "So, what would you have done? If you'd had to ask twice?"

The woman said, "Gary behind the bar there's stepping out with our Derek's Carol. Trevor doesn't want to go crossing me if he wants to keep his local."

There was a family web Sarah didn't want to get stuck on.

"And last thing Trevor wants to lose is his local. Lad's lost pretty much everything else."

The "lad" must have been in his fifties.

Sarah said, "Is this where you tell me his sad story? So I grasp what a noble soul he is?"

She might have saved her breath.

"Once Armstrong's went to the wall, that was his future used up. His wife found a better prospect. He gets four weeks a year at Christmas on the Post. Rest of the time, he's in here."

"I get the picture."

"I'm not sure you do. What were you doing twenty year ago?"

Those robin's eyes had shifted somehow. Still bright, but predatory now.

"Buying your first house? Starting your first job?"

"Not quite," she said. But not that far off, either.

"Trevor was in here. Where do you think you'll be twenty year from now?"

"You've made your point," Sarah said. "Next time, I think I'll just get wet."

The woman smiled at last. "Wouldn't be doing my job if I didn't make you feel worse. Truth is, Trevor was an arsehole when he had work and a wife. Where he'll be in twenty years is his problem."

"And what would your job be again?"

"I'm the local busybody, dear. I'd've thought you'd've worked that out by now."

She picked up her drink — something Coke-coloured, that probably wasn't — and drained the glass. Then winked at Sarah.

Feeling she'd wandered out of one situation straight into another, Sarah suppressed a sigh. "Same again?"

"That'd be grand, pet."

Not a freeloader, though. She bought her round.

She just liked to talk.

"Don't get me wrong, pet. They've rebuilt this city from the ground up. They just forgot parts, that's all."

Sarah said, "It's a process. Not everything gets done at once."

She was on her third whisky. It was still raining. And the bar was still full, though most of the background noise had muffled to an ambient roar. Maybe that was the drink, insulting her.

"And when they reach here, they'll build more fancy housing where the yards used to be. But us who've lived here these forty year'll not be moving into riverside flats."

"Ivy," she said. "Last thing you want is to be moving into any fancy new riverside flat."

"Aye. Be nice to be asked though, wouldn't it?"

She laughed a cackle of a laugh: raw and unabashed.

When Trev had been hassling her, Sarah had suspected they'd had a secret audience. It wasn't so secret now. Ivy played to a crowd.

The door had opened a dozen times: always someone coming in; never anyone leaving. And every time, she'd had to look, just to make sure. And it had never been Barry. She was starting to believe it never would be.

Which didn't stop her looking.

Ivy said, "You'll be having another."

It wasn't a question.

Sarah said, "I should be going."

But she'd got it right first time: it wasn't a question. Ivy had already given the nod to Gary behind the bar, who was stepping out with our Derek's Carol.

A warm fuzz was taking the edge off Sarah's next big issue: what was she supposed to do now?

Okay, so she'd given Alan Talmadge the slip. But all she had with her was her purse. She'd been going to call DS King, but that was before the warm fuzz had wrapped her: she'd need a good hard think before trying to outline the details of the day to a policeman. And besides, so many of those details remained shadows in the dark. Did she need to take another look at the body on the slab? Did she still think it was Zoë? Maybe it was. Maybe Talmadge had taken her mobile phone at the same time he'd taken her life.

The door opened with a now familiar scrape, and she couldn't help herself: she had to look. She knew it wouldn't be Barry but she had to look.

Ivy said, "Are you sure it's just the rain you're sheltering from?"

Sarah said, "It's bound to stop soon. It can't keep this up forever."

"Only every time that door opens, you startle like a fawn."

Sarah couldn't help wondering how many fawns Ivy had encountered on the streets of Walker. Even as she was thinking that, a bell was ringing: Walker. Why was the name familiar?

"Or is Trevor not the only one been making himself a nuisance?"

"Any given day," Sarah said, "we can safely assume Trevor'll not be the only one doing that."

"You're married, then."

She had to laugh. "I have been. Not any more."

"Turned out not what you expected?"

Sarah said, "Not so much being married. More the husband."

"Aye, that's a long road, once you start down it. Men who aren't what they seem."

She tapped her glass. Sarah still hadn't identified her tipple; "same again" had done the trick. But Ivy seemed capable of drinking it forever without a visible twitch.

. . . Men who aren't what they seem, she thought. It certainly was a long road. Mark, her ex-husband, lived somewhere on it; along with, she sometimes thought, every man she'd met since. Which wasn't always a bad thing. Russ was a darling, though hadn't seemed so on first meeting, while Gerard had struck her as a monster. And while that was true enough — he was a monster — he was also human, as it turned out. But they were the mild examples. Barry loomed larger right now: a man who adopted the identity of friendly Australian barman as easily as he tossed a tea-towel over one shoulder. Nor was she the first woman to have been fooled. As Alan Talmadge, he had taken lives. Was it any wonder Sarah startled every time the door scraped open?

And then there was Jack Gannon. A nice guy at a party, who turned out to be the son of the Godfather.

Which was the connection, of course. The Gannons were a Walker family. This was their patch.

Ivy said, "So that's who you're worried about?"

For a moment, Sarah thought the old woman had read her mind and was talking about Jack. Then she respooled the thread of their conversation, and realized Ivy thought Sarah had an ex-husband on her tail.

She shook her head. "He's long gone."

"But someone isn't."

Ivy wasn't the police. She was an old soak in a pub. On the other hand, she had a pair of ears.

Sarah said, "It's a long story."

Ivy called to Gary, "When you're ready, hen."

Their drinks arrived.

She wasn't sure how long her story took. All she knew was that once she'd started there was no slowing; and that what poured forth was pure narrative, drained of emotion. No tears, not even when describing the body on the slab. But as she spoke a valve loosened, and the strain she'd been under since arriving in Newcastle eased. Even the rain seemed to relax; its onslaught on the windows calming to a patter that was mostly drowned by the hubbub inside.

It was the kind of story that brought itself to an obvious conclusion. It ended with Sarah sitting on this barstool, now.

For a while after she'd finished, the two women sat in silence. Ivy had been an unexpected listener. Their conversation so far had mostly involved her own story, which was not so much a linear narrative as a collage of details whose context Sarah had been expected to keep up with, the end result being a sort of pointillist biography; various unconnected dots adding up to a life, provided you viewed them through half-shut eyes. Perhaps, Sarah thought, Ivy wasn't used to things happening to other people. Or didn't accord them importance. But that was an impertinent conclusion, as well as a wrong one. Ivy listened. Ivy weighed things up. Ivy didn't speak until she'd decided what she was going to say.

Which was: "Well, bugger me."

Somehow, Sarah hadn't been expecting that.

"And every word of it gospel. Yes?"

Sarah said, tightly, "Every word. Yes."

"Now, then. It's a reasonable question."

Ivy drained her glass. Sarah had long lost count of how many that made. Her wallet was feeling light, though. As was her head.

"This man, your Barry."

"He's not my Barry."

"Pet, you've got to lighten up."

Which was the first time she'd been given that particular piece of advice by an octogenarian.

"But he's also this Talmadge feller."

"Yes," Sarah said. "I think so," she amended.

"Who's killed your women in the past."

Zoë's women, she thought. Talmadge killed Zoë's women, though Zoë never met them either.

She closed her eyes briefly, and when she opened them, the bar swam in front of her. That's it, she thought. No more to drink.

As ever, that awareness arrived ten minutes after it might have been useful.

Ivy, though. Ivy looked like she could keep drinking until the birthday after next.

"And he knows I know," Sarah said. "Know who he is."

This struck her with some force, and she turned to make sure Barry hadn't sneaked in while she'd been spilling her story. The room boomed before her eyes, then diminished into a miniature version of itself, full of small happy drinkers. She felt Ivy's hand patting her arm, and then her vision was back to normal. She had the horrible feeling she was about to throw up.

"Through the back, pet," Ivy said. She was pointing with an admirably straight arm. Back along the bar — near to where Trev still sat — then through a door marked *Toliets*. Or probably *Toilets*. "You'll feel better after. That's always the way."

As Sarah tested her legs on the floor, she heard Ivy say, "And there's nowt to worry about. Not in here. Your man'll never dare show his face in here."

The next five minutes were not among Sarah's finest. When she re-showed herself in the bar, her face was white and still damp. The dispenser had been out of paper towels, and she'd had to do what she could with her hands. The taste of vomit lingered, and she dreaded to think what her breath smelled like. But there was a glass of water waiting on the bar, next to a mug of black coffee, and while she'd never subscribed to the idea that coffee was a cure for being drunk, she welcomed both. The water helped with the sour taste in her mouth, and the coffee scalded her tongue, but made her feel better.

She began to say, "Ivy, I'm —"

"Hush, man. I'd had your day, they'd need a crane to lift me off the floor."

"I haven't eaten lately either, and —"

"Well, I'd give that a while yet. Let's not run before we can walk, eh?"

Good advice. Even the thought of food made Sarah's stomach threaten to heave again. But she felt better, that was true; and as drunken episodes go, she'd enacted worse. Her memory was intact, and she knew she hadn't danced on the bar or shrieked with laughter. Up until feeling sick, she'd actually thought she was more or less sober.

Now all she wanted to do was close her eyes.

Ivy said, "You've not called the polis?"

"The polis?"

"The polis."

The police, Sarah translated. She drank more water. Funny how having drunk too much made you thirsty. There were sound chemical reasons for this, but still: funny.

She said, "You know — right this minute? Right this minute, the last thing I want to do is talk to anyone."

It was so tempting to close her eyes, and lay her head down on the bar. For all the noise and the heavy wet fug, she'd sleep so peacefully . . .

"Maybe so, pet. But you can't just leave it at that, can you now?" Ivy seemed to be in charge of Sarah's immediate future. "Not that I'm recommending the polis, like. We've little love round here for the blue." A fresh glass of her Coke-coloured drink had materialized in front of her. Gary was evidently under a standing

208

instruction. "For all our Eileen's youngest took the shilling ten years back. He's a sergeant now."

"Ivy —"

"So I made a phone call while you were freshening up. It's clear you're in more trouble than you know what to do with. And this Barry fella — I'd give him a good clip if he showed his face round here. But he's not likely to do that now, is he?"

A good clip. One way of dealing with him. But other facts were struggling for clarification: "Ivy? You called who?"

"Someone who'll know what to do."

Not Eileen's youngest, by the sound of it. Maybe our Derek's Carol. Sarah reached for her water, but she'd finished it last time, so picked up the coffee instead. It was still too hot to drink. The pub door opened, but Sarah didn't turn. A more urgent question had occurred to her, having weaved its way through the whisky-smoke in her mind. "Ivy? What does 'gan canny' mean?"

If Ivy were discombobulated by the change of direction, she didn't show it. "Learning the lingo?"

"I like," said Sarah, "to make the effort."

Ivy said, "Our Derek's pal Tezza, on the buses, he was from St Kitts. He used to say, 'Be careful as you walk.' Instead of goodbye, like."

"Be careful as you walk," Sarah repeated.

"Aye," Ivy told her. "That's what 'gan canny' means, pet."

"Be careful as you walk," she said again.

There was a man right behind her now, but it wasn't Barry. Wasn't Alan Talmadge. Looking at his reflection in the bar mirror, Sarah could say with some certainty that she'd never laid eyes on him in her life.

"He'll see you all right, pet," Ivy said. "No need to worry."

"I'm not," Sarah said.

Which was true. Whatever Ivy had in mind, Sarah knew it didn't involve doing Sarah harm.

"Gan canny, pet," Ivy said.

"This the lassie?" the man asked.

Ivy nodded.

"Had away, then," he said, or something like it.

Sarah got to her feet, none too steadily. The man let her lead the way out of the bar. It was hard not to notice that everyone watched them leave, or that they stopped talking while they did so.

Outside it was dark and still wet. A car was parked at the kerb, hazards flashing. The man opened the door, and Sarah climbed into the back. Then he got into the front, and drove away.

# CHAPTER
# THIRTEEN

"More water?"

"Thanks."

He poured it from a jug. She was a world away from dead-end Walker. The armchair embraced her like a feather bed. She could easily close her eyes and swim into sleep.

"Another Nurofen?"

"Better not. Shouldn't have had that first one." Her words stumbled. "Not after whisky."

Jack Gannon said, "You'll be fine. They put that warning stuff on the packets to cover themselves."

The drive across town was already a blur. Her chauffeur had barely uttered a word, once he'd established that nothing he said met with comprehension. Sarah's attempts at learning the lingo had juddered to a halt.

But there was quite some distance between here and where Jack had grown up, that was clear. This street was quiet, suburban, tree-lined; included, across the road, what was either a school or a convent, with ivy creeping in and out of the diamond pattern of its mesh fence. Tidy strips of grass lined both pavements.

Jack said, "Why go to Walker? Why drop my name in a pub? You could have called."

"I didn't drop your name." She half-laughed. "Didn't even know I was in Walker till I got there. And didn't know you were someone whose name would be picked up that easily."

"No?"

She looked up. He was obviously sober; he came into focus within a second. His living room was a long uncluttered space, knocked through front to back, but he was close at hand, in the matching armchair. "Okay. I knew more about you than you revealed on first meeting. Or second."

He said, "None of us can help our ancestry."

"Ivy asked me my story. I told her. You came into it, that's all."

Jack nodded. There was something different about him tonight. He was still tall and the same kind of thin steel cables were; still had neatly styled dark hair and acne-patched cheeks. But there was something different. Maybe it was to do with being on his own territory.

He said, "The Internet's a sort of jungle pond, don't you think? Jump into it, you never know what you're going to find. Or what's going to find you."

You wouldn't have to bend that too far out of shape to make it a threat. But he didn't look threatening. More rueful, if anything. As if he was all too aware of the details an Internet trawl might drag into the light.

Sarah said, "I take everything I find on it with a pinch of salt."

212

The image threatened to make her gag. Hurriedly, she took another gulp of water.

"But you found some interesting facts nevertheless."

"About your father. Not about you."

"There's always someone'll tell you the apple doesn't fall far from the tree."

Sarah remembered the photograph of Michael Gannon she'd found: heavier than Jack, with an out-of-date moustache. One look, and she'd been sure he was guilty of all he'd been acquitted of.

Jack, though . . . First meeting, she'd liked Jack.

But did she like him enough to be alone with him in his house?

Things had happened too fast. She'd been too startled by what she'd learned about Barry; had backed into a corner she'd tried to drink herself out of. And now she was here, looking for safety. She could almost hear Zoë's voice: *Safety? You don't know the meaning of the word.* She should ask if she could make a phone call. She should speak to Russell; start organizing her departure from this city.

The time it took to think all this, the glass had grown heavy in her hand.

There was nothing spooky about this, though. Nothing underhand in the water. She was tired, that was all. Tired and still drunk.

Jack said, "That aside. This man Barry. From the hotel."

"Yes," she said.

"What I heard from Ivy was a bit garbled."

"You know Ivy?"

"I know a thousand like her. Grew up among them. Basically," he said, "they're all my gran."

She nodded. She could see how that worked.

"He's not who he seems to be," Jack said. "That much I got."

"He isn't," Sarah said. "He's not Australian, for a start."

"He's not from Wallaby Springs?" Jack said. "That's disappointing."

"You didn't believe that anyway," Sarah remembered.

"But how bad does that make him? Maybe he just wanted to be interesting."

"Ivy didn't tell you the rest?"

"She said some stuff. I'd like to hear more."

Sarah took a deep breath. Closed her eyes. The armchair wanted her to fall asleep: that was clear. "There was a man. A few years ago. He was killing women." She stopped. That seemed enough for now. More than enough, even.

After a moment Jack said, "And this is Barry?"

"Yes."

"You're sure?"

She paused. "No. No, I'm not sure."

"But it's possible enough for you to be seriously worried about it."

"Yes," she said. "Seriously. That's the word all right."

Seriously seriously seriously. It threatened to follow her down through the plughole that was even now sucking her in.

Jack put his glass down. She hadn't even noticed he'd been drinking. "You look like you could do with some sleep."

"What time is it?" she asked.

"Early." He looked at his watch and nodded, as if pleased that it agreed. "But you definitely need an hour's kip. Come on. I'll show you the spare."

Maybe something showed on her face, because he gave her a thin-lipped smile. "It locks on the inside."

"I'm sorry, I didn't mean —"

"That's all right. You've had a rough time."

But she said it again. "I'm sorry."

He led her upstairs, into what was recognizably a spare; was too neat to be anything else. A candlestick fitted with clean candles sat on the mantelpiece, and nothing at all sat on the dresser. Best of all, though, it had a bed in it. She turned to thank him, but Jack was already closing the door. Sarah didn't lock it. Nor did she bother getting undressed. Kicking her shoes off, she lay on top of the covers. She closed her eyes. When she opened them again, three hours had passed, and the house was empty.

In the kitchen, she filled a glass from the tap, drained it, then filled it again. Ominously, she had no headache. In most circumstances, a free pass from a hangover would be a blessing, but it felt now like a pain postponed, as if Sarah's future were laying traps. To counteract this, she acted as if the hangover had already arrived. So she drank three glasses of water, and took another pair of Nurofen from the pack on the counter. Then had another look for the note Jack had left, explaining where he'd gone. But it remained invisible.

Sarah found the phone, though, largely because it was unhidden. Sitting, she picked out three-quarters of her home number before pausing, then gently replacing the receiver. She desperately wanted to speak to Russ. But she couldn't do so here, in a strange man's house, with no explanation that wouldn't leave Russ screaming with anxiety . . . She couldn't cope with that. She'd talk to him once she'd left, which she'd do as soon as she'd worked out where to go.

Her bag was at the hotel, but she had her purse, which held her credit card. She'd go to the station. She'd leave the city. But as soon as she'd had the thought, she had a second, which was that leaving would give Barry all the time in the world to do exactly the same.

And one thing Alan Talmadge was good at was disappearing.

She was still by the phone when the hallway grew bright. Headlights crawled up the walls, collided on the ceiling, then abruptly died. Jack, she thought. The car had come right into the drive. It could hardly be anyone else. But the engine choked away, and nothing happened: no feet crunched on the path; no one came through the door. Her hand curled into a fist. Her nails bit into her palm.

Then she shook her head, to clear it of interference. There was a car outside. That was all. She wasn't about to hide under a table. Before she could change her mind, she opened the front door. The car's side window rolled down at her approach. Her reflection sank into the window's recess, revealing the man who'd collected her from the pub.

"Hello," she said.

He nodded.

"Where's Jack?"

"Oot."

Oot?

Out.

"Did he . . . Did he say where?"

He nodded.

This was going to be a long conversation.

"And could you tell me?"

He could and he did. She had to make him say it three times, though. It was unforgivably rude, but she could barely penetrate his accent. And he was making no concessions. Why should he?

At length, in possession of as much information as she was likely to glean, she thanked him and returned to the house. Should she have asked him in? It wasn't her invitation to give. Anyway, he seemed happy enough in the car; like a bear in a mobile cave. And besides, in a sudden access of self-consciousness, she remembered how drunk she'd been when he'd collected her from the pub. Communication difficulties aside, she didn't want that topic taking up space between them.

Front door closed, she leaned against it, treasuring its barrier-like properties. How did she feel? First things first: she felt better for sleep and painkillers. She wouldn't call herself one hundred per cent. But then she hadn't felt that since learning about Zoë; even less so since seeing that body on the slab.

*Oot. On a message.* A word that carried a wealth of meaning up these parts: anything from nipping round the shops to undertaking a quest. *Not be long, like.* Which might mean five minutes or might mean an hour. What was Sarah supposed to do in the meantime? Grab something to eat, she thought.

Good answer.

In the fridge she found cold chicken and a jar of mayonnaise, and made herself a sandwich. Jack wouldn't mind. Ten minutes later, she was considering making another, but that would involve finishing the chicken: maybe Jack would mind after all. So she went back into the sitting room, then got worried she could be seen from the car in the drive. She didn't know the driver's name — also unforgivably rude, come to think of it — and didn't like the idea of being observed by him, so wandered into the adjoining room, where there was no possibility of observation. This turned out to be a study. Bookshelves naturally attracted Sarah, but a few moments with these let her down: rows of volumes called *Project Management* and *Deal-making Done Right* weren't anything she wanted to browse. But there was a computer on a desk by the window. A light on the monitor indicated it was sleeping, and while it would have been pushing the boundaries to turn the thing on herself, if it was already on, that made a difference, yes? Besides, everyone knew you should shut a machine down when you weren't using it. Standby was just another word for environmental damage.

218

When she moved the mouse, the screen came to life. No fancy image, either: just the generic Windows blue, and a few familiar icons.

She wasn't here to creep his private folders, she told herself. She had no intention of doing that. She woke his Internet browser instead, and opened her e-mail account: work-related messages had come pouring in while she'd been away, not to mention a fair amount of spam, but nothing that couldn't wait. Ignoring them, she sent off a message of her own: a quick one to Russ, telling him not to worry, that everything was okay. When the words were on the screen, they didn't look enough. But she didn't have time to polish: she pressed send, and hurled them into the void. Then closed her account down, and opened a search engine.

This was what she'd planned to do before her encounter with Barry derailed her. If that hadn't been Zoë on the slab, it had been somebody else. And Sarah refused to believe this could happen — that you could be dumped and poured into a river — without causing ripples somewhere.

These days, *somewhere* was the Internet. If you couldn't drag a body to the surface of the web, there was nothing left of it to drag.

The first few minutes were spent narrowing down search terms. *Missing* and *woman* were too broad; threw up too much bad poetry, too many Amazon pages. Zoë would have done this better, Sarah thought ruefully. Zoë would have aced this. After ten minutes she wandered into Jack's kitchen and made a cup of coffee. The clock on the wall said it was coming up to eleven. The clock in her body shrugged, and accepted it. You had to accept the ruling of a higher power. Come to think of it, that was one of the rules for those regretting alcohol abuse.

She shook her head. Concentrate on the task in hand. Back at the screen she found a site dedicated to missing persons, and trawled it for giveaway words; words relating to middle-age. But it was mostly children who went missing; teenagers or younger, who'd gone off-reservation. They'd turn up, if ever, in runaway hostels, or when police sweeps netted underage prostitutes. She drank some coffee. It had gone cold: how long had she been sitting here? Time operated differently in front of a screen. Another link dragged her on to an archived news page, and she clattered her search terms into this one too, because she was too far down the rabbit hole to claw her way back to the surface. That was what the web really was. The rabbit hole. It turned us all into Alice: almost everything encountered there was weirdly familiar, but at a tangent to reality. It was a paranoid playground; a —

Hang on.

She'd ploughed through a screen which had triggered something, and had to backbutton to discover what it was. A news story from mid-January, from one of the nationals:

*Concern is growing about the whereabouts of Madeleine Irving, 47, of Moseley, Birmingham, who has not returned from holiday. Ms Irving, who is single, is believed by neighbours to have been travelling in the*

*Lake District over the New Year period. It remains unclear whether she was accompanied.*

The photograph took a moment to manifest, as if the ether itself were struggling to recall Madeleine's image. *Is believed by neighbours.* There was nothing wrong with keeping your travel plans to yourself. The picture shimmered into being; unfocused at first, then sharper, like a memory nudged into the light. Madeleine Irving had a pale face and dark curly hair, though a black-and-white headshot tended to exaggerate such distinctions; she wore thick glasses in a heavy frame that looked as much designed to hide behind as see through. *It remains unclear whether she was accompanied.* She was forty-seven and single: just the type Alan Talmadge favoured. If you took the glasses away, she looked enough like Zoë to be taken for her in the right circumstances. If she'd been left in the water for a while, for example.

Sarah was heading back to Google, armed with this new name, when she heard the front door open.

The streets were mostly empty, and the rain had stopped, but the side window was still freckled with raindrops, which made a blurry miasma of the streetlights. Puddles were pools of light by the roadsides. A wet night was a science fiction film.

"Where are we going?" she asked.

"Back to Walker, like," he said.

She was pretty sure that's what he said.

Jack had called him: she'd got that much. It was worse than being abroad and not speaking the language

— abroad, it didn't matter if you were thought stupid. Ivy, back in the pub, had had enough of an accent that Sarah had needed her to repeat herself a few times, and some of her responses had relied on Ivy's body language and raucous laugh. But this man, Jack's driver: every time he opened his mouth, Sarah was lost. He had no trouble understanding her. But then, to hear someone speaking like Sarah, you only had to turn on the TV. To hear someone speaking like Jack's driver, you had to get in the car.

Which she presumed was returning to Walker, but the route rang no bells. She had, of course, been plastered last time. Now she was in that heightened state of not only being aware that she'd sobered up, but proud enough of the fact to be taking in minor details. They passed a large building with dozens of massive bobbin-like articles in its yard, miles of cable wrapped round them. Then another: this one with boarded-up windows.

"Are we nearly there yet?" she found herself asking.

His grunt was affirmative, she was nearly sure.

Confirmation arrived within the minute. They turned off the industrial estate and came to a halt by a pair of iron gates set in a high fence which guarded no structure she could see. Low points of light to her left trembled as if frightened; they were, Sarah realized, reflections on the river. Higher lights were static. She was near the Tyne; could see clean across it. This must have been where a shipyard stood. Now it was a darkling plain of muddy roughland, at the far reaches of which stood four huge cranes and two smaller ones. More lights strung across their arms picked out ladders in the sky.

The larger cranes took down the buildings, she thought. And now the smaller cranes take down the big ones. Like vultures turning on each other, once the carcass has been stripped clean.

Small flames flickered, a few hundred yards away.

"Jack's in there?" she asked.

He nodded.

The gates had a section missing, where an entrance had been made with a crowbar. She crouched, and squeezed through the gap. He didn't follow. On the other side she hesitated for a moment. Like a candle in a cathedral, the flickering campfire made everything darker.

"Jack?"

"Over here."

Her boots weren't made for terrain like this. They were designed to be worn in wine bars, not for stumbling over rubble in a derelict shipyard. Even as she had the thought, she tripped and nearly fell, but caught herself in time.

"You okay?"

Jack, in front of the campfire, assumed alien proportions: his limbs made stringy and indistinct.

"I'm okay," she said.

The air was cold and damp. The sky was far away, and the river too near. Sarah's breath made clouds that the wind tore away. As she approached Jack, he resumed his normal dimensions. Behind him lurked a squat boxy shape, and her heart beat faster as it twitched.

"Jack?" she said. "What's going on? Why are we here?"

"All will be clear," he said.

Afterwards, she'd ask herself why she hadn't been frightened. And the only answer she could come up with was that her day had taken on a momentum all its own, and she had no option but to be carried along. She was a passenger of ongoing events. The fact that she'd set them in motion herself was a detail, that was all.

The shape behind Jack was a wooden chair, part of an ordinary kitchen set. On it sat Barry. He was naked, and whiter than milk.

"Jack —?"

"Barry and I have been having words."

"What have you done to him?"

"I haven't done anything to him. Have I, Barry?"

"N — no."

"Haven't laid a finger on him."

Sarah took another step forward. Barry wouldn't look at her. Instead he stared straight ahead, as if there were something lurking in the darkness he was keen to focus on.

"Where are his clothes?"

"Where are your clothes, Barry?"

"The . . . the . . ."

"Take your time."

"There. Over there. Where we came in."

No Australian twang here. This was local. This might never have travelled more than yards from the chair where it now sat.

"Would you like me to fetch them for you?" Jack asked.

"I'm — no. No. I'm okay."

"Let him go," Sarah said.

"You can go now, Barry."

"I'm okay," he said again.

There wasn't a mark on him Sarah could see. The firelight dancing on his body revealed no obvious breaks or bruises. And nothing pinned him to the chair. He just sat, not looking at her. Not looking at anything. He was shivering, but so would anyone: naked, in this cold air.

"Barry wants to tell you a bit about himself."

"Jack, I —"

"Don't you, Barry?"

Barry said, "Yes."

From a distance, Sarah thought, they must look like they were fixed in a bubble. A bubble of firelight, its reach barely extending a yard from Barry's chair.

"Go on, then."

Barry said, "My name's Barry Malone. Born in Gateshead. Been from there all my life."

No faulting his logic.

"Been in London, though. Past few years."

His voice shivered too. If he made his sentences any longer, words would break off.

"Bar work mostly."

He still wouldn't look at Sarah; nor at Jack. Skin like milk, Sarah thought again. His skin was white as milk.

She said, "You're not Australian."

He shook his head.

Jack said, "Barry? What did we agree?"

"Answer out loud," Barry said.

"So?"

"No," he said. "Never even been there. Australia."

She couldn't help asking. She ought to be calling a stop to this, but something about the last exchange suggested Jack wouldn't hear of that. "So why did you pretend?" she asked. It was little more than a whisper, but he heard.

"Makes it easier," he said.

"Makes what easier?"

"Getting the job," he said.

Something skittered in the shadows, but Sarah barely flinched. A mouse. Hell, no: a rat. But what was a rat in the big scheme of things? She was talking to a naked man in a derelict shipyard. Half an hour ago, she'd have said he was a multiple murderer. But now he was just a naked man, looking and sounding less like Alan Talmadge than anyone else she'd met lately. John M. Wright, she thought. Was it just today she'd had lunch with John M. Wright? She'd find it easier to believe Wright was Talmadge than that this frightened lump was.

In the circumstances, she wasn't fussed about a nearby rat.

"It's easier," she said, "getting a job as a barman if they think you're Australian?"

"Sometimes."

"Why?"

He shrugged. "Just is."

Maybe this was what it was like with an actor you'd admired on stage. Performing, he'd been full of life, shining with every word. But catch him without a script, and it was like talking to an empty bottle.

"You met Zoë," she said.

He nodded.

"Barry," Jack said softly.

"Yes," Barry said. "Yes, I met her."

"Where?"

"Where I said. Bar. Bolbec Hotel."

"And what happened?"

"Nothing."

"What kind of nothing?"

"We talked. That's all."

"What about?"

He glanced at her for the first time since she'd walked into this circle of light. "Can't remember. Nothing much. Whatever I said we talked about."

She tried to remember — the usual stuff? Something like that. "And she checked out next day."

"I think so. Yeah."

"And you haven't seen her since."

"No."

"Or heard from her."

"Nothing. No."

"Has anyone been looking for her?"

"Only you."

"Did you see her with anyone else?"

"No. But . . ."

"But what?"

"That night in the bar. It got busy."

"Doesn't sound like the Bolbec."

"There was a crowd. Expecting free drinks. Don't know what that was about."

"So she might have been talking to someone else?"

"Might have. I was off my feet."

Somewhere on the far side of the river a car alarm sounded, its *whoop whoop* curving sudden circular slices out of the night.

"But you didn't see her with anyone in particular."

"No."

"You're sure?"

"No. Yes. I'm sure."

The alarm died mid-*whoop*.

Sarah said, "Did you see me in the soap shop?"

And now he looked at her again, confused. "Soap shop?"

"I was there. When you came in."

"Oh."

"I heard you talking to the girl on the counter."

"Oh. Right."

"Your accent slipped," Sarah said.

"Didn't know you were there."

"Obviously. But when I came back into the hotel, you were different."

"Was I?"

"You acted different. Like I knew you were just pretending."

He shook his head. "Didn't mean to."

"You told me to ring Zoë."

"So what?"

So what indeed. She remembered the policeman, Fairfax, delivering something pompous and prepared: *It wasn't necessary to inform the staff that we'd found a body.* If Barry was telling the truth now, he hadn't known Zoë was dead. Which meant he'd hit a target in the dark, that was all. One stray comment about a phone call. The sort of thing anyone might say.

She remembered sitting in her room, phone pressed to her ear. *You've reached Zoë Boehm. Leave a message.* It had convinced her Zoë was still out there, but it wasn't proof of anything, was it? Maybe Zoë's mobile had slipped from her pocket. Maybe it was lying at the bottom of the Tyne. But if so, would her answering service kick in? Sarah didn't know.

Barry said, "It was just something to say."

She'd almost forgotten about Jack, but he was there, hovering on the edge of darkness. It struck her that what he'd done was kidnapping; then, with slightly more force, that what *they'd* done was kidnapping. By asking these questions, she'd made herself part of Jack's crime.

But it was done. That was the point. Barry was here, however much he didn't want to be. And as long as she was here too, she might as well find out what she needed to know.

"What about Gerard? Gerard Inchon? Did he really check out in the middle of the night?"

Barry nodded.

"Barry," Jack said.

"Aye," Barry said.

"Did he say why?"

"He just said he — said he was leaving, that's all."

"But . . ." Sarah trailed away. Gerard had been drunk. "But he was drunk," she said. "He could barely stand when I left him."

"Drunk, aye. But he could stand all right."

The Geordie fell strangely on her ear. Sarah still half-expected Barry's voice to emerge all beach-body: tanned and trunked.

A sudden gust blew sparks from the fire, and a scatter landed on Barry's naked chest, where they died. He didn't flinch. Perhaps he was glad of the warmth.

". . . Did he have luggage?"

"He was already packed."

"What do you mean?"

"His bags were downstairs. He'd left them at reception."

Sarah stared. "You're saying he planned it? When I spoke to him, he already knew he was going?"

"Must've done."

She tried to cast her mind back: what had Gerard been like, apart from drunk? He'd been talking about Paula, about their son. Had said something heart-rendingly ugly: *he looks like a ping-pong ball, balanced on an egg.* Had that been just last night? It was like peering through a telescope with a Vaselined lens. Nothing about their encounter had suggested a man ready to take flight. She could accept that, after his confession, he might have wanted to put distance between them, but not that he'd already planned to do so. That would have meant he had a whole different agenda all along.

But then, Sarah already knew Gerard had lied to her, didn't she? About finding Zoë's card. About not having been in touch with her, when it was clear that Zoë had drummed up the list of invitees to his soirée . . .

"Sarah?"

She blinked.

Jack said, "Anything else?"

She said, "Yesterday morning. Were you in his room?"

"What do you mean?"

"Did you sneak into Gerard's room when he was out?"

He shook his head.

She said, "Last night. When he left. Did he say where he was going?"

Barry said, "No."

"Did a taxi come for him?"

"He was in a car."

"He was *what?*"

"He arrived in a car. It was parked under the arch."

She said, "You let him drive? In the state he was in?"

"How would I stop him?"

He had a point. But not a good one. Sure, Gerard would have steamrollered anyone trying to prevent him doing what he wanted, but it would have been the work of seconds to pick up a phone once he'd gone. This wasn't about tattling to the cops. It was about preventing a drunk mowing down pedestrians.

Which hadn't happened, evidently. Or not round here anyway.

Sarah looked at Barry. His voice had grown stronger, though he shivered still. She wondered what he'd imagined Jack had been prepared to do to him. Wondered at the power of the Gannon name; that it cast such a shadow.

His wasn't the only one.

She said, "Does the name Alan Talmadge mean anything to you?"

"Who?"

"Talmadge. Alan Talmadge."

He said, "No. No, never heard of him."

She waited, as if there were another answer within him, aching to be heard. If so, it kept quiet. All of this, she thought — her panic in the rain; this nightmare interlude — it all came down to a young man thinking an Aussie accent would get him better bar work. Maybe attract better women. It put him somewhere near the park where Alan Talmadge liked to play. But it didn't make him a killer.

"I'm sorry," she told him.

He shrugged.

Jack let him.

"You should go now," she said. "Find your clothes. It's cold."

Jack must have nodded at this, because Barry got to his feet. He opened his mouth as if to say more, but changed his mind. Without a backward glance, he walked barefoot away from them, over the stony, muddy ground, towards the gate where his clothes lay.

It was like watching a ghost dematerialize.

Jack said, "Did that clear things up much?"

# CHAPTER
# FOURTEEN

The wind whistled through an invisible gap. Off in the distance, lights on cranes shimmered.

"Who are you?" Sarah said.

To give Jack credit, he didn't go coy.

"I'm who you thought I was. The one you came to for help."

"Is that what I did?"

"Aye," he said. "That's what you did."

"And what about you, Jack? What did you do?"

He reached inside his jacket. For a moment, she thought he was about to show her a weapon; an explanation of how he'd brought Barry here. But all he produced was a pack of cigarettes.

"You don't, do you?"

She shook her head.

"Sensible." But not so much that he followed her example.

"You haven't answered my question."

"I didn't do anything to him, Sarah. He did it to himself."

"What, he just stripped off his clothes and —"

"Yes."

"— sat down in that chair in the freezing cold, middle of nowhere, and waited for me to —"

"Yes."

"— show up? What do you mean, yes?"

She spat the word. What did *yes* mean? And what kind of man was Jack? He was worse than the one she'd been running from.

Jack said, "I mean, he did it all to himself. Okay, I brought him here. Collected him from the Bolbec. Tank drove. I sat in the back with Barry."

"And he was happy to come along for the ride."

"You know something? I'd not say happy. But he didn't put up a fight."

"What would have happened if he had?"

"He'd have lost." Jack inhaled. "But it didn't come to that. All I had to do was tell him who I was."

"And who are you?" she asked again.

He shrugged; showed his palms. That's what you did when you were open: look. Nothing up the sleeves. Just a cigarette burning between two fingers.

"Jack Gannon. That's who I am, Sarah. I make no secret of that."

"Son of Michael Gannon."

"That's not a secret either."

"Well-known local gangster."

"Now then," he said. "He was never convicted of anything."

"Didn't have to be, did he?" Sarah said. "I walk into a pub in Walker, drop your name, and your pet gorilla's there five minutes later. You might be straight as the

**234**

day's long, Jack, but you know damn well what weight your family carries."

Jack said, "So, Barry might have jumped to a conclusion or two."

"*Might?*"

"What do you want me to say? That I told him I wouldn't hurt him? You thought he was a killer, Sarah. You thought he murdered at least three women."

"Maybe he did."

"Get real. You just saw him. You think *that's* a killer?"

"Talmadge is a chameleon, Jack. Maybe we just saw him changing colour. You certainly provided quite a backdrop."

"He wasn't faking that. He was scared stiff."

"So? Alan Talmadge specializes in pushing middle-aged women into ditches. Second-generation gangsters are out of his league."

Jack shook his head. "You don't think he's Talmadge any more than I do."

"You pretended to be who he thought you were," Sarah told him. "What makes you think he was doing any different?"

"Sarah —"

"There are ways of doing things, Jack. Okay, maybe I don't think he's Talmadge. But that means we've just terrorized an innocent man."

"Everybody's guilty of something," Jack said.

He dropped the cigarette half-smoked, and ground it underfoot.

Sarah simmered. Everything that had just happened had happened on her word. She'd shared her suspicions with Jack, and this was what came of it: Barry naked in the open air, scared for his life. Convinced the next thing coming his way was a sharp knife or a blunt object.

If he had been Talmadge, would she have cared? She didn't know. She didn't know. If he'd killed women then surely he deserved everything he got. But Sarah didn't want to be part of the punishment.

Jack said, "Long and short of it, you were frightened of him. Now you're not. That's a result. Shall we head for the car?"

She said, "It was you, wasn't it?"

"What was me?"

"In Gerard's room. This morning."

Jack said, "What makes you think that?"

"Because when I asked Barry if it had been him, he shook his head. And you didn't tell him to answer properly."

He smiled. "That's pretty sharp."

"And I'm right, too. Aren't I?"

He said, "When your phone went off, I nearly crapped myself."

"How do you think I felt?"

"At least you had the advantage of being in the bathroom."

"What were you doing there?"

"I could ask you the same."

"But I asked first."

He said, "You think someone like Inchon turns up every day? Threatening to chuck money around, asking if you want any?"

"And that's a reason to break into his room?"

"Hell, yes." He smiled again. She distrusted that smile. Jack relied on it too much. "So, okay, it's possible that I picked up a few bad habits. A few family traits."

"You think?"

"I wasn't there to steal."

"I didn't imagine you were. You wanted to know what he was really after, didn't you?"

"We'd just had a meeting, him and Brian Harper and I. We were going to have lunch. But Brian had another appointment first, so Gerard said he'd mooch around town till we were all free. I knew his room would be empty. Or thought it would."

"So what did you find?"

He laughed. "I was interrupted. Remember?"

"How did Gerard get in touch in the first place?"

"He just did. He phoned. Said I might have heard his name — which I had, of course — and asked if I wanted to come to a gathering he was planning."

"Because he was looking for investment opportunities."

"So he said." Jack shook his head. "It's like he was playing a part. You know, I'm a big investor. This is what I do."

"It was strange," she said.

"It was bloody weird. He can sit at home, open his post, and get twenty-seven begging letters a day, all pointing out rich investment potential. He doesn't have to go anywhere. And certainly doesn't have to throw a party when he gets there."

"You were top of his list," she said. "Why would that be?"

"What list?"

"Trust me, there was a list. And you were at the top."

He said, "There's no list of businessmen in this city which would have me up there. Unless you were starting at G. So God only knows where it came from."

God and Sarah. She said, "Ever hear of a firm called Roleseekers?"

"Local?"

"Uh-huh."

"Sound like headhunters. I've never used them."

She was starting to prefer answers that addressed the question. "So you've never heard of them."

He said, "No, Sarah, I've never heard of them." He produced his cigarettes again. For a supposedly once-in-a-blue-moon smoker, he was having a heavy night. "Are we through yet? Because there are better places to have a conversation."

"Oh, I think we're through," she said.

She turned and walked back the way she'd come, towards the faraway gate.

"Sarah?"

She kept walking.

"Sarah? Don't be silly. You've nowhere to go. It's the middle of the night."

"I know," she said. But she didn't turn back.

Jack had called him Tank. He was by the gate, smoking.

"Where did he go?" Sarah asked.

Tank pointed up the road. She started walking. But Barry was nowhere to be seen.

That was probably just as well. Out from under Jack's gaze, he might not be so tractable. Might, in fact, be pissed off.

Besides, what was she going to say to him? Sorry? She'd already said that. It didn't seem enough.

Perhaps he'd go to the police. Any sane man would. He'd been kidnapped, assaulted — whatever Jack said, interrogating someone naked in a derelict shipyard had to count as assault.

Sarah had lost all sense of time. When had Tank driven her here? After midnight? What did that make it now — one o'clock? Later?

The air was still damp, and the streetlamps were haloed with mist.

He wouldn't go to the police, she decided. Because it wasn't what any sane man would do. Or at least, not what any sane man who spent half his life pretending to be Australian would do.

Besides, Jack had stripped him naked. How was that going to look?

*And you're sure this was against your will, sir?*

She'd come to a halt, which was not a sensible thing to do on an unknown industrial estate at night. There was nobody around she could see, but that meant nothing. Jack and Tank weren't far away — any moment now, that sharky car would ease past — and she didn't want to be here then. She hurried to the next junction. There was a car not far up the road, engine running. People were piling out of it; crowding

**239**

into a lit building. Heading away from it, she walked faster.

*Tap tap* said her heels to the pavement. *Tap tap*. So much louder at night.

A sudden burst of sound made her jump. The wind, sending a dustbin lid surfing.

Up ahead, traffic lights hung out their colours.

That noise advancing on her was a car. She didn't look round.

It eased to match her walking pace. A voice called out.

"I'm for the city centre, lady. Any use to you?"

It was a taxi. Not in itself a guarantee of safe transport, but the driver's round black face beamed at her like a grandfather's.

"Thanks," she said. "That would be good."

In her room at the Bolbec, she packed her bag. She'd had to ring a bell to get in, and the young man who opened the door wasn't familiar. A last-minute sub for Barry, she presumed. She wasn't about to get into a conversation about it.

First thing she did was turn her phone on, making it buzz crossly. She had three voicemail messages, all from Russ. The first was puzzled and anxious; the second angry. The third anxious again. She rang him, reached voicemail, and left a loving, apologetic message, or hoped she did. It was always possible she'd left an incoherent, half-crazed one. She'd call again when it was light. With luck, she'd be nearly home by then.

Lying on the floor was the *Big Issue* she'd made Gerard buy. Picking it up, she riffled its pages. Maybe the name would leap out at her: *Madeleine Irving.* 47. Missing. But who would think to announce to the world that Madeleine wasn't where she ought to be? Sarah's impression had been that nobody much noticed her even when she was there. Which was exactly the target Alan Talmadge preferred, of course. And if it was indeed Madeleine, or someone like her, on that slab, then Zoë was somewhere else.

Sarah knew that the odds of having identified a missing woman by chance were slim. But the possibility that Zoë wasn't dead had taken root in her brain.

The room phone rang.

It would be Russ. But it wasn't.

"Sarah?"

"What do you want?"

"Just making sure you're safe. You wandered off in a bad part of town."

"I'm fine. Packing."

"That was the other thing I wanted. For us not to part on bad terms."

She said, "You kidnapped him, Jack. *We* kidnapped him. And making him strip like that, putting him on that chair in the open air — that was torture. You're aware of that, aren't you?"

"He's not going to report it."

"I think you're missing my point."

"No, I get your point. But you made a convincing case for him being a serial killer, Sarah. I think that entitled us to a little leeway."

"I should have just called the police."

"At the time, you had pretty sound reasons for not doing that."

At the time, she'd had too much to drink.

She said, "I was wrong about him. Whatever I said afterwards. He's not the person I was afraid he was."

"Which means someone else is."

There was little point disputing that. Whoever Talmadge was, it was clear he was no one Sarah had encountered.

She said, "I'm sure you were trying to do me a favour."

"I'm glad you get that."

"But don't do me any more."

He said, "People aren't always who you think they are."

She shook her head. It was the middle of the night. She didn't need life-lessons from gangsters.

"Goodbye, Jack."

"Goodbye, Sarah."

"And tell your friend Wright — tell him he's a lousy lunch guest."

"I will. When he turns up."

Sarah said, "What do you mean, turns up?"

"Well," Jack told her. "Before the evening went topsyturvy, he was supposed to be meeting me for a drink. But he never showed."

"I assume you'd have been buying the drink."

"That's the pattern."

"Sounds odd, certainly." It was nice, having a target for venom. "First time I laid eyes on him, he was freeloading. Can't imagine he'd pass up the chance."

"How do you mean, freeloading?"

"At Gerard's do. You brought him along, right?"

Jack said, "Well, sort of."

"What do you mean?"

"He came with me, that's true enough. But Inchon asked me to bring him."

"Gerard did?"

"That's right."

"I'd got the impression he was there on your coat-tails."

"Aye, well. That's not how it was."

Sarah shook her head. What kind of sense did that make? Though it didn't have to. It had happened, that was all. Making sense wasn't part of the deal.

"Sarah?"

She said, "Goodnight, Jack."

Cutting him off, she sat on the bed. Did what she'd just learned make any difference? It had to. She wasn't sure how, but it had to.

She cast her mind back to the paper she'd found in Gerard's room: the Roleseekers list Zoë acquired for him. John M. Wright hadn't appeared on it, and for that reason she'd dismissed him except as a means of discovering more about Jack. Because Jack had been top of the list. She remembered that for sure.

But maybe Jack had only been there because his presence could guarantee Wright's.

So the difference was that everything had just turned upside down. Wright wasn't peripheral to the events Gerard had orchestrated: he was the reason for them. And why was that? Because Gerard really believed

Wright was on the brink of a major medical breakthrough?

Sarah thought about Wright: stuck out on a trading estate near electrical superstores. She couldn't see a break-through happening there. She could believe Wright was some kind of idiot genius — the idiot part took no faith — but not that he was about to come up with a cure for anything. Not in premises like that.

Okay — that was shallow. Genius made its own rules. Or so it would have lesser mortals believe.

And maybe the rubbish premises, the lack of assistance, the below-par computers, were all part of the point. Maybe Gerard had recognized that if he could put these elements right — which only took money — then Wright would flourish and asthma be vanquished.

A victory which would bring, in its wake, a lot more money.

All of which left open the question of how Gerard knew about Wright in the first place. And why he'd approached him with subterfuge. Maybe that had been to avoid alienating Jack Gannon, the only other backer Wright had. But if so, why involve Jack at all? Gerard wouldn't care about alienating someone he never had to meet — he didn't give a noticeable toss about alienating those he was in daily contact with. And Wright wasn't burdened with scruple. If Gerard had waved a cheque book, he'd have come running. Would have forgotten Jack's name before the ink was dry.

No, Gerard could have waltzed in, set Wright up in a dream-factory, then headed back south and waited for good news. There was no need for any of it. No need to have involved Zoë.

And if he hadn't, she'd not have disappeared. Maybe died.

Perhaps she needed to reconsider John M. Wright. She'd written him off as Talmadge; couldn't see any way he might fit. But maybe that was the point. Talmadge didn't fit anywhere, which was why he was able to switch identities so easily.

For maybe a minute, probably less, she gave this due consideration. Then tossed the idea away. John M. Wright, ladykiller? Whichever sense you allotted the word, that could never have happened.

Which meant there was something Sarah was missing. Or something she'd never seen. Either seemed plausible.

Jack's call had interrupted her packing, which she should get on with. Last thing she wanted was to have Barry return before she'd left. If she had to place a bet, it would be that Barry wouldn't come back here today, but she'd lost bets before. There wasn't much to pack. She'd not been planning to stay this long.

The tangerine soap lay on the dressing table, in its paper bag. Instead of trying to fit it into her overpacked washbag, she unzipped her holdall's side pocket to slip it in there, and as she did so flashed back to the last time she'd done this — nothing to do with soap; something to do with a suitcase. Gerard's suitcase. A hot flush of shame washed over her that she tried to hold at bay with rational justification. She'd been trying to find out what had happened to her friend. Searching

Gerard's room had been wrong, but she'd do it again. She might have found a clue.

What she'd found had been a DVD of *Buffy*. And a collection of Internet clippings about orphanages.

Gerard's wife Paula had been orphanage-raised. Sarah had even been, once, to the orphanage in question. That had been another false trail on a different quest; cause for a new flush of shame.

Poor Paula, she thought. Poor Paula, with her poor baby.

"He's called Zachary," Gerard had said. "He has no arms. But then, he has no legs either."

There would be a reason for this. Jumbos don't fall out of clear blue skies. When children are born missing parts, there's a cause, and it's usually discovered.

She thought about Gerard drinking himself into oblivion. And then coming out of it, evidently, before leaving on a mission of some sort. Had he been as drunk as all that? He couldn't have been. Nobody could have been as drunk as she'd thought him and survived a drive anywhere.

And if he hadn't been drunk, why had he told her about Zachary?

She was still holding the soap. She tucked it into the holdall, and sat on the bed again.

Gerard's telling her about his son was one of the reasons she'd thought him so wasted. She couldn't imagine him opening up like that without an alcoholic excuse. But maybe she was approaching this from the wrong direction. Maybe Gerard had needed Sarah to think he was drunk before he could open up. Protective colouring. That sounded male enough to be convincing.

As to why he'd felt the need to open up in the first place . . .

Again, this required male thinking. A woman wouldn't have needed a reason to share; only the opportunity. Gerard, on the other hand, had a motive for everything he did. But even with that track record, he surely couldn't have had a *benefit* in mind when he told her about Zachary. It must have been something else. Something he couldn't be honest about, but needed to express.

She thought: yeah, no, great. That narrows it down, Sarah.

Except, of course, whatever the reason, it all boiled down to the same set of circumstances: Gerard being here, the people he'd met, the things he'd done.

It made no difference. It was too late, in every possible sense. She was going to the station. The first possible train that would take her anywhere near home, she'd be on it. The next move she came up with, she'd manage from there.

The Asian grocery was open; same cards taped to its windows; same Internet connections offered, at 75p an hour. Any city worth the name called itself 24/7, though it remained a hollow boast outside the hotspots. Here, only that same sweet shopkeeper was to be seen, sitting at one of his own monitors, reading an online newspaper in a foreign alphabet. He smiled as she came in.

"You're up early."

"So are you."

"Ah. I've not been to bed yet."

They could have spent a while, she imagined, trading tales of sleeplessness. "Do you have a connection available?"

He laughed. "Pick a stool. Would you like some coffee?"

She'd die for some, but remembered it came from an all-purpose vending machine. But before she could shake her head, he said: "There's a cafetiére in the office. I'll bring some out."

She could have kissed him, but even in the hotspots, that might have been cause for concern. So she just smiled and thanked him, put her holdall down by one of the machines, and sat and booted up.

Five minutes later, he returned to put a beautiful-smelling mug at her elbow. "You're catching a train?" he asked, nodding at her bag.

"That was the plan," she said.

"But you've changed your mind?"

She looked at the screen she'd found. "I've had it changed for me," she said.

There'd be no left-luggage facilities open. Not at this time. And few railway stations had lockers any more, for obvious reasons. But her new friend was happy to keep an eye on her bag, and wouldn't think of taking payment.

"But where are you going? How will you get there?"

"I don't suppose the Metro's awake yet?"

He smiled.

"Could you call me a taxi?"

"Call? I can whistle you one."

"Give me a few minutes? I need to make a call."

"Please. As long as you need."

And he retreated into his back room, so she could talk in private.

He was as good as his word. A whistle was all it took. The taxi driver, an Irishman, was a friend of his, which meant Sarah was the taxi driver's friend too. Perhaps she'd had it wrong about the 24/7 city. Perhaps whole communities were rubbing along in undetected harmony.

"I'll be back later. For my bag. And thank you."

"It's no problem."

It was dark as they headed out of the city centre, but the promise of light to come was painted on the sky. She thought: I can't remember the last time I've seen this side of a morning. Though she could remember being drunk earlier, which went some way towards explaining the growling sensations in her stomach.

The streets were empty, and the journey took no time.

"And you're sure this is where you want to be, now?"

"I'm sure," she said, paying the fare.

"It's awfully quiet."

"There'll be someone to meet me. Really. I'll be fine."

"If you're sure, pet."

It wasn't Irish, that *pet*. It must have rubbed off in his time behind the wheel.

"I am. But thank you."

She watched while he did a three-point turn, and waved as he drove away. His car disappeared round a corner. Then she looked at the building over the road.

Sarah had specified the Metro station as her destination. But it was the cinema she'd had in mind.

At this time of morning, it looked no more inviting. The same security panels were bolted across its entrance; the same peeling whitewash daubed its walls. It still called itself a picture house. And from the row of blackened, book-sized windows at attic-level, no lights showed. Probably it was empty, she told herself. She kind of hoped so. But still, she crossed the road. Pushing the panel from which the padlock hung, she found little give to it. The noise — a hollow clang familiar from prison movies — echoed between cinema and station for a moment.

If she tried that again, it wouldn't be long before someone appeared to complain. That wouldn't help.

Circling the building seemed an idea. There was a back lane to the left; reaching it, she saw a car parked halfway down. It turned out to be one of those hearse-shaped cars with a capacious boot. She had no idea what make Gerard drove, and wouldn't have picked this out of a line-up.

Something dashed from a shadow, and her heart leaped. But it was a cat, or that's what she told herself. It was gone before she could be sure, but still: it was only a cat.

The car was next to a pair of fire-exit doors which had no handles on this side. But they didn't seem flush. Kneeling, Sarah found a glove wedged at the foot of the left-hand door, preventing it from locking. She pushed, and let herself into the cinema; into a corridor leading to another set of doors, presumably to the auditorium. And then the fire door closed, and what little light had filtered in from outside was gone.

Quiet, too. Absolute silence. She reached for her mobile phone. This cast a feeble blue glow which was better than nothing. Its light didn't reach as far as the walls, on which anything might be crawling. But it was best not to think about things that might be crawling.

I could turn and walk out of here right now. Cross the road, and sit on a bench until the first Metro arrives. Ride it to the Central Station, then leave the city behind.

Sarah thought, I could do all of that. But it would involve forgetting that the fire door had been propped open with a glove.

She reached the door to the auditorium, and pushed it open.

When it crashed to the floor, she almost wet herself.

# CHAPTER
# FIFTEEN

The echo explored the dark spaces. It disturbed the spiders, and woke the ghosts.

The other noise, a sudden shriek, Sarah made herself.

Dust rose when the door hit the ground: an old filthiness that made her want to spit. So she spat. The light her mobile cast was useless now. All it illuminated were the tips of her own fingers; making them translucent, as if she were one of the woken ghosts.

As the echoes clattered away silence returned, except for the noises her body made. Her breathing. The rustle of her clothes.

Careful not to trip on the fallen door, she stepped into the pitch-black auditorium. The light switches Brian Harper had thrown the other day were in the lobby. There weren't any nearby, or none her mobile's glow could find.

She could walk up to the lobby. The aisle couldn't be more than a few feet away. Her eyes would grow accustomed to the gloom, and then she could make her way up there.

Past those hammocks of spiderweb. Past the dark ranks of seats, where grey things scuttled.

It was useless. She couldn't do it. She wouldn't step further into the dark.

A muddled noise, halfway between a bump and a whisper, slithered across the auditorium.

"Gerard?"

Her voice startled her. It was an unexpected visitor in this damp palace.

There was no reply. Gerard, if he was here, didn't want her to know.

"Gerard!" she called again.

And this time there was an answering scuttle, which didn't sound human.

Something fluttered past her face, and she yelped a curse, and swatted — it must have been a moth. But it had felt large, and she couldn't stop the picture of a bat forming in her mind. In this picture, the bat had large pointy teeth.

Okay. Enough. There was nothing keeping her here. If Gerard was hiding in this darkness, he was welcome to it.

Though it wasn't simply a matter of hiding. That was the trouble.

But there were other, better ways of dealing with this than stumbling into a spiders' lair. She could find Brian Harper, and bring him along with his key and a torch. Which might have awkward consequences if what she suspected were true, but that wasn't her problem. Her problem was that she was nowhere she wanted to be, and that her mobile couldn't keep the dark at bay.

Her mobile . . . She was holding her mobile.

*Tchah!*

It was the work of seconds to call the number up. For another few moments her thumb hovered over the call button. Perhaps walking away was the best option after all. But the phone was in her hand, and her thumb had its own ideas. It made the call before she'd finished the argument.

Almost immediately, in the darkness on the other side of the auditorium, a phone began to ring.

She jumped: couldn't help it. She'd been half expecting it, but still: she jumped.

The ringing phone switched off midway through its second tone; but not before Sarah had caught the flash of light from its screen. It illuminated a vague shape, halfway up what must have been the furthest aisle. And then there was quiet again, except this time it was bracketed by interruptions. There'd been one noise. There'd soon be more.

She said, "It's a bit pointless pretending you're not there, isn't it?"

A sigh made its way across the darkness. As soon as she heard it, she wondered he'd been able to remain silent for so long.

"Do you have a light?" she asked.

A torch snapped on. Pointing upwards, it momentarily turned Gerard's features into a goblin mask. Then he aimed it at the floor, and used its beam to trace a path to where Sarah stood.

In the fringes of its wavering light she could see the web draped over the collapsed seating, and the scuttling inside it. She swallowed, hard. A moment later, Gerard was in front of her.

254

"Do you know," he said, "I can't say I'm surprised."

"You pretty much invited me."

"Don't be ridiculous. The last thing I wanted was company."

"You're not going to pretend you're here by yourself?"

"I'm past pretending anything," he said. "This is where it all stops."

It was hard to tell with just the torch, but he looked slighter, somehow. A Gerard anything less than larger than life was strange to contemplate, but here he was: trembling like the light. His face a pale idea of its normal self.

Into this face, he now inserted a cigar.

"You're not going to light that?"

"What else do you imagine I'm about to do with it?"

She bit back a suggestion. "Gerard, this place could go up like a pack of cards."

"Now there's an interesting possibility."

"Where's Wright?"

"Who's to say?" Gerard asked. "Where's right, where's wrong? It's so very confusing, this world of moral complexities, isn't it?"

"It doesn't suit you."

"What doesn't?"

"Philosophy. Even the Christmas cracker kind."

He plucked the cigar from his mouth and returned it to his breast pocket. His suit must be filthy, she thought. No one upright could help but be a magnet for dirt in this place.

No one upright.

She said, "What have you done with him?"

"I'm supposed to understand what you're talking about?"

"Don't bother, Gerard. Like I said, I'd not be here if you didn't want me."

"There's something about a woman being so unequivocally sure of herself that just naturally makes me want to contradict her."

"You pretended you were drunk. Or drunker than you were. So you could tell me things you couldn't bring yourself to say otherwise."

"Cheap psychology, Sarah. I'd expect better of you."

"It's not cheap. It's free."

He rolled his eyes. In the torchlight, the effect was straight out of Hammer.

"I'm here, aren't I?" she said. "You think that's chance? I'm here because you brought me with you the other day."

"I thought you'd enjoy a trip to the cinema."

"Now who's making unworthy comments?"

"Please," he said.

He sounded tired. She wondered how long he'd been here, in this dead pleasure dome, and why he hadn't left hours ago. What was keeping him? What had he done?

She had the awful feeling she was going to find out. That she'd arrived too late . . . That whatever had happened had happened hours ago, while she'd been in that pub, drinking her fears away.

"I know," she said.

"Well of course you do," he said. "You wouldn't be here otherwise. Remember?"

"Gerard —"

"So what did you plan to do? Save him?"

"I hadn't got as far as having a plan."

"Or did you hope to save me from myself? That sounds more like you, now I think of it. Little Sarah Tucker. Saving the world, one soul at a time."

"I came because I thought you needed me, Gerard. I couldn't make the bits fit together any other way."

"Isn't that sweet? Shame you're too late."

"Is he dead?"

He shook his head. But she couldn't tell if that was a response, or just a refusal to answer.

She wished they could sit. But she doubted the seats would bear weight, even if they weren't shrouded in cobweb and caked with dirt.

She said, "I found some stuff out."

"Thank you. I'd got that far."

"On the Internet. About Wright. About his . . . research."

Gerard said, "Mentioned by name?"

"Wright? No. No, he wasn't. But the orphanage was."

"I forgot. You went there once, didn't you?"

She probably blushed, but it was too dark to tell. "The Arimathea Home. Not a name easily forgotten. You're right, he wasn't mentioned by name. But I knew it must be him. Asthma research? Using the children as . . ."

"You can say guinea pigs," Gerard said. "It's not like I'm easily offended."

"I'm so sorry, Gerard."

"Do you know, I think the window for apologies closed long ago."

"I meant about the baby. About Paula. It was Wright's fault, wasn't it? She was one of the children he treated. With steroids, or . . . whatever."

"Or, indeed, whatever. He's strangely reluctant to go into detail."

"Is he here?"

Gerard said, "The Church claimed he was acting without its — do you know, I'm going to have to say *blessing*. That he was acting without its blessing. A claim that would carry more weight if the Church didn't have form."

Sarah said, "I found some other stories."

"There's a place in New York. A home for orphans born with HIV, run by Catholic charities. And there were medical trials going on, on children as young as three months, children with no traceable family — they were trialling experimental drugs. And they justified this by — well, fuck knows how." The torch wavered in his hands, then held firm. "There were huge companies involved. GlaxoSmithKline. Others."

"And something similar happened at Arimathea," Sarah said.

"Something happened. But the story never broke like the New York one did. There were fewer children involved, and the drugs were less obviously . . . harmful. There was a stopper on it before the press got wind. Trust funds for the children. That was before any long-term issues came to light, of course." Gerard broke off; looked around, as if he couldn't understand what he was doing here. Then he turned back. "There've been whispers since, but that's all. Smoke and whispers. Nobody talks. The children — well, they're in their thirties now. They could lose their trusts if they started ringing bells. And you'd be surprised how few of them married rich monsters like me."

"So Wright got away with it."

"Well, you won't find his name attached to any of the rumours. But it was him. I showed Paula his photo. She stopped breathing."

"You could have taken it to the law."

He laughed. "Would you listen to yourself?"

"Well, if not you, who? Christ, Gerard, you've got the money, you've got the weight, you've —"

"She said no."

Sarah, who'd been gathering a head of steam, felt it whistle away into the darkness.

"No way was she appearing in a court. Or before an inquiry. Or before anyone at all. And show pictures of our child, as if he were a . . . an exhibit." Gerard took the cigar from his pocket again. She wondered how many times he'd done that already. There was no taste of smoke in the damp, earthy air.

"That was the first you knew of it, wasn't it?" she said, some kind of light showing.

"What?"

"When Zachary was born."

A clanking sound made her jump. Something, somewhere, had rattled a pipe. But Gerard didn't bat an eye. Perhaps he'd grown used to the building's conversation. Nothing it said could surprise him any more.

At last he said, "Paula hadn't told me about it before then."

She found nothing to say in reply.

"Not even during the pregnancy. Of course, we knew things had gone badly wrong." A flash of the old Gerard made itself felt: "Even the NHS would have worked that much out. If we'd gone NHS. Which we didn't."

"But you didn't know why."

"You want to know what I thought? When I saw him, when I first saw him, I thought it was my fault. I'm not talking about God's punishment, or anything ridiculous like that. I mean, quite simply, that it was my fault."

His eyes bore into her. Even in the dark, they managed that.

"I'm used to taking responsibility for my actions."

"I know," she said.

"And that's what this was. We'd put off having children. I wanted to wait until I'd established myself. Does that sound sane to you?"

"Thousands of people do it, Gerard. Everybody tries to be in control of their own destiny."

"Don't tell me the crap you think I want to hear. You're better than that."

"I don't have children, Gerard. You think I'm going to cast stones? Anyway, it wasn't your fault, was it?"

260

He continued as if she hadn't spoken. "What I really meant was, I wanted to use my energy building a business. Not spending nights juggling kids and mopping up sick. I thought there'd be time enough for that later."

"You weren't wrong. There was no reason for you to think you were wrong."

"Paula's younger than me. I doubt you've forgotten that. She didn't mind waiting, or that's what she said. I wonder, though. Whether she went along because she knew that's what I wanted. And whether her tendency to do that has anything to do with being orphanage-raised."

Sarah said, awkwardly, "She's never struck me as —"

"Please," he said. "We went through this the other day. You don't know my wife. You only know what you think you know."

"And that makes me different from anyone else?" It was a sudden flash of anger, gone as soon as released. "I'm sorry. You're right. I don't."

He shook his head. "I told her, anyway. When we found out. Told her it was my fault. That I couldn't give her a healthy child, and that if she wanted to look elsewhere I'd not stand in her way, she could have all the money she needed — anything she wanted. But what she wanted was her baby."

Darkness dropped like a torch cut off mid-beam.

"She wanted him to live a happy life."

Sarah's heart had skipped a beat when the light disappeared; but she'd caught her tongue in time. Now

**261**

Gerard wept, almost without sound — as if he'd had practice — but only almost.

Not reaching out was the hardest thing she'd done today.

At length, he clipped the torch on again, holding it to one side.

"That's when she told me."

"It must have been awful for her."

"If I ever needed to justify what I've done . . ." Gerard swallowed. Then said, "She blamed herself."

"People abused as children often do," Sarah said softly.

"I'm sure you'll appreciate that I don't give a fuck what other people do, feel, or think. That creature force-fed her medication when she was eight years old — eight fucking years old — and now my son needs a machine to breathe in. And there's no machine invented will mend my wife's heart."

The beam in his hand flickered again, but not from anything he'd done. The battery, she supposed. The battery was wearing down, just as her own was. How long had today been going on? And how much longer would it last?

"What did she tell you?" she asked softly.

For a moment she thought he wasn't going to reply, but the circumstances prevailed. Out in the big world, Gerard was his own boss. Here in the dark, among the spiders, where she'd found him, he had to speak.

"Paula never knew his name. She wasn't a patient. Her role was just to turn up in the orphanage

262

sanatorium once a week for a year and a half and be given an injection. Did I tell you she was eight?"

Sarah was expected to answer. She said, "Yes," then cleared her throat. "Yes."

"He never spoke to her. What was there to say? He wasn't interested in her, beyond how she reacted to the treatment he was . . . providing. The children had been told he was a doctor. And because they were children, and were told this by someone they trusted, they did as they were told, and were probably grateful."

"Did she even have asthma?" Sarah asked.

"No. She was part of a control group."

"She told you that?"

Gerard said, "No. I learned that fact today."

The torch flickered again, and at that same moment the clanking noise rang. It crawled up the walls, slithered across the out-of-sight ceiling. There might have been words buried inside it, but Sarah couldn't make them out.

"Wright wasn't a doctor. He has no medical degree. His deal with Arimathea was private enterprise. He approached the man running the home, a priest called Thomas Walsh, and offered him a cut of any profits resulting from patents Wright registered. In perpetuity. That must have appealed to Walsh. Priests deal in the perpetual. I'm sure he got a kick out of having a stake in it."

Sarah said, "He wanted *money*?"

She wasn't sure why this shocked her, but it did. Priests and corruption, she had no problem with, but all the usual scenarios involved sex.

Gerard was ahead of her. "Not for himself. The money was to be made over to the home. I've got a copy of the deed he drew up, somewhere. It's even legal, if you can believe it. In fact, it's probably still binding."

"How can it be legal?" she said. "No part of it can be *legal*. It involved giving drugs to children, for God's sake."

"Not for God's sake," Gerard said. "And nothing he was doing made it on to the contract. It simply said that a percentage of profits arising from patents resulting from Wright's research — details unspecified — belonged to the trust in charge of Arimathea's upkeep."

"He didn't want a record made of what he was up to."

"He was too canny for that."

"But it went wrong."

"There was no disaster." He shook his head. "No, the whole fucking thing was a disaster. What I mean was, nothing hit the papers, then or afterwards. But someone higher up the ladder got wind of what was going on. The church ladder, I mean. They hadn't known about it, you see. Everything that happened was just between Wright and Walsh and the others at the home. Like I said. Private enterprise."

"Must have made it easier to put a lid on," Sarah said.

"The CIA could take lessons from Rome," Gerard said. "In fact, I wouldn't be at all surprised if they do."

Again, the torch beam flickered. This time, Gerard noticed. He slapped the torch with his free hand, and

264

the beam died totally for half a second, then returned full strength.

The pair contemplated the renewed light for a moment.

Then Gerard said: "So Wright went under the radar. Like I said, he'd lied about his credentials. He wasn't a doctor. He could have been open to any amount of charges, not least assault. Assault on children. But the Church wasn't about to put its hands up, so none of that happened. He was allowed to walk away. And had just enough sense to keep his head down."

"But you found him."

"There are gaps. I don't know where he's been all the time since. But he came out of the shadows before I started looking for him, and what do you know? He's been treading the same path all these years."

"Still looking for a cure for asthma."

"He was ahead of the curve first time round. Nobody's found a cure in the meantime. He stands to make a fortune, if he cracks it. But he's not there yet. And he's still crunching the results his work at Arimathea produced."

Sarah remembered Wright whining about needing better computers. *If you don't want the animal rights brigade on your case, you need some fairly sophisticated software.*

You need a licence to use animals in research, he'd told her.

He hadn't needed one to use children.

"What have you done with him?" she asked softly.

She was remembering something he'd said over lunch that day. The four of them talking about the local art gallery, and Gerard saying: *The terrible vengeance of a righteous God.* Looking directly at Wright. Explaining it to him. *We can all learn something from that.*

"What do you think?"

"Just tell me."

"I fed him to a shark."

"Gerard?"

"I sliced bits off him. Small, important bits."

"Gerard . . ."

He said, "Fuck him. Fuck you too. Fuck everybody."

"I'm so sorry, Gerard."

This time, he didn't switch the torch off. Tears rolled down his cheeks, and his shoulders shook. Then something went skittering into the darkness: a rat-sized spider, or cat-sized rat, and Sarah wanted to howl too, but couldn't — she bit her tongue instead, and stepped forward, and put her arms round Gerard. For a big man, he felt insubstantial. Perhaps what she'd heard fleeing into the shadows had taken a piece of Gerard with it.

After a while, he settled.

Sarah thought it best not to speak yet.

Gerard released himself and found a handkerchief. He passed her the torch, and she swept it round the darkness while he blew his nose noisily. The grey webbing that draped everything was clotted as ever, but some of the horror had left it . . . Gerard's story had supplanted it as an image of filth. She remembered her first impressions of John M. Wright: a man so dull, he'd told her his middle initial. Round face; a neatly trimmed beard but no moustache. *A style choice so ill-advised, she wondered if it weren't a medical condition.*

Medical condition: she'd actually had that thought. A less rational woman might wonder if she'd picked up vibrations.

And next time she had nightmares, they'd not be of abandoned picture houses shrouded in cobweb, or of rats' nests built of shredded cushions. No, they'd feature a round face with a ridiculous beard, leaning over her with a sharp needle; as bland and humourless and uncaring as . . .

Which was where her knowledge broke down. She'd have to wait for the nightmare to provide the comparison.

Gerard thrust his handkerchief away, and held his hand out for the torch. She sensed this was more than his need to assert control; he needed to re-establish a sense of self. She doubted he'd cried in front of anyone for a while. Not even Paula. Not even after Zachary was born.

If he had, they'd probably not be here now.

She released the torch into his grasp. "Where is he, Gerard?"

"I don't suppose you'd consider walking away?"

"I'll probably have nights when I wished we had. But I can't. Neither can you. If you could, you'd not still be here."

And he'd not have flown flags for her to see. She'd not be here at all if he hadn't brought her here; if he hadn't told her about Zachary.

"So where is he? You haven't killed him or anything? Shit, Gerard, tell me you haven't killed him."

"I haven't killed him," Gerard said. His voice was dull. A lot of adjectives, Sarah had for Gerard. Dull, though, was a first. "Not because I don't hate him enough. Not even because of the morality of it. He's beyond morality."

Sarah couldn't dispute it. Not wanting Gerard to have murdered Wright had nothing to do with wanting Wright unmurdered.

"But I couldn't face telling Paula what I'd done. She'd know I'd done it for my own sake, you see. Doesn't matter that everyone else would think I'd done it for her, or for our son. No, she'd know I'd done it for myself. And I don't think I could bear her knowing that."

"Where is he, Gerard?"

"There's a room. Behind the stage."

"You'd better lead the way."

# CHAPTER
# SIXTEEN

Something soggy had collapsed at the end of the corridor: Sarah didn't want to know what. The air grew colder, ranker. She wondered how many broken things had crawled in here to die over the past decade, and if any of them had been human. But the building was a valuable property, or at any rate, taking up valuable space. Brian Harper must have the place inspected regularly.

She was careful to step round the soggy something all the same.

They'd reached a door; one secure on its hinges, and with a large rusty key fitted into its lock. Gerard shone the torch on it.

"Did you know this was here?" Sarah asked him.

"Not until this morning." He blinked, and shook his head. "Yesterday morning." He looked at her. "When Harper showed us round, I made sure I could get back in."

"You propped open an exit with a glove," Sarah said. "I found it."

He'd wanted her to find it. He'd wanted not to have to kill Wright.

"How did you get him here?"

"I waved a cheque book under his nose."

That would work, thought Sarah.

She reached past Gerard and turned the key.

It made exactly the screechy noise she'd expected, as if this were a cruel, unusual punishment for a key: being made to revolve in its lock. The door, too, protested when she pushed it.

Sarah fumbled for a light switch, and gave a yelp when it worked. The light that dropped was a filmy yellow that soiled everything it touched. After so long in the dark, Sarah felt it like a physical shock. And when she saw what it illuminated she felt another, duller thump. If she hadn't already witnessed Barry Malone sitting naked on a chair tonight, that thump might have been less dull.

Jack Gannon hadn't laid a finger on Barry. Barry had sat down compelled by nothing more than fear, which had proved powerful enough to hold him in place. Gerard had gone a different road, that was clear. Gerard had used his fists.

Wright was handcuffed to a radiator pipe — he'd been the source of those clanking noises; the spooky echoes that had crawled around the moribund cinema. Earlier, she supposed, he'd have made more noise. Right now, he looked near the end of his tether. He'd been gagged with a handkerchief, and beaten around the face. His jacket lay in a scruffy heap. What had happened to his glasses, Sarah couldn't tell.

He whimpered at her entrance. Whether that meant he hadn't recognized her, or that he had, Sarah didn't want to think about.

**270**

Without a word, she thrust her hand out at Gerard, who was behind her. He dropped the handcuff key into it.

"Wait outside," she told him.

At her approach Wright curled into a ball, and Sarah found herself making soothing noises; the same calming buzz she used on the ostriches when they were fussed by a low-flying plane or high-pitched car. She knelt, still crooning, and unlocked the cuffs. As soon as one wrist was free, he snatched both hands away; the metal bracelets dangling from his left.

"It's okay," she said. "It's going to be all right."

He didn't reply.

Sarah supposed she ought to put a hand on him; offer him comfort the way she would a frightened child, but couldn't bring herself to. Wright wasn't a frightened child. The nearest he'd come was frightening a few himself. Besides, he looked damp.

"Nobody's going to hurt you," she said.

While he absorbed this, she looked around the room, which wasn't large. Paint flaked from the walls, and a stack of wooden chairs seemed to be folding in on itself, as if the chairs aspired to the condition of matchsticks. She wondered briefly why they were here, and then forgot about them. There was a sink in the opposite corner. There didn't seem any great purpose to this either.

There was less cobweb, she noticed. Perhaps spiders saw no reason to confine themselves to a crabbed little room like this when there were wide dark spaces to explore a mere —

Never fails. Before the thought had fully formed, the biggest spider Sarah ever laid eyes on scuttled across the floor in front of her. Except *scuttled* wasn't the word. Strolled, rather. Nonchalantly. As if it owned the place. She was too terrified to speak, let alone scream, so did neither, and two seconds later it had vanished inside that collapsing palace of wooden chairs as if it owned them, which maybe it did.

When it didn't re-emerge to waggle hairy eyebrows at her, she tried to pretend she hadn't seen it, and turned back to Wright.

"Okay. You want to stay in here, that's your funeral. But I'm off."

This got through.

"Don't leave me."

"Then get up."

He said, "That man — that *bastard* —"

"Be quiet," she said. "There's no time for that."

"He's an *animal* —"

"I said be quiet!"

She shocked herself with her own shrill tone. And then unshocked herself by remembering who was who: Gerard had beaten him up, true, but what had Wright done? He'd committed the kind of crime you read about in history books; the kind performed behind barbed wire, in the service of brutal ideology. The kind that made you ask yourself what you'd have done if you'd been there. What you'd have sacrificed to stop it. Up to and including yourself.

She said, "Have you any idea what you did to him?"

"I'd never seen him before this week. He tricked me."

"Maybe so. But have you any idea what you did to him?"

"I don't know who he is. But he beat me. He *beat* me!"

. . . Afterwards, she wondered how she'd have approached this in a debate. Whether she'd have attempted to get Wright to admit being the cause of greater suffering than Gerard had caused him. But nothing about Wright suggested him capable of taking on board other points of view. It was one of the ways you recognized a sociopath. Put a bleeding body in front of them, they'd complain it was in their way.

Wright had never spoken to Paula. He'd simply administered whatever dose he'd prepared for her, then forgot about her until next time. He'd deserved everything Gerard had done, and worse. It shocked Sarah, realizing she thought this. Perhaps it was to do with getting older; seeing more shades of grey.

The spiders scuttling around in the grime were nothing compared to what crawled around some minds.

She said, "You know what happens now, don't you?"

"I'll see him strung up."

Okay, she thought — here we go.

"I'll see him nailed to a wall."

He'd grown stronger in the last few moments. That was what anger did. It rushed in to fill up the spaces fear left in its wake.

"You might want to reconsider that."

A voice behind her said, "I might want to, actually. Reconsider letting him walk away."

"Gerard. Shut up."

"You're sounding braver now, Wright. You want to start again?"

"Gerard!"

Wright said, "Oh, he's brave enough when I'm handcuffed to a pipe."

"You had both hands free when I hit you, you little prick —"

"*Gerard!* Back off. Now."

She could feel his weight behind her. There was a heaviness to his presence above and beyond his bulk: the gravity of a man who'd recently committed violence, and was in the presence of his prey. Events hung on a spider's thread. Gerard had wanted her here, to stop him from doing his worst. But now she'd arrived, perhaps he wanted a witness to his righteous anger instead. That thread might snap.

But didn't.

He said, for her ears only: "He wasn't cuffed when I hit him."

"I believe you."

"He cowered like — I don't know what he was like. Didn't even raise a fist. Just whimpered."

"Gerard, leave, okay? Wait outside."

She could sense him hovering, his rage looking for new vocabulary — as if there were words which would sum up precisely what had happened here, in the hours before she'd arrived; raw-knuckled words which

274

remained beyond his reach. But at last he backed off, and she and Wright were alone again.

Wright said, "He's lying."

"You think so?"

"I know so. I was here. You weren't."

She began again. "Did he mention his son at all? While he was hitting you?"

"I don't know him. Don't know his family. I've nothing to do with his son."

"Oh, believe me, you've got everything to do with his son." An image flashed through her mind: Gerard's description of his helpless infant. "His son needs a machine to keep him breathing. Do you know why that is? *Do you know why that is?*"

She wanted to hit him. Hell, he was on the floor: she wanted to kick him. But held back, because that was a line she didn't want to cross.

Though she knew, in her secret heart, that it was a line she was glad Gerard had crossed already.

She said, "Arimathea."

That caught his attention.

"The orphanage. Did you think I didn't know?"

Wright pulled at the handcuff still wrapped around his wrist. "I'm not supposed to talk about it."

"You're not . . . you're *what?*"

"I had to sign confidentiality agreements. If I talk — they could sue me."

Sarah dizzied with anger. "Is that what you told Gerard?"

"He made me tell him things. He had no right."

She shook her head. Wright was an empty box, she thought, without knowing where the thought came from, or what it meant now it was here. Was just an empty box. She said, "You destroyed a life. Lives. Is there anything inside you, anything at *all*, that's prepared to recognize that?"

"My research is important. And there's no proof, no documentation, that anything I did caused damage to — to that man's wife. Or his son. None at all. The procedures were safe. I'd not have performed them if they weren't. Do you think I'm a monster?"

And he meant it. Jesus Christ, but he meant it.

"I'm not interested in proof," she said. "Do you really think I — oh, fuck, I should have stayed away, shouldn't I? Should have let him kill you. But he's a good man, and he doesn't deserve that. You do, but he doesn't."

"What I'm doing will save lives."

"What you're doing will make you rich. That's all you're interested in." She didn't know that. It might not be true. She didn't care. "And even if it does save lives — you've no right, you had no *right*, to do what you did to those children."

"You've no proof I did anything wrong."

"Really? You think there's no proof? No *documentation?* What you did was covered up because it was in some people's interests to do so." She was thinking on her feet. She wished he'd stop breathing. "Did you think that was written in stone? If the wind changes, you'll be hung out to dry."

"I've done nothing wrong."

276

"And you really believe that? Because if you do, I might just let him kill you."

He said, "Nobody can prove I've done anything wrong," but he sounded less sure about it.

Sarah said, "He's very rich, you know. Well, of course you do. And the only reason he did what he did was because he wanted to feel his fists on you."

"He's —"

"I'm not finished. You really think, if he'd decided to take another route, you'd be a free man now?"

An odd thing to say to a man looped in handcuffs, but he didn't point out the contradiction.

"And that doesn't change just because he slapped you about. Now, you can call the police the moment you leave here, but can you guess what'll happen? They'll talk to Gerard. They'll be very polite. And possibly they'll politely arrest him. I imagine he'll be in custody for all of twenty minutes, don't you? And then there'll be at least two years before any of this ends up in court. And during that time, every penny at Gerard's disposal will be dedicated to establishing exactly what you did at Arimathea. How confident are you that he'll fail?"

John M. Wright said, "I want to go now."

"You'll go when I say you can go."

Something lizardlike flickered when she said that. The same lizard that crawled the corridors of Abu Ghraib. But she blinked twice, and it went away.

"The other children were paid off. Do you really think Gerard can't afford to open their mouths? By the time your story's heard in court, you'll be the one in the dock, Wright."

He looked at her with baffled resentment. A man who really didn't think other people should be allowed to interrupt his view.

"You're a creep. An animal. No, you're worse than that. Animals don't do what you've done. And sometime soon you'll pay for the lives you've destroyed. But tonight you get to walk away, and you know why that is? It's because I can't stand the sight of you a moment longer. Now get the fuck out of here."

She threw the handcuff key. It bounced off his shoulder, and on to the floor. He scrabbled for it, fingers black.

It took him some while to free his other wrist.

When he'd managed she said, "Wright? Next time you turn up at ResearchWorks, you can expect a reception committee."

"I've done nothing wrong," he told her.

"Keep practising that. Imagine saying it in front of cameras."

He glared at her with hatred, but with something else too. As if he really didn't understand her. As if she were an obstacle to all that was true and good and desirable. And glaring back, she knew there'd never be a way of breaking through the walls that minds like his built. Like Talmadge, he was out of step with other people. The only music he'd ever hear was his own.

She let him leave first. In darkness they made their way back into the auditorium, then round to the fire exit. When Wright pushed through the door and emerged into the lane, he looked back once and then ran, as if all this was something he could escape from. As if, by running, he might arrive at a place where he was someone else. She waited until his footsteps had diminished into nothingness, then bent and plucked the glove from the groove where it had held the door open. As she stepped outside the door slammed shut, its noise the finest she'd heard in a while.

Gerard was smoking at last, leaning back against the bricks and looking up at the sky. The rain had gone, and the clouds were chasing after it. The moon pulsed somewhere above them.

She joined him. Stood to his right, so his smoke drifted away from her; still, she could smell its acrid heat. Strange that a man with so much money took his pleasure in such cheap cigars.

She said, "He's gone."

"So I see."

"It's over. He's not likely to make a fuss."

"Sarah. Believe me when I say I couldn't give a fuck what kind of fuss he tries to make."

"You didn't want to kill him."

"Evidently not."

"And I'm glad you didn't."

He said, "Maybe so. But there's nothing I want more than for that bastard to walk under a train. Soon. Very soon. Now will do."

"I don't really think people get away with very much."

"Don't you? Don't you really?"

"No, Gerard. I don't."

"Well, it beats me what world you're living in."

"He's a shell, Gerard. He's a man without a middle. Talking to him was like shouting down a well. You don't think that's a punishment?"

"Sweet God above. That's not a punishment. It's a point of view."

Somewhere, streets away, a door closed loudly.

Sarah ran a hand through her hair. She wondered what kind of a mess she looked like. Then wondered why that mattered.

"You did the right thing," she said.

"Letting him go?"

"It's what Buffy would have done," she said, before she could stop herself.

Gerard opened his mouth, and closed it again. He took another toke on his cigar. Then said, "I'm sure I've no idea what you're talking about."

"Then let's change the subject," she said. "You didn't find Wright by yourself, did you? You had help. You hired Zoë Boehm."

He didn't reply at first. Kept staring skywards, as if expecting a heavenly messenger to be dropping in soon. When he exhaled, it was as if he were talking cloud: a big language, not understood by the earthbound.

"I lied about that," Gerard said at last. "About Zoë's card."

"I know."

"I didn't just find it. It was clipped to the report she sent me."

"Right."

"On the other hand," he said, "you only found out about it by sneaking into my room. So don't mistake an admission for an apology."

Now that sounded more like Gerard.

He said, "That's what brought you here in the first place, isn't it? Zoë."

"What happened to her, Gerard?"

"I don't know. Well, she did her job. She found Wright. Told me about Jack Gannon, his . . . sponsor. It was her who came up with the idea of the party. Gathering. Whatever you want to call it. I'd wanted a look at Wright without him knowing. That was her solution."

"She produced the list of local worthies."

"She got some local recruitment consultants to come up with it. Sarah — all that time, I never laid eyes on her. We spoke on the phone, or e-mailed. But I never met her. I didn't lie to you about that."

"But you hired her because of me. I mean, I'm the reason you'd heard of her."

"Yes," he said.

"And I came here to identify her body."

"Her *body*?"

"Yes, Gerard. Her body."

"She's *dead*?"

"I did say body, Gerard."

"But I didn't — I never — I assumed she'd just . . . I don't know what I assumed. It didn't matter to me. She'd found Wright. By the time I came north, she'd left. She'd done her job. It wasn't as if I needed her to . . . Dead?"

Sarah said, "That's what it looks like."

She wondered that she could say the words so coldly, but after the day she'd had, she was wrung out. All she had was a wall to lean against, and a dark sky overhead in which one or two stars were showing. After the rain, these pinpricks of light. And soon enough would come the morning.

"I'm sorry. I'm sorry she's dead. But I don't think that had anything to do with what she was doing for me."

"That's good, Gerard. So long as your conscience is clear."

That reached a shriller pitch than she'd intended. Some of the higher notes whistled round the dark for a moment.

She said, "So she was gone before you arrived at the Bolbec."

"That's right."

"And you've no idea where she went."

"None at all. The last communication I had with her was that list of names. A fortnight ago. Sarah —"

"The body was found last week. But Zoë checked out of the hotel the week before. The previous night, there'd been a crowd in the Bolbec bar, apparently. That sound odd to you?"

Gerard said, "It's been quiet as a grave while I've been there." Then he thought about that, and added, "Sorry."

She shook her head. Gerard had his own problems. Tonight was like the lancing of a boil: a lot of nasty stuff had poured out, but that didn't mean the healing was done. It meant it was beginning. And whatever had become of Zoë, he knew nothing about it. Because if Alan Talmadge hadn't led Zoë here, he must have followed her. The job Zoë had done for Gerard had had nothing to do with it.

A brief fizz released her from her thoughts. Gerard had tossed his cigar into a puddle. "What now?" he said.

He looked deflated. She wondered how long it had been since he'd asked anyone what he should do.

"Sarah?"

"I take it that's your car?"

He nodded.

"Well, what you do is get in it and drive home." She put a hand on his shoulder. He didn't flinch. "Paula needs you, Gerard. So does Zachary."

"He'll never know what he needs."

"That doesn't mean he doesn't need it."

She expected a harsh comeback to that. Was almost disappointed when none arrived.

"What about you?"

"I could do with a lift, since you ask."

"To where?"

Anywhere, she thought . . . "Anywhere. Somewhere far away, where I can get home from."

"When?"

"Now's good."

"Yes," he said. "I suppose it is."

He patted his pockets for his car keys, and at that exact same moment, a phone buzzed.

"Was that you or me?" Gerard asked.

"It was me."

She fished it out. *One message received*, her screen said. It would be Russ, she thought. Russ, who was awake at five in the morning, wondering where on earth she'd got to.

But it wasn't.

"Anything important?" Gerard asked.

"You might say," she told him.

It was from Zoë.

# CHAPTER
# SEVENTEEN

At the bar on The Sage Gateshead's third floor Sarah was more or less on a level with the nearby Baltic's viewing gallery, which in turn gave a great view of the Sage. She'd heard there were those who thought the very best view of the Sage was from inside it, but anyone who'd done hard time among the concrete bunkers of London's South Bank would have laughed that off. Way down below, the Tyne shifted choppily. On its far bank stood the courts buildings, and to her right, between Sage and Baltic, was the Gateshead Millennium Bridge; a graceful eyelash she'd yet to see drop. About the same distance upriver was its industrial older brother, the Swing Bridge, squatly supported by a jetty-like structure the water lapped at hungrily. And immediately below her, a large white **H** on the concrete apron was a helicopter landing pad for the naval base.

And that was quite enough tourism, she knew, but Zoë was twenty minutes late, and Sarah herself had been early.

*Bar, 3rd floor, the Sage. 11.30. Z.*

As messages from beyond the grave went, it was hardly *I am risen*, but it would have to do. If the woman turned up to put some body behind it, Sarah would have no complaints.

Though if she was pressed, the lack of seating might have been mentioned.

She was leaning against the rail bordering the oval edge of the bar area — the bar itself was no more than a small counter between doors into Hall One — and from here could see right to ground level through the gap between the floor and the glass outer wall. When she arrived, there'd been a band playing near the café down there. Strange thing was, she'd seen half this band before, busking on Northumberland Street. This time the two brothers were performing with two other young men: fiddles, guitar and melodeon. Last Orders, a poster had proclaimed them. They looked like Arctic Monkeys gone folk, and had been joined by a female vocalist as Sarah watched, for a haunting song about whales.

That had been forty-five minutes ago. Then the band had packed up, and a matinée performance had started inside the hall: *A Young Person's Guide to the Orchestra*. Monitors over the doors showed an auditorium full of schoolchildren.

She looked at her watch again. Zoë was still late, and there was still no sign of her.

The text had been a reply, of sorts, to the message she'd left on Zoë's voice mailbox in the early hours, at the Internet café:

"I don't know whether you're listening to this. I don't know whether you're able to. But if you are . . . I need your help, Zoë. I think something really bad has happened, or is about to. And I need to stop it. But I don't think I can do that on my own . . ."

In the end, Sarah hadn't needed Zoë's help. But that didn't defuse her smouldering sense that if she had done, it wouldn't have been forthcoming . . . A sense itself smothered, in turn, by relief that Zoë was alive. Along with anger that she'd been alive all this time, and allowed Sarah to think otherwise.

If you let it happen, conflicting emotions could cripple you.

Take Russ, for example. She'd spoken to Russ at last. It hadn't been a happy experience. He was forgivably pissed off about her extended absence; but less forgivably too pissed off to listen to the reasons for it. She'd had flashbacks to the derelict cinema while he'd been talking. *I didn't want to be with the spiders*, she wanted to say. *I'd rather have been with you*. But because things happened the way things happened, she found herself responding angrily instead. And then the conversation had been terminated, and it had been too late to say anything.

She should call him now. It wasn't really too late to say anything. But if she did, Zoë would turn up next moment, and then Sarah would have to disconnect and it would all be terrible again —

With the thought, she scanned the level once more. But saw no sign of Zoë.

Gerard had left. Was in London by now, or at the very least, in a traffic jam quite near it. He'd given her a lift to the railway station, and had hugged her quite hard on leaving . . . As for Wright, he might be wandering the back lanes near the cinema still, in a daze. Wondering what he'd done to deserve this.

But she didn't want to think about him.

One day soon, she'd call Gerard. Make sure he was okay, or as okay as circumstances allowed. And she'd talk to Paula. Sarah would try to forget everything she'd ever thought she'd known about Paula — *Hello!* magazine; designer labels — and listen instead to the woman she was talking to. She would try to hear the music. And after that she'd talk to Gerard again, to discuss what to do about Wright; something that didn't involve instant justice in a cobwebbed court. If nothing else, there were always newspapers. Even the worst papers would jump all over a story like his. Especially the worst papers.

There was no way a rat like Wright could be allowed to get away with what he'd done.

All of this she would do, as soon as everything else was over.

She'd eaten breakfast after collecting her bag from the Internet café; had eaten two, in fact, to make up for however many meals she'd missed. After that she'd drifted around the quayside, cold and edgy, watching gulls bobbing on the water like they owned the place. She'd wondered where Zoë had been, and invented mental conversations with her. These always closed with Zoë's abject apologies: pointless exercises in self-justification. But hard to resist all the same.

Time dragged when all you had to do was kill it. This was hardly news. She'd been in the Sage for some while. Had checked her bag in at the cloakroom, exactly as if she was here for the matinée performance.

And now she checked her watch, and it was 11.55.

"You'd think they'd open the bar, wouldn't you?"

She started, then recovered herself. It wasn't Zoë, obviously.

"Well . . . It's a bit early."

"I didn't mean for a drink. Just a cup of coffee, you know?"

He was about her age, with neatly trimmed dark hair and rimless glasses, and wore a long dark raincoat. She hadn't heard him approach. He'd come to a halt a careful three yards distant.

She said, "Good point. Coffee wouldn't hurt."

He smiled, then leaned on the rail and looked out at the riverside.

Sarah checked left and right, but there was still no sign of Zoë.

Outside, the skies were blue, or nearly blue, with no trace of yesterday's unstoppable rain. It was cold, though. Next time, if there was a next time, she'd bring a warmer coat, even if it proved less stylish. And thinking so, she brushed again at a smear on her collar, which she must have picked up in the cinema, and which she didn't care to analyse too carefully.

"Do you have someone in there?"

"I'm sorry?"

The man had turned her way again, but was nodding towards Hall One. "Are you a parent? Lot of children in there."

"Oh, right. No, I'm just waiting for a friend."

"I'm not waiting on a lady," he said, and then, at Sarah's confusion, added: "Stones song. Sorry. Bit of a fan."

"Right. Yeah, no. I remember that one."

He grinned, and she knew him. And then the moment passed.

". . . Something wrong?"

"No, sorry. Just remembering something."

Though who she was remembering, she couldn't have said.

Sarah resumed her outward gaze. A chord had been struck, and she was trying to follow the reverberation back to its source. But it all became part of the larger cacophony of the past days: of trains arriving and cars hammering past; of noisy voices in bars, and scuttlings in the darkness. Of hiding behind locked doors while unknown men prowled on the other side.

But that had been Jack Gannon. This man was no one she'd yet seen.

She shook her head. Memory was playing tricks. Something had suggested something else, which had suggested something else again. She was tired, that was the problem. And Zoë was still not here. She reached for her mobile phone, whose battery was so low it couldn't have more than a couple of minutes' life in it. It was hard not to empathize. But she pulled Zoë's name onscreen anyway, and pressed Call. She'd avoided this so far, as if to phone once more would be to push her luck. As if the fact that Zoë had answered once meant nothing, while a failure to answer a second time would definitively indicate her absence.

During the moments it took her phone to respond, she glanced sideways at the waiting man. He seemed oblivious to her presence; had his back to the rail and was looking towards the monitor, presumably hoping for an indication that the performance was nearly over. He must be a parent. *Lot of children in there.* That was what she thought. And then in her ear, she heard Zoë's phone ring.

And two yards away, a tinny Stones riff buzzed in a pocket.

*Dah-dah — da-da-dah — da-da-da-da-da-dah-dah*

She watched, unbelieving, as he calmly reached inside his coat, and pulled out his mobile. Held it to his ear. Pressed Connect.

The Stones died.

At her ear she could hear the same ambient noises that rang around the hall.

Into his phone the man said: "I changed her dial tone," and the words dopplered straight into her ear. "Told you I was a fan."

Sarah lowered her handset.

"Don't stress out," he told her. "It's not a big issue."

And he smiled again, and she knew who he was.

Because things sometimes happen in synch, a noise clattered round the lobbies and landings at precisely that moment: a tray spilt in the café downstairs. Crockery was broken. In pubs and bars, such accidents provoked a communal jeer; here, there was instead a respectful pause, before events resumed their normal course.

Last time she'd seen this man he'd worn dirty blue jeans and a variety of shirts and sweaters, layered one on top of the other. His hair had been dead straw, and his face was grey from huddling in corners.

He'd sold her a *Big Issue* on the instalment plan. Pay now, collect later.

Looking back, she suspected that was a first.

She said, "Where's Zoë?"

"You don't know?"

"Where *is* she?"

That note hit the glass, and bounced off it like candlelight. She was aware of it splintering around the high spaces; of people she couldn't see pausing to wonder what was up. It made her bite her lip. As if public embarrassment remained a consideration.

He leaned across to pat her hand. She withdrew it furiously.

"What have you done with her?"

"Please, Sarah. Don't make a fuss. Not here." He gestured to the Hall behind him, as if Benjamin Britten might take offence. "If we're going to talk, you have to stay calm."

Her mobile phone was in her hand. "The police," she said. "I could have the police here in minutes."

"Why on earth would you want to do that?"

The look on his face was one of genuine puzzlement.

"What have you done with her?" she said again, less sure of herself.

"I haven't done anything with her," he said. "I don't know where she is. And I'm worried about her. Same as you."

Sarah opened her mouth, then wiped whatever she'd been about to say. "What do you mean, you're *worried* about her — you're — you're *you*. You're a killer. Don't think I don't know who you are."

Though she didn't, in fact, know who he was. He was Alan Talmadge. But that wasn't even his name.

He said, "Now there, you see? You've been listening to Zoë. And she's wrong about me, Sarah."

"She's not wrong."

"She's taken certain facts — facts capable of different interpretations — and she's put them together and come up with this wild idea, this crazy story. But it's not true, Sarah. I'm not the person she thinks I am."

"So who are you?"

He shrugged. "I'm what you see."

"So why the disguise — the homeless get-up? Why have you been hiding if you've nothing to hide?"

"Do you always see things in such black and white?"

"You've got her phone, for God's sake — you've got Zoë's *phone*. Where's the grey in that?"

An usher appeared from round the corner — that would have been the moment to make her voice heard; to shout, if not *Rape*, then something equally incendiary. But the woman carried on round the curved wall, and if Sarah raised her voice now, she might lose whatever chance was being offered to find out what happened to Zoë.

He said, "There. That wasn't difficult, was it?"

Sarah looked at him.

"Not shouting out, I mean."

She said, "You've got her phone."

"She left it behind."

"Zoë wouldn't do that."

"Why do you think I'm worried about her?"

"She was at the Bolbec. She was in Newcastle, doing a job. And you followed her here."

He said, "You make it sound creepy. It wasn't like I was stalking her. I wanted to make contact, that's all. And I thought it best if I did that off home ground."

"So where's home?"

"This isn't about me, Sarah. I just want to know Zoë's all right."

"I'm not one of your lonely victims, Talmadge, or whatever you're called today. I trust you as far as I could throw this building. You won't tell me who you are, or where you come from, but I'm supposed to help you? Get a grip."

"I disguised myself, okay." He shrugged. "Zoë has certain ideas about me. As we've established. But she's wrong, Sarah. And it's important to me that she realizes that."

His words, his being here — the very fact of him, when all she'd previously had to go on was Zoë's stories. All of it, put together, amounted to a feeling like a slug crawling over her grave.

"You were watching her."

"I was waiting for the right moment."

"You sent her an e-mail."

". . . You've been looking at her e-mails?"

Sarah said, "I've been looking everywhere I can. Because there's a body on a slab up there" — and here

294

she pointed through the glass wall; over the river; towards the heart of the city — "and it was wearing Zoë's clothes, and carrying Zoë's wallet, and for all I know it was Zoë. Except if it was, you wouldn't be here, would you?"

He looked in the direction she'd pointed, as if the body might suddenly materialize, unshrouded, on the other side of the glass.

Sarah said, "It was Madeleine, wasn't it? Madeleine Irving."

"Who?"

"Madeleine Irving," Sarah repeated, with less conviction. Madeleine Irving. A name she'd plucked from the ether. But when you got down to it, Madeleine was one of many, wasn't she? One of many who went missing, looked for or not. It didn't have to be her. It just had to not be Zoë.

Though whoever it was, she'd once had a name.

She said, "The woman — the woman in the water. You made it look like she was Zoë."

"I don't know where you're getting this from, Sarah."

"You're making noises, but you're not saying anything. There was a body. And you know it wasn't Zoë's. So you know whose it was. You put it there."

"I didn't put anyone in the river, Sarah. I'm just looking for Zoë, same as you. She needs me."

"She *needs* you?"

"Of course she does. She just doesn't know it yet." He looked away, into the glassed distance. "She's lonely, Sarah. It's tipping her over the edge. Why would she do what she did, otherwise?"

"What does that mean?"

Talmadge shook his head.

Sarah said, "She told me what you do." The words were coming out quietly, as if this were their secret, here in this public place. "You worm your way into women's lives. Because they're 'lonely'. And then you kill them."

He was shaking his head again before she'd finished. "It's fantasy. She seems to need a dark figure in her life, someone to unload all her bad stuff on to, as a way of keeping her real feelings hidden. She's not much for self-analysis, is she? If this were happening to anyone else, she'd be the first to tell you what was really going on."

"Oh, please," Sarah said. "Enlighten me."

He looked at her, amusement glittering in his eyes. He was very smooth-cheeked. Professionally so. She imagined that, having finished with his homeless guise, he'd spent half a day getting a professional seeing-to: hair, nails, skin. It wasn't simply that he looked different. It was that you'd never associate this man with the other.

"I think you know," he said.

"Did you talk to her?"

"No."

"You didn't make contact."

He bowed his head: one slight admission. "I sent that e-mail. But she was gone by then. From the hotel, I mean."

"But you were following her. Stalking her."

"You keep using that word."

"It keeps being true. How long were you hanging round the hotel?"

"Just a few days." He smiled suddenly, and a naïve sincerity lit his eyes. If he could fake that, Sarah thought — if he could fake that: yes, he was dangerous. "I wanted to be near her, that's all. Even if it meant being part of a crowd."

"Really? At the *Bolbec*?" But she was remembering what Barry had said: *There was a crowd. Expecting free drinks. Don't know what that was about.* She said, "You pulled some kind of fast one, didn't you?"

"I put up a few posters round town. It was no big thing. But — well, it guaranteed a few punters, you might say."

There was a growing commotion, as if a wave were pushing upriver, and it took Sarah a moment to understand that it was applause. The performance in Hall One had come to an end. On the monitor, the orchestra had taken to its feet, bowing acknowledgement to the clapping crowd. Even as she registered this, the door opened and the first of the erstwhile audience slipped out.

"I hate that," Talmadge said. "It's discourteous. They should stay where they are a few minutes. Let the players know they're appreciated."

And now more people streamed out, the vast majority children, and the noise levels on the landing escalated.

He said, "Well, it was good talking with you. When you see Zoë, tell her I'll be in touch."

"We're not finished yet —"

But it seemed they were. With a nod and a smile that combined pleasure and regret, he moved away so deceptively swiftly that he was among the staircase-bound crowd before she finished her sentence.

She looked round, as if there were someone she could explain this moment to. *Don't let him get away,* she could say. *Don't you realize who that is?* But there was nobody there. Nobody, at any rate, with a moment to spare for Sarah.

There were more doors into the auditorium to her right, all of them disgorging people. Sarah joined the stream, eyes locked on Talmadge's back. He was at the top of the staircase already; had navigated himself into a clear channel where he could take the stairs two at a time without even appearing to be in a hurry. It was hard to believe that just two minutes ago, this building had been full of empty spaces. Now it was raucous and echoey; full to spilling with children who'd been trussed up inside an audience this past hour. Freedom had them bobbing around like balloons.

But Talmadge towered above them, beanstalk-high.

Don't lose sight of him, Sarah, she told herself. That shouldn't be too hard: just don't lose —

"Shit — oh God, sorry —"

Eyes fixed on Talmadge, she'd stumbled over an infant, a boy.

"I'm really sorry, are you all right?"

An adult — a teacher — was zeroing in on her. "Excuse me, do you think you could watch where you're going?"

298

The boy was okay. The boy wasn't crying. The adult, though, looked spoiling for a fight.

"And I'd ask you to mind your language with so many young people around."

"Yes. Yes. Right," Sarah said. She hurried round the group of children who were her immediate obstacle, but Talmadge was nowhere to be seen.

"Shit," she said again.

The staircase was a swarming mass of movements: children mostly, chattering mostly; squawking in some instances. Adults dotted among them were making the kind of calmingly authoritative noises sheepdogs would make if they could talk. But none of the adults was Talmadge.

The pestery teacher had caught up with her. "Do you really think that's any way to —"

"Oh, fuck off," Sarah snapped. She scampered down the stairs, hoping to find Talmadge on the next level. But he was nowhere. How had he *done* that? She couldn't have taken her eyes off him for more than a second, and *whap*! He was gone.

There were more doorways into Hall One on this floor, with more children streaming from each. Talmadge could have slipped inside. It wouldn't have taken a second.

But hiding inside the auditorium would have narrowed his choices. Wouldn't he head for the outside world? She took the next flight down, fetching up on ground level by the café. The ticket counters were to her right; there were loos either side. She wasn't going to find him in a hurry if he was lurking in the Gents.

Think, Sarah.

Hours ago, in a previous life, she'd used her mobile to lure a shape from the shadows. That wasn't going to work here. Half the people in sight had a mobile phone in their pocket. The rest had one in their hands. Even "Satisfaction" wasn't going to make itself heard among this lot.

And standing on the spot wasn't helping. Or was it? If you want to hide in a crowd, don't push your way through it: find somewhere you can stand still without being noticed. Like a queue. She turned to those lining up at the café counter: not there. Then those leaning against the ticket counters; engaged in transactions, or just leafing through pamphlets. They included a lone man, and it might be Talmadge, but it wasn't — already, though, his image was starting to fade, her memory superimposing upon it his earlier incarnation: dead-straw hair; face grey from huddling in corners. What colour coat had he been wearing? She couldn't recall. Black. No, blue.

She was holding her mobile, but couldn't imagine anything useful to do with it. She could call the police, sure. Then spend the rest of the morning explaining what she was talking about.

Somebody bumped into her and she turned, expecting that teacher again. But all she faced was a mumbled apology from a youngish man. She was standing in the middle of the hall, that was the trouble. There were people trying to go places, and she was in their way. She shook her head. Two minutes. It hadn't taken two minutes: that was how much time had passed

**300**

since she'd been standing three floors up, talking to Talmadge. And now he was gone.

But Zoë was alive. That was worth hanging on to. She'd lost Talmadge, but Zoë was alive.

Where she'd got to, and what she was doing there, were questions that could wait.

Jamming her phone into her coat pocket, Sarah headed for the exit on the Millennium Bridge side. Large groups of schoolchildren were being corralled here and there in the wide lobby. She had to thread her way through them.

On the other side of the curved glass walls, a boat made its way upriver, piloted by a man in a bright green life-saving jacket. Gulls rose squawking from the water at its approach, and on the far quay a small child, bulked to a sphere by its padded coat, pointed this out for its mother's pleasure.

There were people on the Millennium Bridge; some crossing; others just taking in the view. A major part of this was the Sage itself, the great glass slug behind Sarah. She fumbled with the collar of the coat, buttoning it in place. On the bridge, a woman's shape lifted a hand to her ear.

Down the steps and halfway across the terrace in front of Sarah, another shape stopped.

# CHAPTER
# EIGHTEEN

She couldn't hear it, but she knew what it would be.

*Dah-dah — da-da-dah — da-da-da-da-da-dah-dah*

A tinny Stones riff, buzzing in a pocket.

She couldn't believe she'd not seen him until he stopped, because there he was in open view, halfway across that neat expanse between Sage and Baltic. As she watched, he too raised a fist to his ear.

Sarah turned back to the woman on the bridge.

Who didn't look like anyone she'd seen before. She wore a calf-length white raincoat, and a tight-fitting black cap. Except it wasn't a black cap. She'd had her hair cut, that was all. A pretty brutal cut, but just a cut.

Not like anyone Sarah had seen before, but it was Zoë all right.

Talmadge's arm dropped, and he turned to face Sarah. For no reason she could have readily explained, she pointed at him. Rude, of course. But ruder to kill women. He shook his head, as if disappointed by her vulgarity, then continued his sweep of the area. He spotted Zoë swiftly enough. Still with her phone at her ear, she began walking his way.

Now Sarah's phone rang.

*I want you back . . .*

"It's important we don't lose him, Sarah."

"Fine, thanks. How about you? Not dead?"

"Can that wait?"

Sarah cut the call.

Talmadge was walking away from them, fast. For someone anxious to know where Zoë was not five minutes ago, he now seemed keen not to encounter her.

But it was all about choosing your ground. Talmadge wanted to control events. So Zoë appearing from nowhere, getting the drop on him — no wonder he was off.

Zoë was coming off the bridge, Sarah advancing from the Sage. The pair of them forming a pincer movement, cutting off Talmadge's lines of escape.

But he didn't glance round. It was as if this was where he'd always been headed: the Baltic; once a flour mill, now a museum of modern art. He was heading inside: shop to his left, café to his right. When Zoë and Sarah intersected, they were about a hundred yards behind him.

Without slowing down, Sarah said, "How did you know where to find us?"

"Fine, thanks. How about you? Not —"

"Zoë —"

"He's got my phone. You'll have noticed that."

"So what, you've got it bugged? Your own phone?"

Zoë looked at her. Her eyes were darker than ever. And with her hair all but buzz-cut, and that white coat — Zoë in white? That's what Sarah called a disguise — she looked like a bruised ghost.

She wasn't dead. But she gave good affect.

Now she said: "My own phone? I might be paranoid, Sarah. But I'm not . . . *fucking* paranoid."

Talmadge disappeared inside the building.

"How many exits does this place have?"

"He's not slipping away," Zoë said. "Not this time."

That smell — Sarah suddenly registered that smell. "You're smoking again."

Zoë said, "A mobile phone gives off a pulse. Everybody knows this."

"I've seen *Spooks*. But how do you —?"

"You don't. But you pay people who do." She snorted. "The Internet's not a toy, Sarah. You can buy any service you need."

And then they were inside too.

"You've been following him."

"I've been waiting for him to stick his head above the parapet."

"So you can cut it off."

Zoë said, "Can I remind you who this guy is?"

The shop had a wide, wide doorway. Zoë stopped as they reached it, and pointed. "Check the café."

"Sir," Sarah said.

But it needed doing.

In the café, a family sat around one table; harassed young parents too busy shushing their infants to pretend to be Alan Talmadge. The rest were couples; a few solo women. No Talmadge. On her way back, Sarah stopped at the toilets. In here? Of course. The women's were empty, an unusual occurrence. Stepping back out, a thought nagged: *what if he slipped past while I was inside?* But what could she do about it if he had? She stepped smartly behind a young man heading into the Gents. He paused to hold the door for her, and executed a perfect double-take.

"He can run," Sarah told him. "But he can't hide."

A man at a urinal looked over his shoulder, bemused, while another paused in the act of washing his hands. Neither was Talmadge. The doors to the stalls mostly hung ajar. The one that didn't swung open at her push.

"Is this a happening?" the young man asked.

"Is it a what?"

"Some kind of art event?"

"Oh. Yes. A sort of installation." She nodded at the urinals. "I'm thinking of having one of them installed."

Back in the lobby, there was no sign of Talmadge. If he'd got past her, he'd got past her. She joined Zoë at the shop's entrance.

"He went inside."

"It's not a small place, Zoë."

"He's not getting away again."

Her voice was tighter than Sarah remembered. As if something were slowly strangling her; its invisible fingers rippling round her throat.

As they headed towards the entrance into the museum proper, Zoë's coat flapped round her knees like a gunslinger's duster.

"I'm taking the lift," she said. "I'll work my way down. You take the stairs."

"Thanks."

"Sarah. This is important."

That was good to know. It was good to know she'd come all this way to identify her friend's body, and it turned out to be important.

. . . Identify her *body*? The woman was right in front of her now, and Sarah could hardly recognize her.

The lift arrived. It was empty.

Zoë said, "Sarah. You want me to owe you forever? Help me catch this man."

She stepped inside and jabbed a button. The door slid shut.

When Sarah turned, a middle-aged woman with a Baltic logo-ed sweatshirt was watching, her jaw hanging slightly.

Sarah said, "It's not as creepy as it sounds."

"Are you a polis?"

"Actually, it is as creepy as it sounds. A man came this way, last five minutes. Long dark coat? Neat dark hair?"

The woman shrugged. "I don't monitor them, pet. I just make sure nobody crawls over the exhibits."

Sarah looked at the stairs, then back at the woman, who had a radio clipped to her belt. "Please call whoever. Security. Tell them what I've just told you. There's a man in your museum, a dangerous man."

"I just tell them that, do I?"

Sarah was heading into the stairwell. "You're probably not his type. But you never can tell."

There were a lot of stairs. More than seemed correct in a six-storey building. But then, these storeys were high-ceilinged.

**306**

And this wasn't the only set of stairs, and Zoë's wasn't the only lift, and there'd be God only knew how many hiding places; places where it would look like you were communing with art . . .

But there was little sense, Sarah told herself through gritted teeth, in giving up before she'd started.

So she took the stairs two at a time, heart racing before she reached the first floor, which wasn't crowded. A couple by the far wall were having an argument, judging by their body language; otherwise there was only a man with a rucksack on his back, which on second look turned into a baby-carrier. Producing a baby at short notice would be setting the bar high even for Talmadge. But she was aware of an ever-growing urgency. Every second put him a little more distant. Even if he remained in this big square building, he'd be slipping moment by moment out of reach, like a fistful of sand.

She checked that the couple hadn't morphed into a single man while her gaze was elsewhere. They hadn't.

Above their heads, a twisted length of neon tubing changed colour. *Eatshitpissdie*, it read.

This was no time for a disquisition on modern art.

But sweet Jesus.

Sarah headed back to the stairwell.

Where she learned again the hard way that exercise was one thing — regular long walks; even regular long walks featuring steep inclines — and running up never-ending flights of stairs another. Her heart was pounding like a basketball before she'd reached the next set of doors: these gave on to a gallery, looking down on the space she'd just left. Nobody had moved. *Eatshitpissdie* was bleeding blue to red. Sarah's legs felt ready to give, and her entire body was wrapped in sweat.

But there were plenty more stairs to climb.

This time she settled for a steady upward propulsion, as if her legs were pistons. Her legs weren't fooled. If she ever got to the top, she'd not be able to stand. But if she got to the top, that would mean she'd missed Talmadge.

The other stairwell nagged at her — there was at least one other stairwell. He could be below her even now, calmly trip-trapping out into the light.

*And I really don't want to be the one to explain to Zoë that he's got away.*

Above her a door slammed, and somebody clattered on to the stairs. Sarah stopped, and pressed against the wall. If it was Talmadge, maybe she could stick a foot out; send him tumbling head over heels —

But it wasn't. It was a young woman whose brown-tasselled boots clashed horribly with her pink jacket. She gave Sarah a twisted smile, unless she was chewing gum, and vanished, heading for an up-close encounter with *Eatshitpissdie*.

An artefact that was definitely taking up too much space in Sarah's head.

She leaned over the waist-high banister and peered upwards. The stairwell still went on forever. But when she looked down, there was quite a drop already . . . Dizzy, Sarah stepped back. Shook her head to release the feeling, then started on the stairs once more.

Another full circuit brought her to another artspace: this one in moody darkness. A series of screens at irregular angles had the same film unspooling on each, at different speeds: a tower block collapsing in a mini-Hiroshima of dust. She knew how it felt. The soundtrack was a playground chant: *Ring-a-ring-a-roses*. There were more art lovers here than downstairs, but Talmadge wasn't among them. She patrolled the room twice, at a canter, and then was back on the stairs.

He was gone. She knew this. He'd been smoke from the moment he entered the building. What had made them believe he was cornered?

Something fell past; a sudden downward rush of noise.

Sarah stopped.

When she looked up, she saw a man hanging halfway into space.

If you wanted a dodgy situation turned into a circus, just add Zoë.

That was the thought banging round Sarah's head in time to her feet on the stairs: If you *wanted* a *dodgy situation* . . . And she might throw up. Another thought, edging its way through the gaps. She might barf without reaching the top.

More noises dropped down the stairwell; muffled and clangy, like a badly judged soundtrack.

Heart in mouth, she reached the next landing and stopped to look down. People were gathering on ground level, pointing. You'd think they'd never seen a grown man hung over a banister before.

*Eatshitpissdie* swam back into her mind. If Zoë lets go of this guy, it's going to make more of a splash than a neon crudity.

Talmadge was a ventriloquist's puppet; a loose-limbed breakable thing half-sitting on the railing, knees hanging over the safe side. The rest of him leaned horizontal, taunting gravity. His fists were wrapped tightly round Zoë's upper arms. His knuckles shone white.

Behind Zoë was a set of doors she must have come through at a whack. Must have leaped without warning; pushed so hard, Talmadge would have gone over if she'd not held his lapels.

"You found him then," Sarah said. The words hurt, coming out. Last time she'd climbed stairs this quickly she'd been younger, and newly in love.

"I found him."

"I'm still here," Talmadge said. "Don't talk as if I wasn't."

To give him credit, he sounded calmer than Sarah. All Zoë had to do was let go. It wasn't even an action; more a cessation. One brief surrender, and Talmadge would bounce off hard edges all the way down to death.

The shaking in Sarah's knees wasn't entirely due to exertion.

A coppery taste rose in her mouth. She said, "Took him by surprise, then."

"He's not used to accidents happening to him. He's usually on the other side of them."

310

"Zoë," Talmadge said. "This is all a mistake."

"Why don't we save the speaking for when we're spoken to?"

"Let me go."

"You might want to choose your words more carefully."

"Zoë. This would be murder."

Zoë flexed her arms, and he yelped.

Not as calm as he'd like them to think.

Zoë said: "A little push here, a little nudge there. People fall under trains, and die in cold ditches. What did you plan for me, Talmadge? If that's what you're called this week?"

Sarah said, "Zoë? Is this the way to deal with this?"

"It's working for me."

"Let go and he'll die."

"That's what I meant."

"What the hell's going on?"

A man wearing one of those Baltic sweatshirts had appeared on the landing above.

Zoë said, "Private chat."

"You're about one inch from killing that man." The newcomer paused, checking his measurements. "An inch."

"Oh, I'm a lot closer than that," Zoë assured him.

Sarah said, "Have you called the police?"

"It's been done."

"Whose side are you on?" Zoë asked her.

"Do you know this . . . woman?"

Sarah said, "It might be best if you backed away. Maybe the other side of that door?"

"I'm in charge here," he told her.

"That's good. But your chances of breaking his fall are slim," she said. "While your chances of making a bad thing worse are looking good."

"The police are on their way," he said. "And an ambulance," he added.

"I'm not sure an ambulance'll help," Zoë said. "A spatula and a jiffy bag might work."

Talmadge said, "You're not going to drop me, Zoë."

"You sound sure of that."

"I know you. This isn't what you want to do."

Sarah said to the Baltic man: "Really. Your presence isn't helping."

"So this is *my* fault now?"

"That's right," Zoë said without turning. "This is all about you."

"I only meant —"

"Just fuck off, okay?"

Sarah said, "It'll be better if you left. Really."

"This isn't some kind of *event*, is it? Because I was never told —"

"This isn't art. Trust me."

He didn't look like he did. But he pushed backwards through the door behind him, on to the viewing gallery.

Sarah looked up. They were one flight below the top. Which wasn't going to matter to Talmadge, if push came to shove. They were too many flights above the bottom for that.

"Zoë," she said. Her legs were shaking. Her lungs ached. She could feel her pulse in her fingernails. "Zoë, this has got to stop."

"Oh, it'll stop. Go and join your new friend. I'll whistle when I'm done."

"I'm not going anywhere," she said.

"Great. How about you, Talmadge?" Zoë flexed her arms, jerking him another inch lower. He dropped his head back; took an upside-down look at what might be his last journey. "Having fun yet?"

"What do you want from me, Zoë?"

And now there was fear. There was no hiding any more. He could disappear in crowded places, Alan Talmadge, but hang him over a banister, and he was all too visibly present.

"You followed me up here. To Newcastle."

"Okay. Yes. I followed you."

"With a woman."

"Are you jealous?"

"You dumb *fuck*, this is not a joke. Do you want to be a splash on the downstairs walls?"

"She was a friend, Zoë. Nothing more."

"She looked like me."

"Superficial." And this was a yelp. "There was a superficial resemblance. Listen, the police are on their way. Do you really want them to —"

"You took my things. Stole my identity. Dressed her up. So you could pretend she was me. Tell me that was *superficial*, you sick fuck."

The light seemed to be growing stronger, Sarah thought. Seemed to be falling on them from above, as if this moody tableau were being incorporated into the museum. Soon the three of them would freeze into place. Future staircase users would ponder their meaning. Talmadge would hang forever, and never fall.

Her head was pounding in time with her heart. The light wasn't growing stronger; her eyes were growing weak.

"You killed her, didn't you?" Zoë said. "Just like you killed the others."

"You know that's not true."

"She was pulled from the river, Talmadge. Don't you read the papers? Yanked from the Tyne by men with poles. Dead as you get. They've already cut her up."

"That's ugly, Zoë. You sound like you're pleased."

"I'm pleased you're not walking away this time. That's what I'm pleased about."

"You're acting like I put her in the river, Zoë. And I didn't even know where she was. Not till they pulled her out. You of all people have to believe that."

"You're missing the point. It wasn't river water in her lungs, Talmadge. She didn't drown in the Tyne. And didn't drown her*self* anywhere else, unless you've a plausible reason for her jumping in the river afterwards." She pushed again. A faraway gasp rose up from way below. "The accident story won't wash this time."

Sarah said, "Let him up, Zoë."

"I want to hear him say it."

"It doesn't matter what he says. Not while his life's in your hands."

"I want to hear him —"

"He could confess to killing Princess Di, Zoë, and it wouldn't matter. A forced confession's about as much use as . . ."

314

"Cardboard wellies?" a voice from above suggested.

DS King was on the landing above.

The lift, thought Sarah. He'd taken the lift.

"Let him free, Ms Boehm," King suggested.

"You don't know who he is," Zoë said, without turning.

"I don't care who he is. You're the one contemplating murder."

"I still haven't ruled it out."

"And I'm sure you're prepared to face the consequences. But can you speak for Ms Tucker?"

That gave Zoë pause.

DS King looked at Sarah. "You came in together. Looking for him. We've got conspiracy and we've got premeditated." He turned back to Zoë, not that Zoë was facing him. "So it won't be just you under the hammer."

He came softly down the stairs as he spoke. He was still wearing trainers, Sarah noticed.

"Are you prepared to send her to jail for murder, Ms Boehm? Along with you? Will you be that good a friend to her?"

There were other policemen behind him, Sarah saw. The uniformed variety, hovering on the edge of the landing.

"Because she was pretty upset back when you were dead, I couldn't help noticing."

Zoë said, "Is this your softly softly? Because I'm not sticking around for your Gene Hunt."

"Zoë," Sarah said. "Listen to the man. Let Talmadge go."

"Don't tempt me."

In that next moment it nearly happened — it would have been a moment's work for Zoë to open her fists, to shrug off Talmadge's grasp. Sarah couldn't see his face, but had no trouble picturing it: his eye-wide shock at having nothing but air to cling on to. The half-second's grace before his body was plundered by gravity.

Zoë pulled him on to the staircase, and sent him sprawling in a heap on the landing.

King nodded, as if she'd done a good thing, then arrested her.

# CHAPTER
# NINETEEN

Looking upwards, it was hard to believe that only yesterday the city had nearly washed away in the rain. Upwards was largely blue; the few clouds a high wadding that stippled into nothingness at the edges. A jet's trail was a brief scratch on the sky's underside. But at Sarah's feet, pools gathered in the cracked brick ground, and a mossy smell lingered, probably from the drainpipes.

Zoë lit another cigarette.

"I thought you were eating apples these days."

"They spray all kinds of crap over apples. At least with these, it says on the packet they kill you."

"That's really good, Zoë. A couple more lines like that, you might win a new lung."

"Can we save the sermon?"

"You let us all think you were dead."

"You saw the body," Zoë said. "You couldn't tell it wasn't me?"

Her voice was still tight, Sarah thought. That invisible grip still flexing itself round her throat.

They were speaking quietly, because there were policemen nearby. A pair of them on a bench on the other side of the yard, sharing a smoke and a joke.

Another just inside the door, waiting for Zoë to finish hers. A slew of butts underfoot spelt out the obvious: this was where the cops came to indulge their addictions. All those films and TV shows where fags smouldered non-stop in interrogation rooms: they were history.

She said, "It wasn't that easy. She looked like you. And she had — there was your wallet, your keys. Everything."

"She could have been wearing a little badge saying 'My name's Zoë'. It wouldn't have made her me."

"So how come you weren't in touch? 'Hey, Sarah? I'm still alive.' Something like that. What would that have cost?"

"He knew I was alive. Talmadge did."

"You thought this was just you and him?"

"If I'd gone to the police, he'd have been smoke."

"Being a private eye doesn't mean you have to sound like one," Sarah snapped.

"Sarah. You know how long I've been after this guy?"

She didn't reply.

"Sarah?"

Sarah shook her head. "I'm surprised they let you out."

Zoë waggled her cigarette, so the smoke looping from its tip squiggled a doctor's signature on the air. "Human rights. They can't deny you life's necessities."

"What will they do to you?"

"They haven't decided yet."

There was nowhere to sit other than that occupied bench, and Sarah didn't fancy leaning against the wall. Her coat had seen enough punishment lately.

"We've only got five minutes," she said. "Tell me what happened."

"I was on a job for your friend Gerard Inchon." Zoë could get to the point when she wanted. "You know that much."

"Yes."

"It was a nothing piece. Find a man he was after, he wouldn't say why. John Wright. Took me a day and a half, tops. Then Inchon wanted to contact him, without it looking like he did."

"So you came up with a list of names he could invite to a soirée. I know about that."

"Busy beaver, aren't you? Anyway, once I gave him the list I was done. But the night before I checked out, it happened."

"The Bolbec bar was unexpectedly busy," Sarah said.

Zoë looked at her.

*There was a crowd*, Barry had said. *Expecting free drinks.*

Sarah said, "Talmadge put up posters round the town. Offering freebies."

"I thought it must have been something like that." She inhaled. Smoke leaked from her lips with her next words: "I was drugged. Roofie in my drink. Something like that. I didn't get drunk."

"I believe you, Zoë."

"That's nice." She threw her cigarette at the drain, where it bounced off a mossy match and fizzled into silence. "When I started feeling groggy, I thought it must be flu or something, so went to my room. Crashed out. Next morning, everything I've got that

**319**

says I'm me has gone. Plastic, mobile, all of it. Plus watch and so on. But he'd left my cash. Now, what did you think I thought about that?"

"You knew it was Talmadge."

"Who else? He's always been out there, Sarah. Always. I've never even known his real name. But I've always known he's out there."

She lit a fresh cigarette.

"But I didn't know about her. The woman he was with. I thought he was trying to spook me, that's all. Not that he was working on his own model. His own version of me."

"You're lucky he didn't kill you."

"That's not what he does, Sarah. The women he's killed, they've all been in love with him. A substitute was the closest he was ever gunna get where I was concerned."

Sarah wondered if Talmadge believed that. *She needs me*, he'd said. *She just doesn't know it yet.* "How did he know you were in Newcastle?"

"Credit card? Mobile phone? E-mail?" A whisper of smoke reached Zoë's eyes, and she flapped it away. "I fly low, but I use my real name. He knows where I live. And it's not like stalking's new to him." She shook her head. "So I dropped out of sight. Figured that was the best way to get him to play his hand. He sent an e-mail the same day."

"Missing you," Sarah quoted.

Zoë stared.

"Vicky," she explained.

320

"That kid'll go far. She should choose her direction carefully."

"Where were you?"

"It's a big city. There's no shortage of places."

"And you just figured that sooner or later he'd, what? Take out an advert in the local paper?"

Zoë said, "Well, he did the next best thing, didn't he?"

Something tapped on glass, and they looked to the window behind them. The policeman inside was pointing at his watch.

"Come in, Ms Boehm, your time is up," Zoë muttered.

"It'll work out all right, Zoë."

"It'll work out all right when they realize the bastard's a killer. Course, they might still be upset about my hanging him over that stairwell."

She gave Sarah a sly grin, and for the first time, Sarah saw her old friend.

"Jesus, Zoë," she said, and shook her head. "What you need is a dimmer switch."

"No, what I need is a hairbrush," Zoë said. She ran her fingers through her close-cut hair. "This itches, you know."

"Mine's in my bag," Sarah said.

"The bastard took mine. Oh well. I'll survive." More tapping on glass: "I'm coming, I'm coming."

The policeman opened the door and Zoë slipped back inside.

Because nobody had said otherwise, Sarah stayed where she was.

It had been a long day. Just forming that thought deserved a prize for understatement: the day had begun, as far as Sarah was concerned, when she'd knocked on Gerard's door at the Bolbec, to find him gone. Then lunch with John M. Wright; then Alan Talmadge in a soap shop . . . She'd bussed in a panic through the rain; holed up in a pub in Jack Gannon's Walker. And there'd she'd slipped off reality's map. The attempt to recapture the ensuing hours produced a Catherine wheel of images: a campfire in a derelict shipyard; a spiders' picnic in an abandoned cinema. All of it meshing into one big helter-skelter carrying her through to daybreak, and the bright glassy newness of Sage and Baltic. Since when, she'd mostly been in interview rooms. Had mostly talked to policemen.

Her main current source of amazement was that she wasn't under arrest.

"Ms Boehm is pretty adamant you just happened to be there."

That was what DS King had said to her, about an hour earlier.

Fact was, Sarah had spent a lot of time lately just happening to be there. If DS King had the full list of those events, he might have reconsidered her non-arrest.

"What's going to happen to her?"

"Charges of assault, I expect."

"But not yet?"

He'd said, "We're waiting for a fuller picture to emerge. It's not often we get a former dead person in custody. So what do you know about it?"

"Until this morning, I thought Zoë was dead."

"So what's kept you in Newcastle the last couple of days?"

"Sightseeing," she'd told him. "What about Talmadge?"

"You keep calling him that."

"It used to be his name. Back when he was killing women. You haven't let him go, have you?"

"No. We haven't let him go."

"You believe Zoë's story?"

"We're considering the evidence."

"And how much of that is there?"

"Not a great deal, Ms Tucker. These, ah, murder victims. You're aware that neither was treated as murder at the time?"

"He's good at causing accidents."

"Well, he slipped up this time, didn't he? A body in the river could get there by accident, no argument. But not if it was dead before it hit the water."

"Nobody gets away with murder forever."

"Do you think so?" DS King had a steady gaze, and Sarah had felt as if he were looking straight through her. "I think you can get away with it for a hell of a long time. But not if you start making amateurish mistakes."

"Well, he's obviously not as clever as he'd like to think. What's he calling himself, by the way?"

"Oliver Cartwright. National insurance checks out. He lives just outside Maidenhead, he says. We're making calls."

Oliver Cartwright. Sarah had rolled the name around her head; had practised it on her tongue. Zoë's bogeyman had a new name.

Perhaps it was the real thing. Perhaps — back against the wall — Alan Talmadge had to slough his other skins, and own up to who he was.

Uncovering what he was would be the next stage.

"What about the woman in the water?"

"Says he knows nothing about that."

"Well, he would say that —"

"— wouldn't he?" King had finished for her.

"So where'd she come from?"

"We know a bit less about that than we did when you identified her as Zoë Boehm."

"I thought that's who it was."

"Really?"

Sarah met his gaze. Tell the truth. "Okay. Not a hundred per cent. But I knew she'd been wearing Zoë's jacket. And Talmadge — Cartwright — stole that jacket years ago. So if it wasn't Zoë, then Zoë had good reason to be hiding."

"And that was enough for you to mislead the police?"

"That was enough for me not to voice the one in a thousand chance it wasn't Zoë." She looked away. "Have you charged her yet?"

"Not yet."

"Can I talk to her?"

"Are you her lawyer?"

She hadn't replied.

324

But a little later he'd asked if she wanted tea or coffee. Coffee. Coffee might save her life. She'd expected him to find someone to fetch her a cup, but instead he'd led her to a lobby with a coffee machine, and left her to it.

The lobby looked on to a yard, and Zoë was out there, smoking.

And now Zoë was gone again, and Sarah still hadn't had her coffee. She slipped back through the door, negotiated a cup of brown liquid from the machine, and returned outside. She took a sip, burnt her tongue, and reached for her mobile. The battery was flat.

I'll call you, Russ, she promised. Soon. I'll see you soon.

At that moment something in the square space of sky overhead made her heart skip a beat. It was a mass of balloons — large bright silver ones — easily two dozen, possibly three, tied to each other but untethered to anything else. A single scarlet tail dragged in their wake. Just for a second she saw this. It was impossible not to smile.

But somewhere, there was a street salesman whose helium-filled stock-in-trade had just taken to the skies. That was the trouble, Sarah thought: everything had a world of detail behind it, and every detail snapped into place in someone else's life. What was that phrase she'd heard lately? Smoke and whispers. Everything was smoke and whispers.

The bench was free now. With all plans on hold she went to sit down, and as she did so DI Fairfax came into the yard. Still tall, with thin elongated features — still with the hint of a developing paunch — he came and sat next to her, cardboard cup of his own in hand.

"You'll want to watch that," she said. "It's hot."

"Trouble is, when it cools down, you can taste it. Cigarette?"

"I don't smoke."

"Good for you. Neither do I."

Sarah said, "But you keep a pack handy for special occasions."

"I don't, actually. It's as well you said no. I'm just doing the nice cop bit."

"Is that supposed to be disarmingly frank?"

He shrugged. "If it works. Ms Boehm have anything interesting to say?"

"What makes you think I'd tell you if she had?"

"Because whatever else is going on here, you're her friend. And the sooner we work out what's going on, the better it'll be for her."

"And for me?"

He drank some of his coffee. If it was as hot as hers, he hid it well. "We've spoken to Mr Gannon," he told her. "He backs up your story. That you've been with him these past few days."

"Sightseeing," Sarah reminded him.

"Strange company to choose."

"But that's not a police matter."

"As you say. I can't remember, are you married?"

"No."

"But you have a partner."

"Is this a crude attempt at blackmail, Inspector? I tell you what you want to know, you keep quiet about what you think I've been up to?"

For some reason, this possibility struck her as rather funny.

He said, "Just making an observation."

"Have you found out who the woman is yet?"

He shook his head.

She could give him a name, Sarah thought. Madeleine Irving. But Sarah had no proof that's who it was. It was Internet-based conjecture, no more. Nothing Fairfax couldn't find for himself.

"And Talmadge — Cartwright — he's still denying all knowledge."

"No idea what we're talking about."

"Zoë's told you he stole her things?"

"Ms Boehm has made that accusation," Fairfax said. "She's failed to back it up with proof."

"He had Zoë's phone."

"Well, he doesn't have it any more."

"It'll be somewhere in the Baltic."

"Or somewhere in the Tyne," he said.

"Have you looked?"

"To the best of our ability." He took another sip of coffee. "Not up to or including dragging the river."

"The last two times, he just walked away," Sarah told him. "Nobody ever came looking for him. Except Zoë."

"Maybe there was nothing to look for."

"Twice?"

"We've only Ms Boehm's word that he knew both women. The way he tells it, he went out with a woman once who fell under a tube train. After they'd split up."

"But this time there's proof."

"I thought we'd established there's nothing —"

"That it wasn't an accident, I mean. Else she'd not have been in the river."

With clean water in her lungs.

Fairfax nodded abstractedly. She'd told him nothing he didn't already know. He finished his coffee, set the cup on the bench's arm, and stood.

Sarah said, "There isn't a bin that can go in?"

He picked it up.

There was something scratching at the back of her mind, but she couldn't tell what.

"My sergeant told you you're free to go?"

He hadn't, in fact, but she'd picked up that message.

"But leave a number we can reach you on."

As he turned Sarah stood, and caught a glimpse of herself in the window. She looked crudely drawn, something a child might have managed with a crayon. Her face had grown new hollows. And as for her hair —

As for her hair.

"The hairbrush," Sarah said slowly.

*What I need is a hairbrush,* Zoë had said. *The bastard took mine.*

Fairfax paused. "What hairbrush?"

"The hairbrush that wasn't." Sarah shook her head. "Sorry. I'm tired. I was playing Kim's Game yesterday — ever played that, Inspector?"

"A memory game, right?"

328

"That's right."

"Is this going anywhere?"

Keys. A watch. A lipstick. Zoë's hairbrush. Zoë's wallet.

"I was trying to remember the things you'd found with the body. And I kept remembering a hairbrush, because that's what Zoë uses. A hairbrush. Except that's not what it was. It was a comb. A tortoiseshell comb."

"And that matters why?"

"Because there'll be hairs on it."

"It was in the river, Ms Tucker," he said.

"And in her pocket. If you don't find any on the comb, there'll be some in her pocket."

He waited, so she spelled it out.

"You can get DNA traces from hair, can't you?"

"We've already got a headful of her hair. It doesn't match any DNA on file. How will more help?"

"Because this won't be hers," Sarah said. "It'll be Cartwright's. It's his comb."

Her phone hadn't magically recharged itself, so Sarah had little to do but sit for the next hour. Every so often, a police officer would wander out to smoke, and looked at her curiously. And every so often she glanced skywards, but no more balloons appeared.

She could leave. Nobody would stop her. More to the point, pretty soon she was going to be asked what she thought she was doing there. But her coffee cup seemed to act as an alibi, and there were enough unclaimed cigarette butts around for her to look like she had purpose. Minutes ticked past. A little over an hour later, Zoë stepped out again.

A policeman closed the door behind her, and took up position by the coffee machine, inside, in the warm.

"You're still here then," Zoë said, lighting a cigarette.

The flare of her lighter underlined the gathering dark.

Sarah shifted to one side, but Zoë shook her head.

"I've been sitting all afternoon." But she leaned against one arm of the bench. "I didn't say thank you."

"No," Sarah said. "You didn't."

"Okay," Zoë said. "I deserve some grief. But can it wait for a less complicated moment?"

"Not really."

"Why's that?"

"Because you knew," Sarah told her.

"I knew what?"

"About the comb."

"I knew about the comb," Zoë said flatly.

"You knew there was a comb on the body."

"Sarah, I asked if you had a hairbrush, that's all. My head was itchy."

"And if it had been an innocent comment, you'd not know what I was talking about."

Zoë said, "So now I'm in trouble for not pretending I don't know what you're talking about? I remember things I say. It's not a big deal."

"So you remember what you said to Talmadge. Back in the Baltic."

"He's called Cartwright. Oliver Cartwright. Can you believe that?"

"Answer the fucking question."

"Yes. Yes, I remember everything I said to him. Which part was so important?"

"The bit where you told him it wasn't river water in her lungs."

Zoë dragged smoke into her own. Then breathed it out again. "That's it?"

"How did you know that?"

"Internet, I guess. Does it matter?"

"It wasn't in the original news story. And I'm pretty sure it's not been reported since. I don't think you saw it on the Internet, Zoë."

"So I must have picked it up somewhere else."

"What, local gossip? Really?"

Zoë didn't answer.

"Speaking of the Internet," Sarah said.

"I'm supposed to be back inside."

"Have another cigarette. I won't tell if you don't."

"Enabler." But she flicked another free of her packet anyway, and lit it.

"You were using a service to trace your own phone. After Talmadge took it."

"Don't make it sound like a special power. Anyone can do it."

"I'm sure. But you found him before, didn't you? Before we were at the Sage, I mean."

"It's not all that accurate, you know, Sare. I mean, it's not like a big red arrow appears with —"

"I'm not interested in the technicalities. That's what you did, isn't it?"

Zoë stood, and moved away a few paces. Her outline blurred into shadow. "I went to ground when he stole my identity. What would you expect?"

"So you wake up and find you've been robbed, and your instinct is to hide? I'd expect you to go to the police, Zoë. That's what I'd call normal."

"I was robbed. But not of my cash. Did you catch that part? The cash was on the dresser. Short of signing his name . . . I mean, what kind of burglar robs you of everything but your money?"

Sarah shook her head. They both knew the answer to that.

Zoë came back and joined her on the bench. There was a memory connected to this: the pair of them sitting on a cold bench, but that time they'd been looking out to sea. Right now, all the waves Sarah knew about were lapping at her heart, and each of them washed it that little bit more numb.

"Yes. I traced him through the phone. He left it on at first. I think he was hoping I'd call, you know? When I didn't, he sent that e-mail. Just in case I hadn't picked up on the big picture. But I already knew it was him."

Pausing, she offered Sarah a cigarette. Sarah shook her head.

"Like I say, the trace isn't that accurate. But it put him on a street in Gateshead, not far from the river. Houses to let. Didn't take long to find out which one had been occupied for all of two days. But not in a man's name, a woman's. Julie Simpson. I tried tracing that, but didn't get far. Probably a fake. But I didn't have many resources available."

"Where were you staying?"

"I wasn't *staying* anywhere. I'd stopped being Zoë." She inhaled. "My wallet was gone. But I keep a credit card in my case for emergencies."

Emergencies, Sarah understood, which didn't need *Zoë Boehm* written all over them.

"I watched a full day. Nobody came or went. And I realized he'd gone. Just like every other time I went looking for him, he'd gone, and there'd be nothing to find. So I went in."

The distance between them hid inside those four words. *So I went in.* Not something Sarah would have known how to go about achieving . . . But even as she had the thought, she remembered lifting Gerard's room key from the reception desk in the Bolbec. If she'd needed to, she'd have found a way.

"And he'd left." Sarah needed to speak, just to hear her own voice. "But she was still there."

"In the bath. I couldn't tell how long she'd been dead. But standing in the doorway, you could read it like a story. There was a soap streak on the floor, and a thin wet wedge of it splatted against the wall. Everything but a big sign reading Join The Dots. She'd run the bath, and was about to get into it when she'd slipped on the soap and bang, game over. The knock on the head might have killed her. But she drowned."

"Yes," Sarah said. "She drowned."

"And he was smoke. Just another accident happening to some other poor woman." Zoë dropped her cigarette

**333**

end, ground it with her boot, then breathed out heavily. It was full-on dark, though lights from the office and corridor windows around them filled the well-like area with passive electricity. She said: "She was fully dressed. Black jeans. Red top. Sound familiar? And she looked like me."

"I know."

"And I'd seen her before."

This was news. "Where?"

"At the Bolbec. The night I was robbed. That's why I didn't see Talmadge doping my drink. He had her do it for him." Zoë shook her head. "God knows what he told her. Maybe that he was a spy. There's always someone ready to fall for a story like that, isn't there?"

There was always someone hungry to hear words no one had ever told them, was what Sarah thought. The kind of words Talmadge specialized in: love and need. Both fed on desperation.

She said, "I think it started with him taking her on holiday. And then it turned into an adventure."

"He picked her because she looked like me."

"Yes. And when he followed you to Newcastle, he took her with him."

Zoë said, "He'd kept my phone, but the rest of my stuff was there. Even my leather jacket. It was like he was laughing at me. As if he knew I'd be first one there."

Sarah said, "Or wanted people to think it was you."

"He's a twisted freak. It's a game to him. The woman was a counter on his board. Nothing more."

As if there were a timer operating, she reached for another cigarette. Sarah put a hand on her arm to stop her.

"No. Finish it."

Zoë glared, but bit back a retort. She placed the packet on the arm of the bench. Then said, instead, "I found a comb."

"In the house?"

"On the floor in the bathroom. I like to think it fell from his pocket when he was arranging her accident."

"And that's why you did it," Sarah said flatly.

"I put her shoes on. Put my jacket on her. It was hanging on a hook by the door, can you believe that? And I carried her out to my car."

"By *yourself*?"

Zoë said, "She was quite petite, really. Smaller than me. You didn't notice that?"

She had looked bigger on the slab, Sarah thought. Had been river-bloated.

"If anyone had seen us, they'd have thought she was drunk. But nobody saw us."

"And you drove her to the river."

"She was already dead."

"And you put her in the river."

"I knew he'd have to come back. He'd need to know what was going on. He might even wonder if it was really me they pulled from the Tyne. It was pretty clear they'd not find her true identity in a hurry."

"So you changed the rules of his game."

"It worked, didn't it? They'll find his hairs on the comb. That'll tie him to the body. And that's when it'll unravel. All those accidents that happen while he's somewhere else. That's not going to work this time."

"And all it took was, you put Madeleine Irving in the river."

A flat-sounding thump meant that Zoë had knocked her cigarettes to the ground. She bent and retrieved them, and had one in her mouth before Sarah could stop her. Her lighter flared. "Was that her name?"

"Yes," Sarah said, forgetting for a moment that she didn't know this for a fact. "She's just a counter in your game too, is she?"

"Of course not. She's the reason I did what I did, Sarah. Her and the others like her. So Talmadge never does this again."

"But meanwhile she's lying in a drawer which doesn't even have her name on it."

"And that's my fault? Sarah, there's more to identity than just a name. Talmadge isn't even called Talmadge. You think it matters to Madeleine, that the cops don't know her name yet?"

"It matters to me," Sarah said.

Zoë didn't reply.

There was a tap on the window; a policeman, beckoning Zoë back inside.

"I've not even been charged yet," she said. "But I'm still at their beck and call." But she took one last drag anyway, then dropped her cigarette.

"Are you going to tell them?" Sarah asked.

"I'll give them the house he was using." The words came out as smoke. "They can match the hairs by themselves. After that . . ." Zoë shrugged. "I'm hoping to avoid some of the finer detail. But if I can't, I can't."

"You're certain there are hairs to find."

"I have faith in science," Zoë said. "Largely because otherwise, I'm fucked." She fitted her cigarette packet into her jeans pocket. "What about you? Going to tell them what I did?"

Sarah didn't answer.

"I won't hold it against you."

The policeman tapped again.

Zoë said, "Dry your eyes."

"I'm not crying for you."

"Take care, Sarah."

Zoë slipped back into the light. Through the window, Sarah watched her say something to the policeman, which made him laugh, then the pair disappeared through a set of swing doors.

After a moment, Sarah followed.

Fairfax caught her by the elbow just before she left the building. "So what did she have to say, then?"

Sarah stared pointedly at his hand until he released her. Then said, "Nothing she won't tell you herself."

"You're sure about that?"

Sarah gave him the goodbye look, then pushed through the doors into the street.

She collected her bag from the Internet café, walked to the station, and caught the first train south. At the last moment, the carriage filled with a noisy group of football fans, but this didn't matter. She wouldn't sleep anyway. It didn't matter.

As the train crossed the bridge, Sarah saw tiny shadows moving inside the bright-lit flanks of the Sage; saw the oblong box of the Baltic, which in the dark resembled the mill it had once been. The eyelash curve of the Millennium Bridge, underlit in deep red, formed a trembling oval with its own reflection, through which the river ran. And further away, beyond the water's bend, some of those lights in the sky would be cranes standing sentry over abandoned shipyards; yards that in time would blossom into spanking new apartment blocks, beneath whose windows the same river would keep on running, casting back the overhead lights as waterbound stars that twinkled black and white, and black and white.

"Gan canny," Sarah whispered through the glass. Though whether her words were aimed at the river, at Zoë, or at herself, she couldn't tell.

338

# The Maze of Cadiz

## Aly Monroe

Sent to Spain by British Intelligence to arrest a rogue spy, agent Peter Cotton expects an easy first assignment. But just as he arrives in Cadiz, his quarry turns up dead. It's 1944, and as war in Europe draws to a close, formerly neutral Franco is edging closer to the Allies — but things are not what they seem.

It appears all of Cadiz has been expecting Cotton. In a hotbed of international conspiracy, shifting political alliances and murder, what Cotton unearths amid the stifling heat and dust could just tilt the emerging balance of post-war power.

ISBN 978-0-7531-8394-6 (hb)
ISBN 978-0-7531-8395-3 (pb)

# The Mind's Eye

## Håkan Nesser

Janek Mitter stumbles into his bathroom one morning after a night of heavy drinking to find his beautiful young wife, Eva, floating dead in the bath. She has been brutally murdered. Yet even during his trial Mitter cannot summon a single memory of attacking Eva, nor a clue as to who could have killed her if he did not. Only once he has been convicted and locked away in an asylum does he have a snatch of insight — but is it too late?

Drawing a blank after exhaustive interviews, Chief Inspector Van Veeteren remains convinced that something, or someone, in the dead woman's life has caused these tragic events. But the reasons for her speedy remarriage have died with her. And as he delves even deeper, Van Veeteren realises that the past never stops haunting the present . . .

ISBN 978-0-7531-8376-2 (hb)
ISBN 978-0-7531-8377-9 (pb)

# Hard Evidence

## Mark Pearson

Jackie Malone has been murdered. Her body lies in a pool of blood in the north London flat where she worked as a prostitute. Deep knife wounds have been gouged into her corpse and her hands and feet are tied with coat hanger wire. For Detective Inspector Jack Delaney this is no ordinary case. He was a friend of Jackie's and she left desperate messages on his answerphone just hours before she was killed.

Just as Delaney begins his investigation, a young girl is reported missing, feared abducted, and he is immediately tasked with finding her. But he is also determined to track down Jackie's killer before the trail goes cold. However, his uncompromising attitude has made him some powerful enemies on the force, and this case may provide the perfect opportunity for them to dispose of him, once and for all . . .

ISBN 978-0-7531-8350-2 (hb)
ISBN 978-0-7531-8351-9 (pb)

# Reconstruction

## Mick Herron

When a man with a gun breaks into her school, nursery teacher Louise Kennedy knows there's not likely to be a happy ending . . . But Jaime Segura isn't there on a homicidal whim, and he's as scared as the hostages he's taken. While an armed police presence builds up outside, he'll only talk to Ben Whistler, an MI6 accountant who worked with his lover, Miro.

Miro's apparently gone on the run, along with a huge sum of money. Jaime doesn't believe Miro's a thief — though he certainly had secrets. But then, so does Louise, so do the other hostages and so do some of those on the outside — those who'd much rather that Jaime was silenced.

ISBN 978-0-7531-8150-8 (hb)
ISBN 978-0-7531-8151-5 (pb)

# The Last Voice you Hear

## Mick Herron

When a woman dies beneath the wheels of a train and her newly acquired love fails to turn up at the funeral, private investigator Zoë Boehm is hired to find him. And in attempting to unlock the secrets of a woman she's never met, in search of a man who might be anyone, Zoë only finds more questions: Where did Alan Talmadge come from? Why does he appear to have no history? How did he meet Caroline Daniels? And has he killed before?

Zoë is accustomed to finding answers to the questions she asks; accustomed too to finding the people she looks for. But as her search leads her nearer to two different kinds of criminal, she starts to wonder if the man she is looking for has found her first. And if he has, is that going to make her another victim . . .

ISBN 978-0-7531-7341-1 (hb)
ISBN 978-0-7531-7342-8 (pb)

ISIS publish a wide range of books in large print, from fiction to biography. Any suggestions for books you would like to see in large print or audio are always welcome. Please send to the Editorial Department at:

**ISIS Publishing Limited**
7 Centremead
Osney Mead
Oxford OX2 0ES

A full list of titles is available free of charge from:

**Ulverscroft Large Print Books Limited**

**(UK)**
The Green
Bradgate Road, Anstey
Leicester LE7 7FU
Tel: (0116) 236 4325

**(Australia)**
P.O. Box 314
St Leonards
NSW 1590
Tel: (02) 9436 2622

**(USA)**
P.O. Box 1230
West Seneca
N.Y. 14224-1230
Tel: (716) 674 4270

**(Canada)**
P.O. Box 80038
Burlington
Ontario L7L 6B1
Tel: (905) 637 8734

**(New Zealand)**
P.O. Box 456
Feilding
Tel: (06) 323 6828

Details of **ISIS** complete and unabridged audio books are also available from these offices. Alternatively, contact your local library for details of their collection of **ISIS** large print and unabridged audio books.